NIGHTS IN WHITE COTTON

'White,' he said softly as my panties began to come on show. 'You often used to wear white ones, that or pink.'

I nodded, unable to speak for my choking mix of arousal and shame as I slid my jeans lower, showing off my taut panty seat, my cheeks bulging in the tight white cotton. With my jeans held down I stayed as I was, showing off the full width of my bottom with just my panties to hide me as I managed to find my voice.

'Is that nice?' I asked. 'Is that what you like to see?'

'Don't move an inch,' he answered me, and I heard the soft rasp of his zip being pulled down.

Again I nodded, looking around as I held myself out for inspection, feeling more of a tart than ever, standing with my panties on show for him to get off over. He had his cock out, still limp in his hand, but quite big, and resting on a bulbous scrotum thickly grown with milk white hair. I managed a little smile for him as he began to masturbate, his eyes fixed on my straining panty seat.

T0316113

Why not visit Penny's website at www.pennybirch.com

By the same author:

THE INDIGNITIES OF ISABELLE
THE INDISCRETIONS OF ISABELLE
THE INDECENCIES OF ISABELLE
(Writing as Cruella)

PENNY IN HARNESS
A TASTE OF AMBER
BAD PENNY
BRAT
IN FOR A PENNY
PLAYTHING
TIGHT WHITE COTTON
TIE AND TEASE
PENNY PIECES
TEMPER TANTRUMS
REGIME
DIRTY LAUNDRY
UNIFORM DOLL
BARE BEHIND
NURSE'S ORDERS
JODHPURS AND JEANS
PEACH
FIT TO BE TIED
WHEN SHE WAS BAD
KNICKERS AND BOOTS
TICKLE TORTURE
IN DISGRACE
PETTING GIRLS
NAUGHTY NAUGHTY

NIGHTS IN
WHITE COTTON

Penny Birch

This book is a work of fiction.
In real life, make sure you practise safe, sane and
consensual sex.

First published in 2005 by
Nexus
Thames Wharf Studios
Rainville Road
London W6 9HA

www.nexus-books.co.uk

Typeset by TW Typesetting, Plymouth, Devon

Printed and bound in Great Britain by
Clays Ltd, Elcograf S.p.A.

ISBN 978 0 352 34008 5

MIX
Paper | Supporting
responsible forestry
FSC® C018179

You'll notice that we have introduced a set of symbols onto our book jackets, so that you can tell at a glance what fetishes each of our brand new novels contains. Here's the key – enjoy!

 cp (traditional)

 cp (modern)

 spanking

 restraint/bondage

 rope bondage/hojojutsu

 latex/rubber/leather/enclosure

 fem dom

 willing captivity

 medical

 period setting

 uniforms

 sex rituals

Author's Note on Erotica

To many people erotica must be restrained in order to have any claim to value. The nude must be less than fully displayed, the sentence cloaked in euphemism. Otherwise, we are told, the work descends into pornography.

I disagree. This is an argument of the bland, the mediocre, of those too frightened to face their sexuality in reflection. To give free rein to one's expression is not a descent at all, but an ascent. Let no word be considered unacceptable, no act of pleasure beyond description, and if the result must be called pornography then I wear the word with pride. A quote from *Nights in White Cotton*:

'– so good, so completely and comprehensively filthy, the behaviour of a dirty, depraved, lewd little slut, a girl whose behaviour is an outrage to everything decent and proper and prissy and dull. To be used so badly, as a butch dyke's sex toy, and to delight in every single instant of my ordeal. It was me, through and through, and I would never want to be any other way.'

Consider Gustave Coubert's *The Origin of the World*. I have heard it dismissed as 'just a dirty picture', as if taking a woman's vulva as the subject immediately destroys all possibility of greater worth.

1

Surely this is a shallow view? In the same way, openly sexual expression in a novel does not preclude a subtext. For those who consider *The Origin of the World* just a dirty picture, *Nights in White Cotton* will no doubt seem a morass of unrelieved filth. Perhaps it is, but for some it may be deep enough to drown in.

Penny Birch

One

I was first turned across my aunt Elaine's knee at the age of sixteen.

Every excruciating detail remains vivid in my memory, from the first awful moment when I realised I was to be spanked to the last guilty tremor of my virgin orgasm. Since that day, more men and women than I can number have had my panties down and smacked my bottom. I *need* to be spanked.

Most people not only do not understand, but *cannot* understand, any more than somebody who has been blind from birth can understand the beauty of a sunrise. They may be hostile – this is violence, the coercion of woman by man, and a relic of our darker past fit only for pity and disapproval. They may be offended – what a traitor I am, to want to be treated like that, and how utterly inappropriate in our modern world. They may be condescending – how sad that in our brave new world my mind should be so bent out of shape that I should be unable to enjoy a normal, healthy sex life. They may be amused – how quite absurd, after all, for a grown woman to want her knickers taken down and her bare bottom smacked! They may be liberal – perhaps they may even come to appreciate the warm glow of a pair of well-smacked bottom cheeks, the rush of blood and endorphins.

To me, spanking is all these things. I want to be held down and punished by somebody stronger than me. I want to feel the stinging shame of complying with an inappropriate act. I want to be kinky, and naughty, and rude. I want to be made ridiculous, an object of laughter and derision with my panties at half mast and my bottom on show to the world. I want the hot pain and the urgency in my sex, to be made to lick pussy or suck cock as I say thank you for my punishment, and to come under busy fingers as I do it.

Yes, I want to be spanked, I need to be spanked, and I wouldn't have it any other way. The more the circumstances go against what the conventional world views as right, the better it is for me. Order me to dress in nothing but a light summer dress and crisp white panties, take me out on the concourse of Paddington Station, strip my bottom bare and spank me until I howl. Yes, Paddington Station would be ideal, public and open, so that I have no choice whatsoever in who sees my punishment. Do that, and I will be your devoted sex toy, for just as long as it takes to leave us cuddled together in the afterglow of ecstasy.

Only I won't, because long before we get to that point we'll have been arrested. That is the problem. Being confident in who I am and what I am is one thing, but expecting the rest of the world to adapt to my personal requirements is simply not realistic. I need to earn a wage, to eat, to keep a roof over my head, and preferably not the roof of a police station or a mental institute. In short, I may need to be spanked, but I also need to compromise with the real world, which is why I found myself walking briskly along a Berkshire lane one bright spring morning.

I'd come by train and walked up from the station as a deliberate choice, partly so I could enjoy a glass of wine with the Sunday lunch I knew Aunt Elaine would be cooking, but mainly so that I could soak up the atmosphere and so fully appreciate what was to be done to me. Our agreement, ostensibly, was to fulfil a need in me. In practice, although never admitted, it was to fulfil a need in both of us. Between the time the joint went into the oven and when the vegetables had to be prepared, I would be given a very English, very discreet, very ladylike spanking.

It was always across her knee, and always on my bare skin, a routine that varied only according to what I happened to be wearing and the time of year. In the winter, I was generally done in front of the fire with my jeans and knickers at half-mast, or perhaps a thick woollen skirt raised and the underwear beneath rolled down to my thighs. During the summer, I was more likely to be done outside, in the walled kitchen garden, dress up, panties down, and my bottom warm and bare in the sunlight. Afterwards, I would go upstairs, to cry out my feelings and bring myself to an orgasm that invariably left my soul as satisfied as the subsequent lunch would leave my body.

The routine was also important to me, a reassuringly fixed point in a changing world: the guarantee of a bare-bottom spanking each Sunday during term-time, and otherwise on Tuesday evenings. It had now been happening for over four years, since shortly after accepting my post as Senior Lecturer at the university, and had become as familiar and comforting as the house itself and the countryside I'd known since childhood.

I still felt apprehensive. As I walked, my bottom cheeks would tighten occasionally in anticipation of the coming exposure and pain, while my tummy was fluttering badly. After all, I would shortly be having my panties pulled down and my bottom smacked, and just because I needed it and just because I was given the same shameful treatment on a regular basis didn't mean my feelings weren't strong.

By the time I came in sight of the house they were boiling, so intense I had to stop for a little. It wasn't just the prospect of my spanking either, but a powerful nostalgia. The view ahead of me was exactly as it had been on the day of my cousin Kate's wedding, the day I got it for the very first time, over my aunt's knee in my pretty pink bridesmaid's dress. Maybe some of the trees were a little more grown, and there was a For Sale sign outside what had been Colonel Aimsworth's house, along with a large white receiver dish on the roof, but otherwise I might have stepped back in time. My aunt's eccentric red-brick house, the moss-grown tiles, the air of sleepy wellbeing, all was exactly as it lived in my memory.

As I walked forwards, I had recaptured that same sense of helplessness I'd felt then, of having no choice in what was done to me. The feeling grew stronger still as Elaine opened the door to me and I caught the delicate scent of her perfume, blended with the smell of roasting beef. A single, demure peck in greeting and I was inside, my aunt speaking as she moved towards the kitchen in the brisk, no-nonsense manner I knew so well. 'You're rather late, Penny. Other people will be here soon.'

'Other people?'

'Other people, Penny, yes. Geraldine, Kate, everybody. Didn't you get my mail?'

Her voice was a trifle stern, carrying the sense of mild exasperation with my behaviour that reminded me so strongly of my mother – the last person on Earth I wanted to catch me across her younger sister's lap.

'Maybe we shouldn't –' I began, only to be cut off.

'No, no, better to get things over and done with, don't you think?'

As always there was a hint of a sigh in her voice. She understood my need to be spanked, and felt that if it had to be done then she was the best person to do it, a family member I could trust. Yet there was always that touch of disapproval for my inability to control my needs.

I nodded and swallowed hard as she walked across to the kitchen table. A chair had already been pulled out, probably in readiness. She sat down on it and patted her lap, her mouth set in a little firm smile, full of sympathy and understanding yet anything but weak. I hitched my skirt up a little, just the exposure of a few inches of thighs setting my stomach into a tight knot that grew tighter still as I laid myself gently across her lap and into spanking position. She took hold of my skirt as I braced my feet on the floor to lift my bottom and let her get me bare. My whole body was trembling, and I closed my eyes to savour my own shame as I was made ready.

'Just as well to be in a skirt,' Elaine remarked as the garment was eased gently but firmly up my legs. 'Those jeans you always seem to wear are very awkward.'

My mouth opened to answer, but there was a bubble of mucus in my throat and no words would come, only a strong shiver as my skirt was pulled up over my hips with a single sharp tug. With my panties showing behind, big and taut and white around my bottom, I felt the first of my tears start to grow, moist in the corner of my eye. I thought of how right she was, and how I'd deliberately dressed to make it easier to spank me.

I'd begun to sob, and Elaine gave a little tut as she adjusted me into a more comfortable position across her lap, half-sympathy, half-disapproval. Her voice was the same as she spoke. 'Now then, let's have your knickers down and we'll soon have you dealt with.'

Her thumbs pushed into the waistband of my white cotton panties, and they begun to come down, not slow, nor fast, just a good practical speed to get my bottom bare for punishment. I felt every instant, blissful humiliation so strongly it made my throat hurt and set me choking back tears. She took them right down, too, all the way to my knees, making sure the chubby globe of my bottom was laid completely bare, completely vulnerable, and showing everything, the way a spanked girl should.

I'd begun to cry as she took me firmly around the waist, exposed and helpless, lying bare bottom across my aunt's knee in the kitchen, and about to be punished. Her hand settled on my bottom, lifted, came down again, and it had begun. It wasn't all that hard, but it didn't need to be hard, just a firm, purposeful spanking applied to my bare bottom. That was what mattered: that I was bare, that I was punished, my panties taken down and my bottom smacked.

It soon got harder, enough to make me kick, just a little, my legs turning up and my thighs jerking in my panties. I knew it made me show behind. I knew it made me look even more ridiculous, with my feet waving and the wet tart of my pussy peeping out between my thighs. That was right. I was supposed to look foolish. I was supposed to have my modesty stripped away. I was supposed to have my bare sex put on display and, as Elaine began to spank harder still and the stinging pain grew worse, that rudest, most intimate detail of all, my bumhole.

Elaine gave another little disapproving tut as my cheeks began to come wide and I'd given in completely, bawling my eyes out across her lap, as she spanked me with fast, stinging slaps, peppering the full spread of my behind. My legs were kicking wildly, my hips bucking to splay out my wobbling bottom cheeks and show the rude brown hole between, a full-blown spanking tantrum. I'd begun to howl, too, and gasp and squeak, all to the tune of her hand on my bottom flesh, smack, smack, smack, so loud in the quiet, drowsy air of the kitchen, with only the faint sizzle of the roasting pan to compete.

She kept on, now spanking as hard as she could, bringing all my emotions to the surface, making me blubber pathetically across her lap, without the slightest shred of modesty or restraint. I was as I should be, a spanked brat, over my auntie's knee with my panties pulled well down and my hot bottom on show to the world, well punished, and now reduced to that abandoned condition that comes no other way.

A last bubble of frustration and shame burst in my head and the pain had begun to turn to warmth. My sobs and gasps gave way to sighs; my bottom began to push up and I was truly beyond caring, brought on heat in the way only a really good spanking can, all my bad feelings smacked right out of me. Elaine knew immediately, but gave me another round dozen to finish me off, then stopped. 'I trust that's what you needed?' she asked, as I climbed unsteadily from her lap.

'Thank you, yes,' I answered, and kissed her.

I was still snivelling a bit, my vision hazy with tears and my mouth salty with the mucus running from my nose, dizzy too. For a moment I had to lean on the table, but Elaine gave me a couple of purposeful pats on one still naked cheek. I nodded and snatched for my panties, clutching them in one hand as I ran for the stairs and up, with my bare red bottom wobbling behind me. She'd tucked my skirt up into its own waistband, and I stayed bare all the way to the room I used.

The instant I'd shut the door behind me I was on my bed, face down as it all came together in my head. I stuck up my bottom and turned to face the wardrobe mirror, admiring the view; my snotty, tear-stained face, my turned-up skirt, my lowered panties and my bare, rosy cheeks between. My hand went down under my tummy to find my sex, wet and ready, my clitoris an aching point between swollen lips. I began to masturbate, letting my feelings go as I ran over what had been done to me in my head.

My aunt had spanked me, my own aunt, over her knee with my panties dropped, the way a naughty girl should be spanked. Just to think about it sent a shiver through me, so delicious, so addictive I had to masturbate again, with a touch of my clitoris each time – spanked bare bottom across my aunt's knee ... spanked bare bottom across my aunt's knee ... spanked bare bottom across my aunt's knee ...

I started to come, but held myself back, right on the edge, deliberately tormenting myself. My spare hand went back to my bottom to stroke my smacked cheeks, feeling the warm flesh, sensitive and ever so slightly roughened. It felt so good to have it bare, to see it pink in the mirror, exposed between panties and skirt, showing off, because I didn't care. I'd been spanked and I was glad I'd been spanked.

My hand burrowed between my cheeks to touch my bumhole, as I thought of how I'd let my cheeks come open, how I must have looked, a grown woman, a university lecturer, with her panties down and her bottom spread to show the rude, pinkish-brown dimple between as I was punished. It was so gloriously, exquisitely humiliating, to have my own aunt pull down my panties and spank my bare bottom with my bumhole on show . . . pull down my panties and spank my bare bottom . . . spank my bare bottom . . .

This time there was no holding back. I pushed my finger in up my bottom just as my ring began to tighten and I was there, coming in a long, tight orgasm with my fingers working on my clitoris and in my bumhole, my eyes tight shut and my mouth wide, the image of myself laid bare across Aunt Elaine's knee fixed firmly in my mind's eye. It was as good as ever, not only ecstasy, but also cathartic, leaving me with all the tension of mind and body washed clean away.

I was still on the bed, absent-mindedly teasing my pussy and bumhole, wondering if I should come a second time when I heard the bell. Until that moment I'd completely forgotten the rest of the family were due to turn up, and I was panicking more than a little as I ran for the bathroom with my knickers still half-down. As I washed and made a few hasty adjustments to my appearance, I heard voices downstairs, first my mother's commanding tones, and then Elaine, softer, suddenly switched from domestic disciplinarian to little sister.

The thought of my mother downstairs in the very room in which I'd just been punished set me blushing, and I took a moment more to splash water on my face and tidy my hair into its neat black bob. A single deep breath and I felt ready, no longer a naughty little girl but a grown, respectable woman. Downstairs, my mother and Elaine were already in the kitchen, sipping dry sherry. I accepted a glass before sitting down in the very same chair over which I'd been spanked.

We'd barely exchanged a word when the bell went again, this time for my cousin Kate, her husband Jeremy and their daughters, Pippa and Jemima. Immediately the house was full of laughter and conversation, and it stayed that way as I helped Elaine with the vegetables, scraping carrots and chopping cabbage while she did the Yorkshire pudding.

I hadn't seen Kate in a while, but she was the same as ever, full of life and talking about everything under the sun. It was even longer since I'd seen the two girls, so long in fact that I had to change gear a little, accepting them as young adults rather than older children, Pippa especially. She was taller than me for a start, with a slender, womanly elegance more in keeping with her grandmother than her mother, although her hair was just as curly, if darker and worn short. Jemima was slimmer still, with a skinny awkwardness and a rebellious scowl that reminded me of Susan, her aunt and Kate's little sister. When Susan herself turned up, just as we were putting the dishes out on the dining-room table, I was even more struck by the resemblance.

For the next half-hour we were all deeply involved in the ritual of British Sunday lunch, with Jeremy carving the rib of beef and the seven women coping with everything else. I still felt a little warm behind, but otherwise had forgotten about my spanking, first trying to follow a conversation about the latest bands between Susan and Pippa, then listening to my mother explain to Elaine why it was too early to plant delphiniums out. Only when we'd finished the beef and the scent of baking apple pudding had begun to replace that of roast meat did Elaine ask us all to pay attention. 'You may have seen the sign opposite,' she stated when we'd all finally shut up, 'so you'll know that what used to be Colonel Aimsworth's house is back on the market.'

'What happened?' Kate asked. 'It was only sold, what, two years ago?'

'Nearly three,' her mother corrected her, 'but, in any event, the new people have moved on, and not before time.'

I nodded agreement, remembering the raucous parties and the sight of broken bottles in the road.

'Quite. Ghastly, noisy people,' my mother agreed. 'Every time I came they seemed to have the builders in.'

'I believe he played football for a living,' Elaine went on, her tone suggesting that she'd have preferred a pimp or a blackmailer as a neighbour, 'and so he has presumably gone to another part of the country –'

'Uh, uh, Mum,' Susan broke in, 'he was Billy Watts, striker for the Royal Blues. He got sacked for spit roasting a girl, in Cardiff.'

'Spit roasting?' my mother queried in open horror.

'Not real spit roasting,' Susan said, laughing, 'it's just an expression for when two guys have a girl from both ends at once, like she's on a spit.'

'I do not wish to know, thank you, Susan,' my mother answered, as Jemima burst into giggles.

I hid a smile behind a sip of wine, remembering the last occasion for me, ruder still, shared between two girlfriends with oversized strap-on dildoes, Jade's in my mouth as Sophie fed hers in and out of my pussy. It was not a memory I intended to share, not even with Elaine, who had carried on talking after a tut of admonition for her daughter. 'In any event, they are gone, and the house is on the market. This time, I suggest we buy the house ourselves, which will prevent any such nonsense in future.'

'What were you thinking of?' Jeremy asked. 'Because I'm afraid Kate and I simply can't risk any further exposure on our mortgage.'

'Nor can I!' Susan added. 'I can barely make my payments as it is.'

'It's not an option for me, either, I'm afraid,' I put in, 'not on my salary.'

'If you were to sell, Geraldine –' Elaine began, only to be cut off by my mother.

'Absolutely not! I'm very comfortable where I am, thank you, Elaine. Nor do I have any desire to live in such a vulgar house. They've ruined it completely.'

'We looked in at the windows,' Kate supplied. 'All the appliances are pink, even the cooker, so are the carpets.'

'The false Greek portico's bad enough,' Jeremy put in.

'There's a swimming pool,' Pippa added, only in a very different tone of voice, 'shaped like a football.'

'Well, I certainly can't afford it on my own,' Elaine went on, now somewhat terse, 'but at least I am prepared to contribute. If you're not prepared to sell, Geraldine, although Purley is hardly what is was when we were children so I can't imagine why not, then Penny can –'

'Me?' I interrupted. 'I can't possibly, my salary –'

'– is quite sufficient to allow you to increase your mortgage to cover the balance,' Elaine insisted.

'I doubt it,' I pointed out, 'and I'm really quite comfortable in my flat.'

'I think you'll find you could manage, Penny,' Jeremy remarked. 'I'm happy to advise and can get you a great deal.'

'Yes, but I really don't want to –'

'You always loved it up here,' Kate pointed out.

'Yes, but I really don't –'

14

'And your flat is rather poky,' Susan added.

'Yes, but I really –'

'And you're not in a very nice area,' my mother agreed.

'Yes, but I –'

'We could use the swimming pool!' Pippa and Jemima said in chorus.

'Yes, but –'

'We'll be right opposite each other,' Elaine put in.

'Yes –'

I bought the house, leaving myself with just a 25-year mortgage and about enough disposable income to live on bread and dripping. It wasn't even particularly difficult, because most of the people who came to view it had been put off by the Watts' taste, which went beyond anything mere redecoration could sort out, or by their apparent inability to be satisfied with what they'd got, which meant that half of it was a building site.

The rest of it had been stripped bare by the time I came into possession, apparently to help cover the Watts' enormous legal bills. At least the pink cooker was gone, but my own possessions were barely sufficient to make the kitchen, the living room and one bedroom habitable. They'd also left both bathrooms complete with baby-pink tiles and gold fittings.

For an entire week I camped out at Elaine's, and drove into work every morning letting the removers and assorted workmen get on with it. I didn't even get a chance to have my bottom smacked, what with endless comings and goings and questions to answer and decisions to be made, not to mention my mother's habit of dropping in to offer critical advice at all hours.

On the Saturday morning a week after technically becoming the new owner, I at last moved in, and for once could look forward to a bit of peace. Elaine and my mother had gone into London, so I was entirely alone, and able to explore at leisure. It was an odd sensation because, even after the changes the Watts had made, being in the house provoked a feeling that I was doing wrong.

I could remember Colonel Aimsworth well, a liverish man with a red face, bulging eyes and a penchant for topiary. He'd also had several fruit trees, which were still there, and although Kate and Susan had perfectly good ones in their own garden it had always been far more fun to pinch the Colonel's. The three of us had fought a running battle with him for years, and I'd twice been hauled from his garden by the ear. Being in his house felt very odd indeed and despite the fact that I now owned it I found myself treading carefully and expecting his angry bark to ring out at any moment.

Telling myself not to be silly, I began to wonder what I could do to make the place my own. With so little money to spare, ambitious projects were out, but the pink and gold wallpaper had to go; so did a lot of other things, in due course, but at least I could strip wallpaper and paint without paying any workmen. Jade and Sophie had promised to come up and help so that could wait. For the moment I could remove the gigantic receiver dish from the roof, because it was a serious eyesore, I had no intention of using it and I wouldn't need to buy any more equipment.

It was fixed right beside one of the attic windows. Going up seemed more sensible than climbing a ladder, so I made my way upstairs to where a trapdoor opened into the roof space above the landing. There was no obvious way up, and a prod with a broom revealed that it was painted in. A second, harder prod showered me with flakes of paint and it was loose. A third and I had it lifted with a squeak of unoiled hinges.

I fetched the step ladder and climbed up, taking some tools with me. Pushing the hatch back revealed a long, dusty space so heavily criss-crossed with beams that it was no real use for anything but storage. Bright sunlight flooded in from the windows at either end, showing that it had been lagged relatively recently, while the workmen had piled up a number of trunks and chests near the window I needed to get at.

Pulling myself up, I made my way cautiously along the planks, only to discover that, like the trapdoor, the window was painted into its frame. Unlike the trapdoor, I couldn't budge it, even by sitting on a trunk to brace myself and pushing as hard as I could. All I got for my trouble was a dusty bottom, but as I turned round to pat myself down I saw the name on the trunk – Capt. L. Aimsworth.

I was immediately intrigued. He had been retired when I'd known him, so presumably he was a Captain during the Second World War, or shortly afterwards. A gentle shake of the trunk revealed that it was quite full, and so were the other boxes and chests in the pile. All were evidently his, left behind when the house had first changed hands.

Not to investigate them would have been impossible, and I quickly sat down on the boards and pulled up the hasps. The central one was locked, but the wrench I'd brought up to remove the dish soon took care of that, and with a deliciously guilty thrill I was pulling up the lid. Inside were several old-fashioned box files, the marbled paper discoloured with age and peeling back from the cardboard beneath.

I opened the first, expecting old documents, perhaps interesting ones. One thing I did not expect was a large black and white photograph of a girl standing beside a pond in the act of removing her only garment, a pair of large pink panties. She was maybe five foot tall or a little more, to judge by the fence behind her, with shiny black hair cut into a short bob, slightly built and compact, her breasts small and turned up, a slender waist and a distinctly chubby bottom – me.

For a long moment I could only stare, my mouth falling slowly open as the implications of what I was seeing sank in. I remembered the occasion well, very well, the summer after my first year at university when I'd come to keep Kate company after the break-up of her first marriage. The pond was a flooded gravel pit, a place we'd known all our lives, a place so secluded we'd thought nothing of stripping off to swim. I remember being disturbed as well, once we'd been swimming for a while. We'd glimpsed somebody on the lip of the quarry, looking down, but it had never occurred to me for a moment it might have been Colonel Aimsworth. He was just too respectable to do such things.

Immediately I was burrowing through the rest of the photos, which filled the whole file, and with every one my sense of shock grew stronger. There were an extraordinary number from that day at the quarry alone, ones of Kate and me undressing and swimming together, even scrambling out of the pool after we'd been seen, with me halfway out of the water, one leg cocked up, my pussy flaunted for all the world to see and my bumhole showing pink in the hair between my open cheeks.

There was more, every single one of the files packed with photos and neatly labelled with the year they'd been taken, from when Kate and I were in our late teens to the year before the Colonel's death, assuming he *had* died. I got off relatively lightly, the picture of me climbing out of the water just about the rudest of all, but with only about one picture in ten showing me at all.

Kate and Susan got a great deal more exposure, mainly taken on the lawn opposite. Most were innocent enough, showing them in cut-down jeans or bikinis, sunbathing or just minding their own business. Elaine had never approved of the girls going naked, even in the secluded kitchen garden, despite her habit of taking *my* pants down for *al fresco* spankings, but in a few pictures Kate had her top off and her full breasts naked to the sun, and to the lens of Aimsworth's camera.

I could tell from the angle where they'd been taken from, too, the very window I was sitting in, presumably with a tripod set up and a chair, probably a table too, for a plate of biscuits or a glass of beer, to judge by the length of time he'd obviously spent spying on us. Nor had he restricted his activities to the house. Just as the old quarry had been a favourite spot of ours, so it had been of his. In addition to the ones with me in them, there were plenty of Kate and Susan undressing, skinny dipping and lying naked on the grass as they dried off afterwards.

Once or twice he'd really got lucky, and some were anything but innocent. Kate's first husband, Toby, had always been a dirty bastard, and a show-off. I knew he'd occasionally made her suck him off outdoors, but I was still shocked to see a picture of her doing it, down on her knees with her cheeks bulging and her fingers tickling underneath his balls as she sucked. She'd had her top and bra pulled up too, her heavy breasts lolling naked beneath her chest.

That wasn't the worst. The worst was of Susan, in the living room, across Elaine's knee in what had always been her father's favourite chair. Her school skirt had been turned up and her long, coltish legs were kicked apart at a ridiculous angle, trapped at the level of her knees by the pair of plain white panties she'd had pulled down. Her bottom was bare, and open, showing off her pouted sex and her anus. She was being spanked.

By then my hands were shaking so badly I had trouble holding the photos. I couldn't get over what he'd done, over so long, and so skilfully. I could even see why he'd put so much effort into his topiary pigeons, because it gave him an excuse to look over the hedge into Elaine's living room and across at least part of the lawn. If anything looked likely to happen, all he had to do was nip upstairs and he could photograph us at his leisure. He'd have been able to see the garden gate too, and when we left with towels under our arms he would have been able to install himself above the quarry before we got there, simply by nipping across his own land and along a single hedgerow.

When I finally managed to pull myself together, my first thought was to burn the lot, along with everything else of his that remained in the house. Most of the other chests and boxes held what I'd imagined in the first place, old documents, but they'd entirely lost their fascination. There was also a collection of ancient pornographic magazines, and a few more rude photographs, some very old indeed and taken in all sorts of places, but not of anybody I knew.

I was feeling distinctly numb as I moved everything to the trapdoor hatch, only to realise that I had a problem, the sheer bulk. Getting it down from the attic was going to be hard enough, as I could not possibly climb down the ladder while supporting a large trunk and so would have to lower each item individually on a pulley. Even once I'd done it and stacked everything in some suitable part of the garden, it was going to take ages to burn, make an enormous quantity of smoke and need to be tended to until I was sure every last piece was gone.

The sensible thing to do was to burn the photos and leave the rest until I had somebody to help me, but by the time I'd stacked all eight of the old box files on the kitchen table I'd realised that I simply couldn't bring myself to do it. The pictures might have been taken by a Peeping Tom, but they still involved me, and some held precious memories of which I had no other record. To have burnt them would have been like destroying part of my own life.

I sat down and had a coffee instead, trying to rid myself of the parade of pictures moving in front of my eyes, of Kate, Susan and myself in various states of undress and Colonel Aimsworth's leering face in the background. It was impossible, especially his bulging eyes peering at my naked body, enjoying my nudity and the thrill of peeping. So often I'd thought I was secure, swimming naked with my cousins or sunbathing on their lawn in just a bikini, and all the time those bulging red eyes had been peering down on me, caressing my body with his gaze, exploring every contour, lingering on my breasts and bottom, even my pussy as I'd pulled myself from the water that time.

By the time I'd finished my coffee, I had the pictures spread out on the table and was feeling distinctly guilty about what I was going to do, masturbate. I tried to tell myself that it wasn't important, that he hadn't done any real harm, but there was no denying the effect it was having on me. It was both erotic and intensely humiliating, for me, a fatal combination. I knew he'd have masturbated

21

over them too, it was naïve to think otherwise, holding my picture as his eyes feasted on my body and he tugged at himself. The one of me taking my panties down at the water's edge was distinctly dog-eared at one corner, where he'd obviously held it while he pulled at his dirty old cock. It had evidently been a favourite, perhaps second only to the one of Susan taking a spanking across Elaine's knee.

It really was hopeless, something I could no more resist than hunger or thirst. I knew where I wanted to do it as well, down by the old quarry. Just thinking about it had me so full of shameful, sexual thoughts that my fingers were shaking as I put my coat on. It was shameful too, so shameful. I mean, what kind of dirty little tart masturbates over the thought of being peeped at?

All but two of the photos went back in their boxes, which I stacked in a cupboard behind my ironing board. The two that stayed out were my favourites, and had been his, Susan being spanked and me taking my panties down. I was going to take both, but changed my mind, feeling bad for Susan. Hers went into the drawer of the telephone table, safe for the time being. Mine I slipped into a magazine.

I left the house, locking up behind me just to make doubly sure nobody could come across the road and find the pictures. Outside, bright afternoon sunshine had made the day tolerably warm, not warm enough to go nude maybe, not like the July day on which the photo had been taken, but warm enough to pop my panties down and take a long, lingering orgasm over what had been done to me.

Instead of going by the lane, I followed the route Aimsworth must have taken to peep at us, through the back of the property. The strip of trees behind the house had become badly overgrown with nettles and brambles, but I picked my way through to where a gate opened in the rusting iron fence. It has seized up long ago and I had to climb over, into a band of scrubby elder and hawthorn less overgrown but liberally dotted with cow pats.

I knew I was trespassing, which added a pleasant touch of naughtiness and vulnerability as I made my way along the hedgerow. The field belonged to one of Elaine's neighbours, a Mr Cudrow, who'd known me from childhood and probably wasn't going to mind now that I was a neighbour too, but, knowing what I was up to, it would have been intensely embarrassing to meet him. Fortunately, I didn't, nor anybody else, as I followed the muddy path to the far side of the field and through a barbed wire fence on to the scrubland above the quarry.

Everything was as I remembered it, the long, rough grass and gnarled bushes of gorse and butcher's broom, the high trees beyond, and the still, open pool beneath the low cliff where the quarrymen had opened up the hillside. I wanted to take my time, and first went to the place Aimsworth would have stood to photograph Kate and myself as we stripped and swam.

It was a Peeping Tom's delight, so much so that I was surprised we'd noticed anyone at all. The gorse bushes grew right up to the lip of the quarry, leaving him looking down from about twenty feet above the water. The little patch of grass where we'd liked to undress and sunbathe or have our picnic afterwards was clearly, blatantly visible. I took out the photo, imagining him watching as I peeled off, as I took down my panties, to send a strong shiver through me.

At the time it had upset me, even though I'd had no idea who he was or how much he'd seen. Now it was different, still a little frightening, but in a safe way, a way that allowed me to fantasise, and to play. First, my panties had to come down, just as they had on that day, and properly, so that my bottom was bare in the sun and I could imagine him watching me.

I climbed around and down to where the shelter of the low cliff made the air warm and still, just as I remembered it. Putting my coat and the magazine on the grass I stepped close to the water's edge, my sense of nostalgia growing with my excitement. It took a moment to get over the feeling that I was just being silly, and then my hands had gone to the button of my jeans. Just undoing them felt exquisitely vulnerable, more so as I peeled my zip down, and more still as I pushed them low, right down to my ankles.

My panties were showing, the sort I like to be spanked in, full cut and plain white cotton, something I'd come to associate with punishment over the years. They were tight too, taut across the back where the tuck of my bottom peeped out under the tail of the old blouse I'd put on to work in, and at the front, a low, soft bulge of white cotton all that concealed my pussy. Just to be like that was a delight, and I put my hands on the back of my head, stretching in the sunlight. I imagined myself being watched, Aimsworth's goggle eyes fixed on my panty seat, hoping I'd take them down, praying I'd take them down.

I did. I had to. My thumbs went into my waistband and I closed my eyes, savouring the sensation as I slowly exposed myself, easing down my panties inch by inch over the swell of my bottom and my pussy mound at the front. I was trembling hard as I came bare, and when I had them right down I held them there, low enough to show everything, bottom and pussy on parade, just as he'd seen me.

Only not quite. I'd gone nude, stark naked, with not a stitch to cover my body, unconsciously showing

24

off to be photographed. It really had to be done, but I hesitated before telling myself that if I could strip naked outdoors at seventeen then I could do it now. There was nobody about anyway, and I couldn't possibly be seen except from the top of the quarry, where I'd just been.

Knowing I was safe didn't calm my nervous excitement as I fumbled open the buttons of my blouse, all the while with my jeans and panties down and very conscious that I was making a deliberate exhibition of myself. My blouse came open, and off, leaving my bottom fully bare, and then my breasts as my bra followed. Now showing everything, I hurried off my shoes and socks, stepped free of my jeans and kicked my panties away.

I was naked, gloriously and completely naked, just as I had been, just as Colonel Aimsworth had seen me. There was no waiting. I had to come and quickly, but nude is one thing, nude and masturbating is quite another. That wasn't going to stop me, but I had to get some privacy. It seemed quite likely that there was somewhere among the bushes I could do it, and I began to explore, feeling ever more vulnerable and ever more agitated as I walked about in the nude. I knew the gate to the lane had been fenced off years ago, and a big notice put up warning of the supposed dangers of the quarry. It was still possible somebody would come, for whatever reason, maybe even somebody who knew that girls had been in the habit of swimming naked there.

It was an alarming thought, and I very nearly ran back to my clothes, but I was too excited to give up. Nowhere among the bushes was any good, all too exposed, or too prickly, or too muddy. One place was OK, just about: the top of the old concrete ramp where it led up from under water. A bank screened it from one side, bushes from the other, but it was open to the pool and right next to the overgrown track leading up to the lane. It was also a good hundred metres from my clothes, but I didn't care, telling myself I'd be quick as I sat down on the warm concrete.

My thighs came wide and I put one trembling hand to my pussy, the other to my breasts. It felt so naughty, naked outdoors as I played with myself, stark naked and thoroughly rude as I imagined being peeped at by a dirty old man. I realised I'd left the photo behind, but it was too late to go back, while I had no trouble at all in holding the image in my mind.

As I teased myself my mind had gone back to how I'd been at seventeen, shy, not at all sure of myself. I hadn't minded stripping off, not in front of Kate, but I'd been desperately embarrassed to discover we'd been seen. It had only been a glimpse, then, but now I knew the truth, and could imagine how I'd have felt if I'd known at the time. I'd have been mortified, so ashamed of myself and so guilty, even blaming myself rather than him.

He'd run away, no doubt feeling guiltier still, but I couldn't help but speculate on what might have happened had he been bolder, perhaps had he somehow known how I felt about it. Maybe he'd even have had the courage to accost us in the lane, to tell us off for being so dirty, despite having a roll of film with our naked bodies well and truly captured. It would have been an incredibly arrogant thing to do, and hypocritical as well. Only I wouldn't have known that. I'd have felt he had every right to tell me off for letting my knickers down in a public place.

Good girls didn't do that sort of thing, and he'd tell me so, with a very clear implication that I ought to be spanked. Maybe he'd even say it, relishing his words as he told us we ought to have our knickers taken down and our naughty bottoms smacked. Not that he'd expect us to submit to anything so undignified. He'd expect a stream of invective, even be ready to have his face slapped. We'd never have done it, not after all those apprehensive visits to his garden for illicit fruit. We'd have run.

Kate would have got clean away and I'd have been caught. It was just the sort of thing that happened to me. Maybe I'd have tripped over or twisted my ankle, because otherwise there was no way he could possibly have outrun me. Whatever happened, I'd have been caught, and in the excitement of getting his hands on me he'd have thrown caution to the wind and decided to do it.

He'd have had me by the ear, telling me to be a good girl and take my medicine, in that same stern, military bark he'd always had. I would not have been good; I'd have been an utter brat, yelling and screaming and making a truly pathetic fuss about it as I fought to stop myself getting the spanking I so obviously deserved. It would do me no good at all. I'd be bundled across his knee, squealing like a stuck pig as my bottom was exposed for punishment.

On the day I'd been in jeans shorts, really quite rude ones, showing a little cheek around the hems. By the time I'd been bent over his lap with my bottom thrust up in the air, I'd have been showing a lot of cheek, plenty enough to spank me on. My shorts would have come down anyway, his hand fumbling under my tummy to get at the popper as I struggled to escape and begged him not to be done bare. My miserable wriggling and my wretched pleas would have only made him all the more determined to get me stripped.

27

I was right on the edge, my finger pressed to my clitoris and one nipple in a firm pinch, my mind focused on the awful, wonderful sensation of having my bottom exposed for spanking. It would have been so easy to come, perhaps as I imagined the intense shame as my panties followed my shorts and I was laid bare, but I wanted more. In my head I was seventeen again, on that hot July day, only not splashing carelessly about with my cousin, but held down over old Colonel Aimsworth's knee with my jeans shorts around my thighs and my panties about to follow.

My shorts would have been down, yes, well down, my hand slapped to make me let go and tugged clear to leave the seat of my panties on show, pink panties, ones he'd just photographed me taking down, and now he was able to do the same for himself. How I'd have fought to keep them up, both hands clutching at my waistband, kicking and screaming, struggling furiously to preserve my final shred of modesty. How I'd have fought, and lost. He'd have slapped my hands again, hard. I'd have let go, and my precious little panties would have been jerked straight down, showing off my bare bottom to the world, to him, his horrid goggle eyes caressing my flesh, examining my pussy where my lips stuck out from between my thighs, plump and hairy and pouted, loitering on my anus as the little brown hole began to wink to the desperate jerking of my body and the agonising shame in my head.

It wouldn't just be his eyes either. He'd have a good grope, making some lame excuse as he fondled my bottom cheeks, enjoying the feel of my flesh and my frenzied sobbing as he explored me. Maybe he'd tell me he needed to see if I'd wiped properly and would hold my cheeks apart to inspect my anus more closely. Maybe he'd ask if I was a virgin and spread my pussy open to see if I still had my hymen. Maybe he'd finger me, chuckling as he amused himself with my twin holes. Definitely he'd spank me, and hard.

He'd show no mercy at all, really laying in, my body contorted into a dozen ludicrous postures as I blubbered my way through it, a hard, purposeful spanking, to punish me, and to make me pliant for his dirty lust. To me it would be punishment, pure and simple, what was done to bad girls, down with their panties and smack, smack, smack, a firm hand applied to a bare, wriggling bottom. Not to him. To him it would be a turn on, making his cock hard in his pants.

By the time my bottom had been well and truly roasted I'd have given in, completely, lying passive across his knees, tear-stained and snotty as I snivelled out my feelings and wondered how it was possible for my pussy to feel so desperately in need. I'd be lost, and he'd take advantage of me, full advantage. First he'd make me go down on him, sucking on his erection, my tear-stained face full of cock, my panties still down behind, my bottom bare and rosy in the hot July sunlight, my cheeks well spread, my bumhole and pussy on show. Then he'd fuck me, on my knees in the long, warm grass, his thumbs peeling my bottom cheeks open to stretch out my anus as he slid his dirty old cock in up my pussy hole.

He have been only the second man to do it, which was a shame. Better still if he'd caught me a few months earlier, spanked me and fucked me, taking my virginity as I knelt for him, red bottomed and sobbing, not understanding why I felt so excited even as my precious hymen pushed in to his cock head. What a way to go, fucked on my knees by a dirty old man who'd just spanked

me. How impossibly shameful, how impossibly nice
. . .

I came, holding the picture in my head, of myself at seventeen, kneeling with my spanked bottom thrust up to Colonel Aimsworth's cock, my hymen pushing in as he thrust, and tearing, my precious virginity gone, taken by a dirty old man, a dirty old bastard, a dirty old bastard who'd had the guts to smack my bottom for me and take me where no other man had dared.

The orgasm was every bit as long and as tight as I'd hoped it would be, and so much better for the slow build-up before letting go. There was a touch of shame as I came down, for being such a slut, stripping off and masturbating over the memory of what a Peeping Tom had done, and what he might have done had circumstances been different and spanking young girls caught skinny dipping been an even remotely acceptable thing to do. Shame, yes, but there was a rueful smile on my face as I hurried back to where I'd left my clothes, to find Pippa Bassington-Smyth sitting cross-legged on the grass, my magazine open in her lap, the picture of me pulling down my panties to swim in her hands.

Two

There have been some seriously embarrassing moments in my life, but finding my teenage cousin looking at a picture of me undressing must be a contender for the worst of all. Not that she could possibly have realised the full implications of what she was looking at, let alone what I'd just done, but I was stark naked at the time.

I did the only thing possible, plunged into the water, which at least explained my nudity, if not the picture. It was freezing, not just cold, but bitterly, numbingly, cold. The spring sunshine might have been warm enough to make the air pleasant, but it had done nothing for the water in the quarry. Once in, I had to stay in, or look a complete idiot. So I splashed about, telling Pippa how marvellous it was and wondering if a heart attack would polish me off before the hypothermia got me.

Pippa watched for a while before delivering her verdict. 'You're nuts, Auntie Penny, it must be so cold!'

'Oh no,' I assured her, 'it's lovely!'

'Well, you won't get me in there! What's with the porno pic?'

She'd picked it up, giving me a split second before she spoke to decide what to say. I couldn't, and dived deep in a frantic effort to avoid the question, also making a fine display of my big, wet bottom as I went under. The water was crystal clear, and as my brain began to go numb I could see the floor of the quarry, flat smooth save for the rusting corpse of some ancient car a good twenty feet below me. I'd never realised it was there, all the times I'd swum in the quarry, any more than I'd realised Colonel Aimsworth had been watching us, any more than Pippa needed to know the truth.

I came up spluttering and gasping for air, now so cold I knew I was going to have to get out. Pippa was still looking at the picture as I swam for the bank, her face set in a cool smile, perhaps amused by my antics, or my embarrassment. I hauled myself out, careful not to make too rude a display of my bottom, despite being absolutely one hundred per cent certain that this time Colonel Aimsworth was not behind me with a camera. 'It's not pornographic,' I said as I found my feet, 'just an old photo I found that reminded me how nice it used to be to come and swim here.'

'In summer, sure,' she answered. 'Do you want your towel?'

She reached out for the pile of my discarded clothing, only of course there was no towel. My first thought was to pretend it had been stolen, but I was only going to be digging myself into a hole. 'I'll forget my own head next,' I said blithely.

'How are you going to get dry?'

'Oh don't worry, I'll soon dry off.'

'You must be freezing, Auntie! Hang on, I'll run back and get one.'

'OK, thanks.'

She was right. I was freezing. My teeth were chattering, my entire body was covered in gooseflesh and my nipples had popped out. I still managed to be

32

pink faced with embarrassment as she disappeared towards the lane at an impressive speed, her long legs kicking up behind her. Alone, I hugged my body, feeling extremely foolish but trying to look on the bright side. For one thing she seemed to take my behaviour completely casually, aside from thinking I was mad. For another there was absolutely no reason she should connect the photo with Colonel Aimsworth. For a third I hadn't been spanked recently, so didn't have to worry about displaying a red bottom or bruises to add to my woes.

Only then did I realise that I'd been altogether too casual about the photograph. Pippa might not connect it to Colonel Aimsworth, but Kate might. At the very least Kate would want to know who had taken it, and there had been nobody else there, only she and I, and Aimsworth up on the cliff, assuming she remembered the incident at all. Pippa was sure to say something, because she obviously thought it was funny and she was close to her mother. Kate would be at the house too, because Pippa was very unlikely to have come up alone. That in turn would mean that Elaine was back, so there was at least a chance of the whole family finding out.

I drew a heavy sigh, imagining the extra spanking I would get the next time I was put across my aunt's lap. Not that it was my fault her neighbour had been a Peeping Tom, but she took a very old-fashioned attitude to such things and would undoubtedly see swimming nude in the quarry as provocative. Besides, I was the only person she was in a position to take it out on. I'd enjoy it, obviously, but, as people who don't like being spanked can never understand, that doesn't make it hurt any less, or reduce the humiliation of having it done.

By the time Pippa got back I was beginning to dry off, and also seriously apprehensive, imagining the family scandal that was about to break. She had not one towel, but two, plain white ones I recognised as Elaine's. She also had an impish grin on her face, making my heart sink as she drew close to where I'd partially concealed myself behind a gorse bush. I had to ask. 'You didn't tell your mum I was stupid enough to forget my towel, did you?' I laughed as I took one.

'Mum's not there,' she answered. 'I came to see Granny, but nobody was in so I came here.'

'How did you get into the house?'

'I know where she keeps the back-door key. She's back now anyway, and so's your mum.'

'You didn't tell them, did you?'

'No way! I just sneaked the towels out. You know what Granny's like.'

I did, only too well, and flushed with relief as I began to dry myself properly. Yet there was still a problem. Pippa evidently didn't feel comfortable enough with Elaine or my mother to tell them, but she did with Kate, and with Susan too. Sooner or later it would come out, and I didn't want to risk upsetting anyone. The sooner the pictures were burnt the better, but I was going to have to take Pippa into my confidence, at least partially, and pray she had the sense to keep a secret.

She was certainly pretty cool, sitting cross-legged on the grass and reading my magazine as she waited for me, moving only occasionally to turn a page or to flick one of her unruly black curls away from an eye. Not for the first time she reminded me of a particularly pretty pixie, with her pale skin and the splash of freckles across her cheeks and turned-up nose, an impression made all the stronger by the mischievous smile she turned to me when she'd finished her article. 'So, Auntie Penny, how come you found a picture of you stripping off in old Colonel Aimsworth's house? Was he a peeper or something or what?'

I'd known she was bright, but I hadn't expected her to figure the situation out that easily. Yet I knew I'd have done the same. After all, I'd admitted I'd found the picture, it had to be recently or why would I have come out to the quarry, and she knew I'd been doing up the Colonel's house. The only other place I could possibly have found it would have been Elaine's, which was highly unlikely. It didn't take Sherlock Holmes to figure out that the picture had been taken from the top of the cliff, either, which was highly suspicious. Suddenly it was no longer my decision. 'I think we need to talk,' I told her.

'OK.'

She said it quite casually, and I'd already begun to dress, so I finished first, allowing myself to get my thoughts in order. I didn't want to lie, but I didn't feel it necessary to go into too much detail either. Certainly there was no point in mentioning the other photos, unless she asked, in which case it was probably best to admit that some existed, perhaps the tamer ones. 'I found the photo in the attic,' I admitted as I knotted my shoelace. 'I'd gone up to take that hideous dish down and I found a pile of old Aimsworth's stuff. The photo was in the first trunk I opened.'

'Just the one?'

Trying to conceal things from her was obviously going to be difficult. 'No. There were others, mostly of your mum and your aunt Susan in the garden. There's nothing too bad. In fact, this is about as rude as they get.'

'Susie always said he was a dirty old bastard.'

'So it seems. Anyway, I'd rather you didn't tell Susan, or your mum. I don't want to upset them.'

'Mum might be upset. Susie would just laugh.'

Not when she saw the one of her across Elaine's knees she wouldn't, I thought, but that was going to be first on the fire. 'Maybe,' I went on, 'but I still think it's best if nothing's said.'

'You're like Granny.'

It took me a moment to answer. 'Me? Like your granny?'

'Sure, what is it she always says, "Least said, soonest mended".'

The voice she'd put on was so like Elaine's I gave an involuntary little start. I had to admit there was some truth in it too, if only because, like Elaine, I prefer not to make a fuss over things, being spanked excepted, which is different. 'I suppose so,' I admitted, 'but, believe me, it's best in this case. Colonel Aimsworth's dead, for one thing, so there's nothing we can do about it.'

'No, he's not. I don't think so, anyway. He went into a home or something.'

'He did? He must be in his nineties even if he is still alive, his eighties anyway, so let's let bygones be bygones. I'd rather you didn't tell your sister either.'

She didn't answer, which I took for assent, and began to walk beside me as I started up the slope towards Mr Cudrow's field. I obviously had to get the photo safely out of the way as quickly as I could, and made for Colonel Aimsworth's house, or rather, *my* house, a concept I was having serious difficulty taking in. Pippa seemed to know the way, and no doubt had explored the local woods and fields just as extensively as I had, only a decade or so later.

It was a bit of a scramble at first, up the slope among dense gorse and broom to the edge of the field, where both of us stopped, instinctively scanning the horizons for Mr Cudrow. I laughed when I realised what she was doing. 'I don't suppose he'd mind.'

'I don't know. He's a miserable old bastard.'

'Cudrow? He's not so bad. I remember he used to let us watch the milking.'

'Yeah, but he's only a few years older than you –'

'Ten, at least.'

'– and he probably fancied you, and Mum.'

'Maybe your mum.'

We'd reached a muddy patch, and had to go in single file for a little way. Neither of us spoke until we'd reached the hedgerow and an easier path.

'I'd have thought it would be Cudrow who was the peeper, not the Colonel.'

'Do you think so? Why?'

'Cudrow's a right perve. The Colonel just seemed to be angry most of the time.'

'Yes, but you were only little. I don't think he's like that at all. So what makes you think Mr Cudrow's a pervert?'

'Just the way he looks. He always dresses in that long brown coat, and sticks his hands in the pockets, likes he's going to flash.'

I had to laugh at the image she was conjuring up, a ridiculous picture, with Mr Cudrow's heavy florid face, which always seemed so serious, and his coat open to show off his cock and balls. It was impossible to take seriously. 'I'm sure he's never done anything of the sort!' I told her, still laughing. 'Who can tell, though? I never suspected Colonel Aimsworth either.'

'Susie did. She says he used to peer in at the living-room window when he was clipping his hedge.'

'She was right. He used to keep a look-out while he was doing his topiary, then go up and sit in the attic window with a camera. I never even guessed, but then I suppose I was a bit innocent. Now I think about it

I remember seeing him out with his telescopic lens, bird watching, supposedly.'

'Amazing what some blokes'll do to get an eyeful.'

'I don't suppose he had much else to do.'

She nodded, a little doubtful. I wasn't. I knew perfectly well the lengths men, and women, can go to for sexual satisfaction. I'd just never thought of Colonel Aimsworth as a Peeping Tom. Yet at Pippa's age I'd been more naïve still, not even fully understanding how men saw me.

I realised I had company before we even reached the trees, from a peal of laughter instantly recognisable as Jade. Sure enough, she was sitting on the low wall Watts had built around his swimming pool, her long brown hair in a pony-tail, her overabundant curves largely hidden beneath a baggy purple jumper. Sophie was with her, also demurely dressed in black slacks and cream-coloured roll-neck. I hurried forwards as they waved, quickly pressed my finger to my lips before either of them could say anything disastrous in front of Pippa, and pressed the point home as I returned their greeting. 'Hi, this is Pippa, my cousin Kate's eldest daughter. Pippa, meet Jade and Sophie.'

'Who've come up to help her redecorate,' Jade responded, 'all the way from London, only to find she wasn't in. Bad girl, Penny.'

'Tomorrow,' I pointed out quickly before either of them could make any humorous remarks about spanking me, 'you were supposed to come up tomorrow.'

'I told you so,' Sophie put in. 'She wouldn't listen, Penny. Where have you been anyway? Why's your hair all wet?'

'I've been swimming,' I admitted.

'Swimming?' Jade queried.

'Yes, there's an old quarry –'

'What's wrong with your pool?' Sophie asked.

'Nothing, I – um,' I stammered, now blushing with confusion and feeling a complete idiot. 'I just wanted to – there are memories, and –'

Pippa had sat down on the wall, saying nothing, but taking it all in, and I could see exactly how Jade's and Sophie's minds were working as they shared a smile. Every choice I could make seemed likely to lead to trouble, and I hastily changed the subject. 'Come in anyway. I'll put the kettle on.'

I unlocked the patio doors and went inside, tossing the magazine casually on to the living-room table as if it was of no particular consequence. Unfortunately, it didn't stop, but slid clean across the polished surface and off the other side, fluttering open as it fell, to deposit the photo of me taking my panties down face up on the floor. Jade had picked it up before I could do anything. 'Very arty,' she remarked, examining it, 'have you two been taking dirty photos then?'

'No! Don't be silly,' I answered her, hastily snatching the print back, my face now burning with blushes. 'It's an old photo, that's all.'

'Cute,' Sophie remarked. 'How old were you?'

'Seventeen,' I admitted, 'but never mind that –'

'Whatever,' Jade answered, at last realising that she was making me uncomfortable. 'We've got paint and stuff in the car. Do us some coffee and we'll fetch it.'

They made for Sophie's car, leaving me alone with Pippa and wondering how I could even begin to explain what the girls had said. She didn't even know I was bisexual, let alone the things Jade and I were into. I had no idea how much she might have guessed, and she was far too bright for me to attempt to fob her off with some flippant explanation, so all I could

39

do was change the subject again as we went into the kitchen. 'Tea or coffee?'

'Coffee please, black, two sugars. Are they your students?'

'Jade and Sophie? No, just friends. They're going to help me decorate.'

'Can I help?'

'Sure, but get into some old clothes first or I'll never hear the end of it from your mum, never mind your gran.'

I began to make coffee, leaving Pippa to wander around the house, and was still doing it when Jade and Sophie returned, lugging a thirty-litre tub of sky-blue emulsion between them and each carrying a bulging B&Q bag. We began to discuss the house as we drank our coffee, walking around at the same time, and I managed to keep the conversation well clear of swimming, Peeping Toms and my own nudity.

We'd carried everything up to the main landing and Jade was trying to persuade me to keep the pink wallpaper when the phone rang. It was Elaine, asking if Pippa was with me and whether I'd be coming over for tea. I explained I had guests and Pippa disappeared across the road. Sophie rounded on me immediately. 'Skinny dipping with your cute little cousin, showing her rude pictures? You are a disgrace, Penny Birch!'

'You might at least have invited us!' Jade added.

'She's not my cousin,' I replied hastily, 'well, only my first cousin once removed, and I was not swimming with her. I was swimming on my own and she turned up out of the blue. It was really embarrassing.'

'Why?' Jade demanded.

'Because – because she's my cousin's daughter for starters, and – and, look, that photo was taken by a

Peeping Tom, the old boy who used to live here, Colonel Aimsworth. He used to peep at me, and Kate, and Susan, who you've met. Kate's Pippa's mum, you see, so –'

'Hang on,' Sophie interrupted, 'so why take the photo down to swim?'

'To have a frig over it, any money!' Jade chimed in.

'OK, yes,' I admitted, blushing scarlet. 'It just got to me. Pippa nearly caught me, too, and she saw the photo, so I had to tell her about Aimsworth. I had no clothes on, and I had to find some sort of excuse, so I jumped in the water, which was freezing –'

'But she wouldn't come in with you?' Jade interrupted. 'Shame.'

'No!' I insisted. 'It wasn't anything like that.'

Both of them laughed and Jade smacked my bottom as she went on. 'Come on, Penny, admit it, you'd love to have her out of her knickers, wouldn't you?'

'No.'

'Why not? I would. She is so sweet –'

'Don't even think about it, Jade Shelton!'

'How can I help it, with those long, long legs and her little round bum at the top? She's an absolute poppet!'

'Jade! She's my cousin!'

'What about it? You've been to bed with Susan.'

'That's different!'

'No, it's not.'

'Yes, it is!'

'No, it's not.'

'Yes – look, never mind that –'

'She's old enough, isn't she?'

'Yes, but that's not the point.'

'She seems fun too,' Sophie added.

'That doesn't make her a slut, so you can both put her right out of your minds, now.'

Jade stuck her tongue out at me, but I ignored her and began to unload the bags of DIY equipment, a pack of plastic trays, a huge sponge and a large paintbrush as she spoke again. 'I reckon I could have her.'

'Leave her alone, and don't be such a trollop,' I warned.

She gave a mocking laugh. 'What are you going to do about it, spank my bottom? Go on then, and make it hard.'

Sophie laughed as Jade stuck her bottom out, a juicy ball of flesh in her tight, low-rise jeans, with the top of a pair of scarlet knickers showing above the waistband. It was too good a target to miss, and I smacked the paintbrush down hard across her bulging cheeks. She gave a little purr and wiggled, making Sophie laugh again. I put the brush down. 'Right, you asked for this, Jade.'

Before she could react I'd grabbed her, with her bottom in my lap and my fingers pushed deep in under her armpits. Her squeal as I began to tickle her would have put a piglet to shame, and she immediately began to struggle. I clung on, tickling all the harder, even as she collapsed on the floor, already fighting for breath, so that her voice came in between broken giggles and urgent gasps. 'No, Penny – please – stop it – stop it, you bitch! I – I won't touch her – I swear – Sophie, help! Sophie!'

Sophie was laughing herself, at Jade, who was squirming on the floor with me straddling her back. Her whole body was shaking with helpless convulsions, and her muscles twitching beneath me. I knew she'd probably have an accident if I tickled long and hard enough, but I was enjoying myself far too much to stop. Sure enough, after just a few seconds more, her laughter broke to a fresh squeal, a gasp of self-disgust as it happened, and a stream of invective as she wet herself over the floor. 'You bitch! You bitch! You bitch!'

I just laughed, still tickling to make sure she couldn't stop it, even as I felt her wet patch where I was straddled across her bum. Sophie was in hysterics, Jade thumping the floor with her fists and kicking her feet, utterly unable to stop herself as the pee squirted into her panties with every jerk of her muscles. She'd done lots, soaking right in, and when I finally took mercy on her and stood up the whole seat of her jeans was dark with piddle and a pool of it had begun to spread out beneath her.

She was so far gone she couldn't even get up, but lay gasping in the slowly expanding puddle she'd made on the wooden blocks of the floor. I took the big paintbrush and gave her a couple of hard smacks on her wet bottom, but she barely reacted, close to indifferent to the pain of spanking, for all her complete inability to control her bladder when she was tickled.

'That'll teach you,' I told her as she finally managed to pull herself to her feet.

'Look what you made me do!' she protested, looking down at the long kite-shaped wet patch over her pussy and down the front of her jeans, also the pool on the floor.

'You asked for that,' I pointed out. 'Now clean up, we've got work to do.'

'Me clean up!' she retorted. 'You clean it up, you made me do it!'

'You wet yourself, you clean it up!'

'It's your floor.'

'It's your pee. Now do it, or I'll make you lick it up, Dumplings.'

'You and who else, Miss Muffet? Getting a bit big for your boots, aren't you?'

'Sophie?' I asked, knowing full well I couldn't do it on my own, any more than she could do me.

'Leave me out of this,' Sophie said, laughing. 'You're both going to need to change anyway, so toss a coin and the loser gets to mop up with her panties.'

Both of us turned to her.

'Oh yes?' Jade asked. 'Well, as it happens, mine are already wet, and I think Penny's may be a bit too, but I know whose aren't.'

'Hey, come on, I –' Sophie began, starting to back away, but too late.

We both grabbed her, all three of us laughing almost too hard to do anything as we struggled in the middle of the floor, Jade trying to hold Sophie so I could undo her trousers. She was complaining bitterly as they came loose, and down, but I was beginning to get turned on and was not letting her off. Soon Jade had her pinned over the table and I'd got her slacks off and her shoes with them, leaving her in socks and a pair of red polka-dot panties below the waist.

'Right, down they come,' I told her, and hauled.

The look of consternation on her face as she came bare was delicious, and I took them right off before delivering a couple of firm swats to her distinctly cheeky bottom. 'And that's for making rude suggestions about my cousin. Now mop up Jade's puddle, or do we have to make you lick it?'

'I'll mop,' she answered, grudgingly but with more than a hint of arousal.

She got down on the floor, crawling along with her bare bottom wobbling behind her as she mopped up Jade's piddle with her own panties. They were soaking in no time, and she had to wring them out twice before the mess had been reduced to a sticky smear. I took over, fetching some water to finish off properly.

Jade had taken off her wet things and stuck them in the washing machine along with Sophie's, leaving both of them bare from the waist down, with the tuck of their cheeks showing underneath their jumpers.

'You can work like that,' I joked, 'now, come on, enough messing about.'

They looked at me, then looked at each other, but I'd already picked up the tub of emulsion and a bag, ignoring them as I went to the nearest of the bare rooms. I had no idea what Billy Watts and his wife had used it for, but it seemed to have required fuschia-pink wallpaper, which I began to scrape away as Jade and Sophie followed me in. There was a three-pack of scrapers, but they didn't take them, instead coming to stand behind me with their arms folded. Jade spoke first. 'I said she was getting a bit big for her boots. If we have to work bottomless, Penny, so do you.'

'Yes,' I answered, 'I know that's fair, but what if somebody came over from –'

'Then you can put your clothes back on and go to answer the door,' Sophie pointed out.

I hesitated, really quite keen to work with my bottom bare, a gentle humiliation that would let my feelings slowly build up. On the other hand, if I had to go bare, far better to be made to do it.

'Just get on with it, sluts,' I ordered, and turned back to my scraping.

They both grabbed me immediately, hauling me out into the middle of the room. I was laughing so hard I couldn't have struggled if I'd wanted to, but also squeaking in pain as Jade twisted my arms into the small of my back. Sophie ducked down, her hands went to my fly and my jeans were open, then down. I shut my eyes as she hooked her thumbs into the waistband of my panties, relishing my sense of helplessness as they were taken slowly down, and I

45

was bare. She took it all off, leaving me just as they were, with my bare bottom peeping out from beneath the tail of my blouse and my pussy showing at the front. But Jade didn't let go, speaking instead. 'I think she needs a lesson.'

'A serious lesson,' Sophie agreed.

'Come on, we haven't time!' I protested.

'A good spanking would be a start,' Jade suggested, ignoring me completely. 'On your knees!'

She twisted my wrists, forcing me down into a kneeling position, then on to all fours, still protesting feebly as they took me around the waist and pulled up my blouse to get my bottom properly bare. Sophie began to spank me, telling me off as she slapped my bottom, and Jade had twisted around to reach for the bag of bits and pieces.

'Not the paintbrush, Jade, please!' I begged.

'You did me with it!' she answered. 'Here's yours, Sophie.'

'Hey, no! Ow! Jade, that hurts – Sophie – ow!'

They both began to spank me, the big paintbrushes smacking down on the meat of my bottom, a cheek apiece, and far more painful than I'd have expected. I was kicking immediately, and wriggling in their grip, but it only encouraged them, and they laughed as they punished me. It was noisy too, with the smacks of the brushes on my flesh and my squeals, which I couldn't keep down. The window was open, too, and, while nobody could see in, anyone who came out into the road was likely to hear.

'Stop it, please – seriously!' I begged the moment they paused. 'Somebody will hear. My mother's in the house across the road!'

'Good!' Jade answered, but Sophie stopped.

'Stop it, Jade,' she said, 'after all, it wouldn't be funny for her mum to know we spank her.'

'No, it wouldn't!' I agreed with feeling.

'Ah, doesn't baby Penny want Mummy to know she gets her botty smacked?' Jade teased. 'I'd love to do that to you, panties down in front of your whole family, your mum, and your aunt, and Pippa. How you'd hate it!'

She'd stopped spanking me, but she was still using the brush on my bum, stroking it up and down over my cheeks and between. It tickled crazily, making me wriggle and kick my legs even if, unlike her, I knew I could control my bladder. What she was saying was far, far worse, and she knew it, her voice thick with glee as she continued. 'Oh, yes, Penny, wouldn't that be fun? Spanked bare in front of dear Mummy and Aunt Elaine? Wouldn't they be shocked to know what their demure little daughter gets up to? And Pippa, oh yes, and Pippa, wouldn't she look shocked as I peeled down your big white panties and began to spank your naughty little botty?'

As she finished she brought the brush down hard across my bottom, making me gasp and jerk. Sophie was in hysterics, and they very nearly lost their grip as I lurched frantically to the side. I managed to crawl a little way, even as both of them again frantically belaboured my bottom with their paintbrushes, but it was no good. Sophie caught me by the hair, twisting it hard in her grip, and I was squealing and kicking in my pain as they laid in.

Eventually they stopped, after maybe fifty or sixty hard smacks, leaving me hot bottomed and panting, my skin prickly with sweat and my pussy swollen and juicy. They held on, too, Jade once again pretending to paint my bottom as Sophie slipped a hand under my chest to feel my nipples. 'Stiff as corks, I thought so,' she confirmed. 'What a slut!'

'What shall we do with her now?' Jade asked. 'Spank her some more? Take turns sitting on her face?'

I didn't reply, now too turned on to want it to stop and thinking of the exquisite humiliation of having to lie on my back while they took turns to put their bottoms in my face, making me kiss their bumholes before licking them to ecstasy. The paintbrush no longer tickled either, but was making me want to push my bottom up for more, until Sophie spoke again. 'I say we push her face in the paint.'

'Sophie, no!'

'Sounds good to me!' Jade agreed. 'Hold her down while I get the lid off.'

I started to struggle as Jade let go of me. 'No, please, you two, not the paint – not the paint – anything else, but –'

'OK,' Jade cut in, 'you get the paint or ... or we take you out and give you an enema with the garden hose.'

'Don't be silly, the lawn's in full view of my aunt's house!'

'You want the paint then?'

'No!'

'The enema?'

'No!'

'Well, make up your mind, Penny!'

'I – I don't –'

'Shut up,' Sophie ordered. 'You get the paint. Now for your next choice. Your face goes in it or we paint your bum blue, like one of those baboons.'

I could just picture it, and was immediately begging for mercy. 'No, please, Sophie, Jade, you can't do that! Just sit on my face or something, I'll lick nicely, I promise!'

'No, I want to see you get the paint. Now choose, or you get both.'

'No! Come on, please. I'll never get it out of my hair, and it's probably not safe –'

'Don't be such a baby.' Jade laughed. 'It's only emulsion.'

'Non-toxic,' Sophie added. 'It says so, right here.'

As they spoke she'd pulled the big tub close, so it was right in front of me as Sophie pointed out the details on the label.

'Yes, but –' I began.

'No buts,' Jade answered me, as Sophie tightened her grip in my hair. 'What's it to be, in your face or on your bum? Choose now, ten – nine – eight –'

'OK, OK, stop. Do my bum, if you really have to do it at all!'

'We do,' Jade said. 'Hold her, Sophie.'

Sophie grabbed my wrist again, twisting it up into the small of my back, still with her handful of hair held tight. It hurt, filling me with helplessness and self-pity as Jade pulled the tub of paint behind me and tugged the lid off. I'd begun to pout as I twisted my head around, expecting to see her dipping the brush she'd just spanked me with. She wasn't, she was retrieving my discarded panties. 'What are you doing?' I demanded.

'You'll see,' she said, chuckling.

I thought the panties were going in my mouth to shut me up, but my feet were lifted a little and she quickly stretched them over my toes, then began to pull them up my legs. If she got paint on them they were going to be completely ruined, and I began to wriggle again. 'Jade, no – what are you doing? You'll ruin my panties!'

'Stop whining, Penny!'

'Yes, but, Jade –'

'No buts, we said. I want to tip some paint down your panties, like those clowns with the big trousers do. Hold her pouch out, Sophie.'

'Jade, no, come on –'

It was too late, almost, she'd got my panties back up, all the way, and was lifting the big tub. I began to panic, kicking my feet and thumping my fists on the floor in helpless frustration as Sophie let go of my hair to pull out the waistband of my panties. 'Not down my panties, please! No!' I wailed, one last pathetic effort as Jade began to tip the tub of paint.

I gasped as the cold slimy mess hit my flesh, right down the seat of my panties to splash over my bottom, quickly filling my pouch and squashing in up my bum crease and over my pussy. It felt absolutely disgusting, and I'd screwed up my face as it was done to me, a good couple of litres poured into my panty seat before Jade had to stop because she was laughing too hard to hold the tub. My waistband snapped back against my flesh as Sophie let go of my waistband and I was done, my bottom and pussy thoroughly soiled, my panties ruined.

'Yuck!' Sophie said with glee. 'That looks so gross, Penny!'

It certainly felt gross, as if I'd soiled myself, a big wet bulge hanging heavy in my panty pouch and squeezing from around my leg holes. They didn't let go, either, but held me in place, giggling as my panties began to sag with the weight then peeled slowly down off my bottom. Finally Jade spoke. 'Wicked! That is so messy! Now her face, come on.'

'Hey, no!' I protested. 'You said my bottom or my face! You said –'

'Shut up,' Jade responded, as she pulled the tub around again, 'we're only having a bit of fun with you.'

'Yes, but not in my face, Jade, please! It's just not fair! Ow! Sophie, that hurts!'

'Doesn't she whine?' Sophie remarked, twisting my arm tighter still behind me. 'Not her panties, not her

50

face, not this, not that – she still hasn't learnt her lesson, has she?'

As she spoke she went back to spanking me, slapping the brush on to my soggy bottom, where my ruined panties were now halfway down my slippery blue cheeks. I began to struggle again, as Jade took me by the hair and began to press my head down towards the slick blue surface of the paint, in genuine panic, but unable to break their grip and still babbling entreaties. 'No, please! Stop – not my face! Not my face! Stop!'

She stopped, my head held just a fraction of an inch above the paint, my nose already in it, just, so that as I pulled back a single drip remained hanging from the tip. Sophie stopped spanking and my panties fell down behind, to slop paint down my legs and on the floor and leave my bare blue bottom stuck naked in the air.

'She does look like a baboon, doesn't she?' Jade commented. 'And I'm sure they have blue faces too, so here goes, three – two – one –'

'No!' I protested, and I could hear the whining note in my own voice. 'You said my bottom *or* my face. This isn't fair!'

'What do you think, Sophie?' Jade asked.

I was waiting for Sophie to speak, completely off guard, and suddenly she pushed down, thrusting my face into the tub so fast I was caught with my mouth open, and it filled with paint. She held me down, as I blew bubbles in the paint and drummed my feet on the floor in pathetic remonstrance, and Sophie began to spank me once again. Both were laughing wildly, and more wildly still as my struggles took on a desperate edge.

She pulled me up, and I was gasping for air, my whole face plastered, my hair soiled, filthy and dripping. Sophie's spanking grew harder and I was struggling to breathe, spitting paint and blowing blue-coloured snot from my nose. Down went my head again, ducked deep in the paint until my nose hit the bottom, the level well up the back of my head. Still Sophie spanked me, both of them in fits of laughter as they amused themselves with my body, smacking my bottom and repeatedly dunking my head, until at last I was pulled gasping from the tub and held up by my ruined hair.

'OK,' Jade said happily, 'almost done. Now open your legs a bit more and stick your bum up. Come on, or your face goes back in.'

I gave a single, feeble nod and obeyed the order, setting my knees as wide apart as my filthy panties would allow and pushing up my bottom. My cheeks came apart with a disgusting sucking noise, making Sophie giggle as she pressed the paintbrush handle to my bumhole, and pushed. I gasped, clenching my cheeks, but my ring was slippery with paint, and there was nothing I could do. My anus spread easily to the thick handle, which went up with a soft squelch as Jade gave a crow of delight.

Sophie began to bugger me with it, easing the handle in and out and laughing at the squashy, sucking noises coming from my bumhole. Her hand slipped in under my tummy to find my sex and I was being masturbated, her fingers rubbing in the slimy mess of paint and pussy juice. I knew immediately I was going to come, my humiliation complete as I was brought to orgasm in such a sorry state.

Jade's fingers groped for my blouse, to rip it wide and jerk up my bra, leaving my tits hanging down to be fondled and soiled as I was buggered and masturbated. My head was immersed again, pushed well in under the paint and immediately pulled back. Sophie

52

began to bugger me harder, my gaping, slippery ring taking the brush with ease, the handle a rigid pole inside me. I began to squirm on it, as my bottom cheeks began to tighten and I thought of how I'd look, filthy with paint, my face and bum as blue as any baboon's, my sodden panties pulled well down, a brush stuffed up my bottom hole, my face dripping, my hair ruined, but not fighting, not resentful, not even all that sorry for myself any more, just utterly, deliciously humiliated as my soiled body was brought to orgasm under my girlfriend's fingers.

Just as I was starting to come, my head was thrust deep in the paint, one last time, blowing bubbles under the surface as my breath blew out in silent climax, long and hard and wonderful, with Jade groping at my breasts, my fat blue bottom wriggling on the brush handle and Sophie's hand doing wonderful things to my filthy cunt.

Three

Our little game with the paint served to reinforce a serious problem with living in what I still thought of as Colonel Aimsworth's house. I was quite simply too close to what had become the social focus for my entire family. Aunt Elaine wasn't too bad, because she at least had some inkling of what I was like and shared the secret of my sessions across her lap.

Kate and Susan I didn't mind at all, but Jeremy regarded me as a thoroughly respectable and highly qualified geneticist, maybe even a bit of a blue-stocking. I wanted it to stay that way. It was still hard not to think of Pippa and Jemima as little girls, even though they weren't, and as such the sort of things I got up to with Jade, Sophie and other playmates were utterly inappropriate for them to know about.

Worst of all was my mother. She had always looked on me with an air of faint exasperation that would be fully justified should she discover the true details of my sex life. It was bad enough that I'd yet to be offered a Chair or make any major break-throughs in my field, without her discovering that I liked to be spanked and humiliated for fun, never mind the rest.

It had been bad enough at my old flat, but at least I'd been able to have Jade and Sophie to stay without attracting undue comment. Now, it was going to be impossible to come and go without being seen, by Elaine if not the others, and even for her the idea of my living in a lesbian *menage à trois* would be a bit much. Possibly it would only mean harder punishment spankings, which both excited and scared me, but that was small consolation.

After three whole hours spent cleaning me up, we'd been too exhausted to do any decorating, or even to sort out the room they'd dealt with me in and the bathroom. Both were an utter mess, which was sure to raise eyebrows, and the Sunday morning, which should have been spent decorating, had to be given over to a major rescue operation. I didn't even get my weekly spanking, what with my cousins being in the house and Jade and Sophie staying until merely midnight, although I felt I needed it more than ever.

I had at least managed to suggest to Aunt Elaine that I might come over for 'supper' on the Tuesday, but when I finally went to bed on the Sunday night I was feeling far from satisfied. Aside from the difficulties with my sex life, I felt uncomfortable in the big, almost entirely empty house. It wasn't mine. All my memories of it brought back the ghost of Colonel Aimsworth, while immediate reality belonged strongly to the Watts. Both were powerful influences completely at odds with my own tastes.

What I needed was a complete clean out, and as I sat in the comfortably familiar surroundings of my room in the department on the Monday morning I decided that the first thing to do was to lay to rest the ghost of Colonel Aimsworth. Not that he was dead, Aunt Elaine having confirmed that he had merely gone to live in Worthing, but he definitely haunted the place. I would burn both the photographs and everything else.

Unfortunately, back at the house I simply couldn't bring myself to do it. The picture of me by the pool might be evidence that I'd been peeped at, but it was too nostalgic for me to be consigned to the flames. I told myself I'd keep it and burn the rest, then that I'd just keep the ones with me in them, then that I needed a cooling-off period before making the final decision.

The rest was easier, or should have been. I'd had Jade and Sophie help me get the boxes down from the attic, and everything was piled in one of the empty rooms. There was a lot, and it seemed sensible to go through it just in case there was anything of real value. I brought a chair in and began to sort, intent on making two piles, a little one for valuable and a big one for the pyre.

Two hours later I was still seated, reading in rapt fascination, letters from the Colonel, then Captain and later Major Lionel Aimsworth, as he fought his way from Normandy to the Rhine, where he'd received what he described as a 'Blighty wound' and returned to England. The impression was anything but what I'd expected, of a very brave, very compassionate man with a genuine belief in the principles he was fighting for.

It left me close to tears, feeling very small and very selfish. Here was a man who had risked his life again and again to help preserve exactly the sort of freedoms I so enjoyed, and I had thought of him only as that most contemptible of things, a dirty old man. I shouldn't have been humiliated by him watching me and photographing me, I should have been deeply honoured. Even if he had taken my virginity the way I had imagined at the very peak of my fantasy, it would have been a tiny, unimaginably trivial sacrifice beside what he had already sacrificed for me.

By the time I eventually went to bed I felt deeply humbled, so much so that I wanted to beg forgiveness for even thinking about him the way I had. It was so selfish, so comprehensively petty, precious, prissy to mind him looking at my body. In the circumstances I should have offered, happy to strip and pose, to let him take pictures of me in any rude position that took his fancy, and to feel privileged to be doing it. I should have sucked his cock and felt honoured to take a mouthful of his spunk and swallow it down. I should have let him fuck me, on my knees to allow him to appreciate my open bottom as he enjoyed himself with me. I should have let him bugger me, and come on his cock, with my bumhole in contraction to suck his come out up my bottom before I licked him clean in grovelling gratitude.

I went to bed nude, knowing exactly what I was going to do. With the covers kicked down I spread my thighs, teasing my pussy and tits as I imagined how I'd have offered myself to him. First would have come an afternoon of photography, perhaps with me doing a striptease out of my school uniform, exhibiting my panties with my pleated skirt lifted as I bent down before peeling them down inch by inch to show him my bottom. Any rude pose and I'd have adopted it, showing off with nothing on under my school skirt, or in just my panties, socks and my school tie. I'd have shown my tits, my bottom, my pussy, spread my lips to show him my hymen, put my finger in my bumhole and sucked it, masturbated in front of him, and that would have been just the start.

My fingers were working hard on my clitoris and I was at the edge of orgasm, imagining him watching me as I did it in my dishevelled school uniform, but I stopped, not wanting to rush my orgasm. Flipping myself over, I stuck up my bottom, thinking of how much he'd have enjoyed my rude rear view and wondering if he'd have liked to spank me. The answer was almost certainly yes, and of course I'd have let him. I'd have been privileged to let him, over his knee as he lifted my school skirt and took down my panties to get me bare, as he fondled my bottom and held my cheeks open to inspect my bumhole and my virgin pussy, as he spanked me hard and told me how naughty I was and what a bad girl I'd been to pose nude for him.

This time there was no holding it. I snatched back, to push a spit-wet finger in up my bottom hole, imagining it was his, pushed up inside me to get me ready for a buggering after I'd been spanked. Once he's got me open, I'd get down on my knees, as I was, with a finger up my bum as I sucked his cock hard for my own buggering. I'd stay down too, with my cheeks held wide to show off my dirty, slippery little hole. He'd push his cock up, deep in, making me gasp and grunt.

He'd bugger me, long and slow, and me still with my red tartan school skirt lifted and my big white panties pulled down, to frame my nude bottom and the straining hole of my anus with his cock shaft pushed deep up. I'd frig off for him, rubbing my wet little cunt until I came, making my bumhole contract on his erect penis, milking his spunk into me. Or maybe not. Maybe my orgasm would take him right to the edge. He'd pull his cock out and pop it in my mouth, telling me what a good girl I was as I sucked down the taste of my own bumhole and a mouthful of thick, salty, slimy spunk.

As I came I had to bite the pillow to stop myself from screaming so loudly I'd not only have disturbed my aunt across the road, but the Colonel himself down in Worthing.

On the Tuesday morning I felt a great deal better, and had a whole new outlook on things. I wasn't going to burn anything. I had no right to. Colonel Aimsworth was still alive and as such had a right to his own property, and the only acceptable course of action for me was to return it, even if he had left it behind when he moved. Besides, I didn't even know what circumstances he'd moved out in, whether he had family or not, what his health had been like, or anything.

The photographs were another matter. For the ones showing me, it had to be my own choice, and despite my vivid fantasy of the night before I couldn't really see myself turning up at the residential home in Worthing and handing him several dozen large and glossy prints of me in various states of undress. He wasn't likely to thank me anyway, as the staff might well find out and would certainly give him a hard time. With those showing Kate, Susan and others, I simply had no right to show them to anybody and decided to burn them at some convenient time.

My day was busy, with three lectures, a tutorial and a seminar, so much so that I managed to put my overdue spanking to the back of my mind for most of the day. Just occasionally it would surface, just a slight, apprehensive niggle, for something I needed, was due to have, but which I could never, ever take casually. I'd driven in, so had to fight my way out of town on the 329, which built up a fair head of tension by the time I got back. It still felt as if I was taking an unspeakable liberty in using Colonel Aimsworth's garage to park my car, so that as I walked across to Elaine's house I was feeling both frustrated and guilty, ideal conditions for a smacked bottom.

The first thing that hit me as I came in was the smell of cooking, another thing that had become closely associated with my weekly punishment. My feelings had begun to soften straight away; my need for punishment became immediate, and I was hoping there would be no delay as we walked back into the kitchen. 'Are you ready for me?' I asked.

'Just a minute, dear,' she answered, taking up an oven glove. 'Pop your clothes off and I'll be with you in just a minute.'

'My clothes?' I queried. 'Everything?'

'Everything,' she said firmly. 'It's a nice evening, and I thought I'd deal with you outside.'

I nodded and began to disrobe, my sense of chagrin rising as my clothes came off, with the thought of having to go naked while she remained fully dressed, naked outdoors and to be punished. As I'd come straight over, I was still in my work clothes, smarter than usual because I'd been at the seminar, a skirt suit of blue grey wool over a crisp blouse, a slip, stay-up stockings, sensible shoes and a pair of spanking panties, which I wore as a matter of course.

Having to go fully bare really brought home the change in my status, from smart, professional woman to naked, naughty girl. I did it slowly too, letting my feelings build as I folded each article carefully on one of the kitchen chairs, and hesitating only when I was down to just my panties. Elaine hadn't even looked round, dropping dumplings into the pot of delicious-smelling stew she was making for dinner.

'Should – should I take my panties off?' I queried.

'Of course,' she answered. 'Naked is naked. And do say "knickers", Penny. You're not an American.'

'Sorry – it's just that you know I like them taken down for me –'

'No nonsense, Penny. Knickers off and into the garden with you, this instant.'

There was a rueful expression on my face as my thumbs went into my waistband, but I did as I was told, taking my panties right off and folding them with my other clothes before stepping out into the kitchen garden. It was fairly warm, but not as warm as it might have been, not when I was stark naked. My nipples had popped out almost immediately, and I was feeling both embarrassed and resentful as I went to sit down on the bench were I was usually given my *al fresco* spankings.

Nobody could see me, the high walls of crumbling red brick and the house itself sheltering me from all possible observers, yet I felt intensely vulnerable as I waited, shielding my pussy and tits and wishing Elaine would hurry up and get me done. By the time she did come out I was in a fine state, feeling absolutely tiny and thoroughly ashamed of myself.

I was put straight over her knee, tipped up with my bottom high and my legs sprawled apart, one on the bench and one on the ground. She'd begun to spank me before I had a chance to get into a less indecent position, and as the stinging slaps began to rain down it was too late. My legs were kicking, in a dozen ludicrous postures until she trapped one with an irritable tut, holding me spread with one leg caught and one still waving wildly in the air.

She had put a hand on the small of my back, holding me down, and I stayed like that as I was punished, my pain rising to every smack and constantly aware of my spread rear view. Stark naked in the garden, helpless, deeply humiliated and with my bottom aglow, wriggling pathetically across my aunt's knee with my heat rising with my feelings, and it wasn't long before the full strength of my arousal kicked in. I began to buck and squirm, sticking my bottom up for more, but it was quicker than usual and she wasn't satisfied.

Her grip tightened; she pushed me down, pressing my bare open pussy to her leg, and as the spanking grew sterner still I was rubbing on her, every slap jamming my clitoris to the tweed of her skirt and sending a jolt of ecstasy to my head. There was nothing I could do. I was going to come on my aunt's leg, a realisation that pushed my humiliation up tenfold, to make the impossible indignity a certainty. My mouth came wide as I tried to speak, to tell her what was about to happen, but all that came out was a wet, bubbling noise and it was too late.

I was there, coming on my aunt's leg as she spanked me, my emotions so raw that there was as much self-pity as ecstasy in my full-blooded scream as I let go. She didn't even slow down, never mind stop, spanking me with every ounce of her strength as my bottom spread and clenched in the violent contractions of an orgasm that simply would not stop. I nearly fainted, it was so strong, and when she finally paused for breath I was left hanging limp across her knees, my legs still cocked wide, the air cool on my burning bottom cheeks and overheated pussy, my juice dribbling down and so copious I could smell my own excitement even in the open air. She gave a disapproving tut when I finally managed to rise, and I saw that I'd spread my cream all over her smart tweed skirt, sending hot blushes to my face. 'Sorry,' I managed, my voice barely audible. 'I – I didn't mean to do that.'

'I think we both understand,' she answered. 'Now run and get washed for dinner. I had better change.'

'Sorry,' I repeated.

I'd begun to cry, and was wiping my tears as I followed her back inside, feeling deeply ashamed of myself, while the spanking had been a great deal less cathartic than usual, despite the undeniable pleasure. Fortunately, Elaine being Elaine, she wasn't about to make an issue of it. I was still snivelling a bit as I washed and dressed, and couldn't help repeating my apology when she came back downstairs, now in a thick cream-coloured towelling bathrobe.

'I understand,' she told me again, 'it's simply what some women need.'

'Yes, but –'

'Sh! It happened, so it happened. Now be a dear and take the stew out for me, would you?'

'Yes, of course. Only – only, would you mind spa – doing me again, perhaps after dinner?'

She simply nodded, understanding if a trifle stern, and I went about serving dinner. It was simple but delicious, a beef stew with dumplings in it and served with excellent wholemeal bread liberally spread with butter. As usual when I ate with her, it was going to mean an extra hour in the university gym, although the physical and emotional exertion of my spankings did a lot to compensate.

As I served up, she went about opening a bottle of wine, a strong Australian Cabernet that went beautifully with the stew and did a great deal to help me relax. She'd said she would spank me again afterwards, and I knew I didn't have to ask twice. The less said the better was always her rule. Instead, I quickly brought the conversation around to the Colonel, choosing my words carefully to avoid any implication that his behaviour might not have been entirely respectable. 'You mentioned that Colonel Aimsworth went to live in Worthing. Do you know the address?'

'I have it somewhere. Why do you ask?'

'I found some of his things in the attic, old correspondence mainly, from the war. The letters are very personal, so it seems only fair to at least ask him if he'd like them back.'

'That's very kind, I'm sure. I don't suppose he had a chance to take them, not after his fall.'

'His fall?'

'Yes. That was why he moved out. Don't you remember?'

'No. That was before I moved back down.'

'Of course. It was a tragedy, of course, but it might have been a great deal worse. He slipped and fell, down at the quarry, and it was only luck the Harrison girls happened to be about. He'd broken his leg, and I don't suppose he could have got help, not at his age.'

I nodded sagely. It made perfect sense. With the trunk full of evidence of his career as a Peeping Tom in the attic he'd have been unable to ask anyone to go up, and it would easily have been overlooked in the stress and confusion. I was trying to remember who the Harrison girls were as Elaine continued. 'I dare say you'll be very welcome. He always remembered you fondly.'

No doubt he had, particularly my bottom and tits, along with Kate's, Susan's and the Harrisons', assuming they were the young women who'd belonged to the Post Office. If so, they were blonde, so alike they might have been twins, and what used to be called 'pleasingly plump', with plenty for Colonel Aimsworth to feast his eyes on, so much so, presumably, that he'd gone over the lip of the quarry.

I got my second spanking, a pleasantly intimate one laid across Aunt Elaine's lap in her bedroom with my work skirt turned up and my panties well down. Unlike the earlier one, it was slow and very much a pure punishment, leaving me with a lovely glowing bottom and a full sense of catharsis, also intensely aroused. Elaine seemed particularly pleased, and I came within an ace of offering to go down on my knees for her, but held back at the last instant. When she punished me she was completely in control, never betraying her own feelings, and I was sure my offer might break the precious spell that had built up between us over so long.

Having brought myself to orgasm in the privacy of the spare room, I went home for the best night's sleep since moving into Colonel Aimsworth's house. In the morning I felt refreshed and ready to tackle the day, even coping with a sick colleague's botany practical, a subject on which I knew almost as little as the students. My mood lasted for the rest of the week, striking a minor glitch only when Elaine told me that we'd have to postpone my next session until the Tuesday again as Kate and her family were coming up for Sunday lunch and were expected to stay until late.

I'd got all the Colonel's letters ready, along with every other paper he might conceivably consider of importance, and had been planning to go down to Worthing on the Saturday and return on Sunday morning in time for roast lunch and punishment. I was invited anyway, and could have made it, but when Jade rang to suggest going out on the Saturday I decided to postpone my trip.

Knowing Jade, the evening was likely to be anything but tame. We were going to Whispers, her favourite Soho lesbian bar, with a back room in which just about anything could happen. I went into London ready for trouble, expecting at the very least to be stripped, tied and whipped by some of her butch friends, maybe a lot worse. What I got was precisely nothing. Whispers turned out to be closed for refurbishment, and Sugar Babes, the noisy and very definitely ersatz dyke bar we went to instead, was no substitute at all. There was nobody there we knew, and when I playfully pulled Jade over my knee we were politely but pointedly asked to leave.

We'd both been hoping somebody would take control of us, and despite going head to tail back at her flat for a loving and mutual orgasm, it was no substitute for the rough treatment we'd been hoping for. The only advantage was that I felt relatively fresh in the morning, so much so that I deliberately got off the train at Goring and walked back to the village to improve my appetite for lunch.

It was a pretty route, and one I knew well, through the little town and along the Thames before striking up the hill along a maze of lanes and overgrown footpaths. In my younger days I'd used a rather different route, following the railway and running helter-skelter across the great arched Brunel bridge to get over the river. Seeing it put a smile on my face, and it didn't seem to have changed at all.

I'd meant to do some more decorating in the afternoon, as I'd barely started, but what with convivial company and a generous supply of wine I was in no mood for it and readily accepted the idea of walking across to Yatten with Kate and her family. Only when Elaine said she wouldn't be coming did I realise I might have stayed and spent a few minutes across her knee instead, but by then it was too late, adding to my underlying frustration as we set off.

The route lay down the lane past the quarry, up on to higher ground and across a landscape of open, chalky fields, woods and copses. Having already walked three miles before lunch, I'd soon fallen back, along with Pippa, who seemed keen on my company. Not that our conversation was in any way out of the ordinary, with her questioning me about the rival merits of different universities, at least until we reached the point where the lane opened out to a large field of rough pasture.

Our path moved off to the right, along a hedgerow, and Kate, Jeremy and Jemima were just passing out of sight around a bend a couple of hundred metres distant. I began to mount the stile, but Pippa had stopped at the field gate and spoke as she climbed up on to the lowest rung. 'Look, there's Cudrow. What do you suppose he's up to?'

'Working, I imagine,' I answered, steadying myself on the signpost and craning my neck to see where she was looking.

Mr Cudrow was at the bottom of the field, unrolling a spool of bright-orange wire. A box was attached to his Landrover, from which a long double line of tracks led back to the gate on which Pippa was standing.

'He's putting up an electric fence,' I said, 'for whatever he's got in that box, probably a bull.'

'Oh, no,' she replied, her voice a little high, perhaps from the claret she'd been drinking at lunch, 'that's not what he's doing at all. He's going to catch some girls and pen them in so he can come here at night and do unspeakable things to them!'

I was more than a little taken aback, but I didn't want to seem shocked or prissy and let my laughter come out at the idea, even though it was uncomfortably close to some of my less orthodox fantasies. My cheeks were a little hot as I imagined myself penned naked in the field, perhaps hobbled so I had to crawl along like a farm animal, perhaps with some hairy Neanderthal type let into the field once a week to cover us . . . me.

The thought had come into my head unbidden, of not just myself naked and crawling as I waited to be fucked by whatever oversexed male was let loose in the enclosure, but Pippa too, with her slim body quite naked and her pussy showing behind, ready for fucking. I put the thought firmly aside, my cheeks now bright red with embarrassment for my own dirty mind, but fortunately she seemed oblivious, watching Mr Cudrow in the distance as she went on. 'I bet he would, you know, if he could. Give any guy a chance and he'll try to collect himself a harem.'

'Do you think so?' I asked, wondering where her ideas were coming from.

'I know so,' she answered. 'Every guy wants as many girls as he can get. It's only natural, 'cause that way he gets to have the most babies, so his behaviour gets passed on.'

'It's not that simple. Do you know about game theory?'

'I've read *The Selfish Gene*.'

'That sets out the theory in populist terms, but –'

I began to explain as we walked on, glad to have changed the subject. Talking sex with Pippa felt extremely awkward, not that I'd normally have minded, but she seemed to have an uncomfortable ability to spark my fantasies. Explaining the intricacies of natural selection was a welcome chance to concentrate on something else, but it was impossible to keep my mind entirely free of inappropriate thoughts. She was just so clever, and so full of life, her brain as agile as her body was lithe, taking in everything I was saying and asking more intelligent questions than many of my students did, even as she balanced her way along the trunk of a fallen tree, giggling in carefree, girlish pleasure.

She was like a pixie of sorts, full of mischief, never still, alert to every sight and sound, every nuance of what I was saying. I wondered if men found her intimidating, so pretty and so pert, yet so intelligent, with her Argyl scholarship and string of A* results. It was a problem I'd had at her age, and later, really until I'd learnt to show my submissive side. I'd also assumed, for some years, that the lack of male attention was because I was small, shy and, frankly, didn't have much to show in the way of tits. Nor did Pippa, but it was hard to imagine her as socially inept as I'd been. As we reached the ridge she asked a question I wouldn't have dared put to Aunt Elaine at Pippa's age, or even to my tutor at college. 'So how do you account for homosexuality then? Surely that can't be passed on?'

'Not at all,' I managed, quickly focusing on the question rather than the implications of Pippa and homosexuality. 'It might seem that way, and within the confines of our modern social system it often does function that way, but that's a consequence of human society, which has advanced far too quickly for natural selection to keep up. There are a dozen factors involved, and as many theories, but consider, for instance, a primitive society in which a proportion of males have strong loyalty bonds reinforced by sexual activity. They will make excellent warriors without disturbing the social fabric of their community, while it only takes a few males to keep the females pregnant. Thus the social system, and the underlying genetic system, will tend to be propagated and it doesn't matter if a proportion of the males fail to breed, as you only really need one and the characteristics can be passed down the female line in any case.'

'And lesbianism?'

I had to swallow before I could answer. Pippa and lesbianism was worse than Pippa and homosexuality in general. 'Again, the potential failure to reproduce applies only in our modern society. Through the vast majority of human history women will have had little or no choice when it comes to taking a male partner, and therefore reproducing. You have to remember that the sort of social structures we're familiar with

70

are very, very recent, while our species has been around for at least a million years and the evolutionary basis that dictates our sexual behaviour is probably older by far. Any trend that stimulates female arousal is likely to lead to increased reproduction in the long term, sex between females included, and after ten million years that's not going to change in a couple of generations.'

'So it's normal?'

'Yes. By definition. If you have a biological imperative towards a given act it cannot be considered abnormal. Immoral in terms of a given society or religion, maybe, but these are simply human constructs, essentially impermanent and therefore trivial in comparison to the urge to reproduce, even when indirect.'

'OK,' she answered, 'so what if I feel the urge to toss off old Cudrow's bull? That can't help me reproduce.'

I nearly swallowed my tongue. We'd reached the ridge, where the thick blackthorn hedge briefly gave way to a section of wooden fencing. She'd climbed up, and was standing on the rail with her legs pressed to the one above, looking back down the big field. As I joined her, I saw that Mr Cudrow had completed his electric fence, enclosing part of the field by the brook at the bottom, and was now leading a great red bull from the box. He, the bull, was a real monster, huge and shaggy, with a mane like a bison, also a pair of heavy, pendulous testicles dangling between his hind legs and a long pink penis half-extended from its sheath, grotesque yet undeniably and intensely virile. To think of Pippa taking the awful thing in her hand was enough to set my stomach tight. 'Yes it can,' I managed eventually, when she turned an enquiring glance my way. 'It's all to do with responding to

71

visual cues, and he may not be human, but he's certainly male, olfactory cues too, because male pheromones don't vary all that much between different mammals.'

To my intense relief she simply nodded and jumped down from the fence, walking on to where the path came out over the ridge, opening out to above a great spread of fields and woods, with the downs rising in the distance and the spire of Yatten church showing among spring green oaks and beeches in the valley. I paused to admire the view, drinking in the soft beauty of the English countryside and trying to ignore my stiff nipples, fluttering stomach and the uncomfortably wet sensation in my panties.

The others were completely out of sight, and the long white line of the footpath led down to where a stile gave access to the woods, quite empty. Pippa came to stand next to me and took my arm, a perfectly normal gesture of cousinly affection that sent a sharp tingle the length of my spine. A picture came into my head from nowhere, of how it would be to go down among the soft grass by the hedgerow and have her wrap her long, coltish legs around my head as we licked each other to ecstasy. I forced it away, telling myself I was just drunk and horny, that it meant nothing, but the touch of her arm on mine was electric and I knew it was a lie. She spoke again as we started down the hill, casual, playful, but full of wicked humour. 'I bet Cudrow would love to watch, the dirty old bastard. Can't you just see it?'

In answer I managed what was supposed to be a mildly disapproving laugh but came out as a choking sound. I could see it all too easily, her squatting down with her jeans tight over her neat little bottom and the huge bull cock in her hand as Mr Cudrow watched, leering, his own cock standing proud from his dirty overalls as I sucked him, Pippa's top up to show her little tits, her hand down her panties, teasing her pussy . . .

I shook my head, desperately trying to clear the awful thought away and thinking what an utter slut she'd think me if she knew that what she was saying turned me on. To her it was just a joke, a dirty joke, but a joke, nothing to get horny about. That sort of reaction was reserved for dirty old men like Cudrow, while she, no doubt, appreciated the sort of clean-cut young men of her own age or a little older.

She wasn't like me, she couldn't be; it was just my own dirty mind twisting her words. Her generation wasn't like that, they were free, not repressed, not hung up on the perverted echoes of Victorian morality. Her fantasies would no doubt focus on film stars, maybe footballers or other sportsmen, nice, clean, socially acceptable choices, not like mine, not bare-bottom spanking, not being used and humiliated by butch dykes and dirty old men, and certainly not fellating Mr Cudrow while he watched her toss off his bull.

'We'd better hurry,' I suggested. 'The others will be wondering what's become of us.'

'So?' she answered. 'I'd rather talk to you, and watch Cudrow and his bull. Shall we go down and talk to him?'

'I'm not sure –'

'Come on, you said he doesn't mind us.'

'Yes, but –'

'Come on.'

She began to steer me off the path, as mercurial as ever as she headed back the way we'd just come. I wasn't at all sure Mr Cudrow would appreciate our presence in his field, but Pippa quickly climbed the fence and I had little choice but to follow. She took

73

my arm again as soon as I'd joined her, full of life as she pointed out a brimstone butterfly to me and pretended to chase it, pulling me after her at a run.

Mr Cudrow looked around at the sound of Pippa's laughter long before we reached him, but finished closing the door of his box before turning towards us. For a moment he didn't seem to recognise us, but even when he did his scowl softened only marginally. I struggled for something to say as we came within earshot. 'That's a very fine bull, Mr Cudrow. Is he yours?'

'He's mine,' he answered. 'Mind the fence. It's on.'

'Yes, of course. Thank you.'

'May I stroke him?' Pippa asked.

'He's not a pet,' Mr Cudrow answered, his voice surly if a fraction short of openly hostile.

'Oh go on,' Pippa urged. 'He's beautiful.'

'He's beautiful and he's dangerous,' Mr Cudrow answered as he twisted the switch on the electric fence to off. 'Now, if you don't mind, I've work to do and, when you leave my field, use the gate. That's what it's for.'

'I'm terribly sorry,' I answered, deeply embarrassed by my *faux pas*.

Not Pippa. 'Lighten up, we only climbed the fence,' she answered him. 'Come on, Penny.'

She turned away again, and I followed, walking towards the distant gate. He ignored us, climbing into his Landrover and manoeuvring it through a gap before getting out again to close it off and reset the switch. By the time he reached us we were halfway up the field, but he didn't overtake, instead driving very slowly twenty metres or so behind, which was distinctly disconcerting.

'What's he doing?' Pippa asked. 'Herding us out, or ogling our bums?'

'Both, probably,' I answered, none too pleased with his behaviour.

'A miserable old bastard as well as a dirty one,' Pippa answered me. 'Come on.'

She broke into a run, too fast for me to keep up, with her long legs flashing behind her. I followed, and so did Mr Cudrow, only a little faster than before. Pippa had reached the gate in no time, but she didn't open it, climbing over instead with deliberate insolence. She stayed on the far side too, her feet on the middle rung and her thighs pressed to the top two, balancing with her hands free. It took me an instant to realise what she was doing, even as she stuck her tongue out and jerked up her top, flashing her pair of tiny, up-turned tits at Cudrow, just for an instant as she called out, 'Hey, Cudrow, is this what you want, you dirty old bastard!'

I was almost at the gate, but Mr Cudrow was right behind me and I had no choice but to scramble over as fast as I possibly could and follow Pippa down the lane, cursing her for her behaviour as I ran. Inevitably Mr Cudrow would come and complain, and inevitably I would be the one who got the blame, as I'd been with her. I'd probably have to go round with her and apologise, a ridiculous thing to have to do at my age, while Elaine was sure to use it as an excuse to take her hairbrush to my bottom.

Only there was a more immediate problem. There was a good quarter of a mile of lane between high hedges before we could reach the road, and Mr Cudrow was sure to catch up with us. I had no idea what I could say, other than stammering apologies, and as I heard the clang of the gate behind me I was earnestly wishing I could take my hairbrush to Pippa's bottom.

There was only one thing to do. Feeling extremely foolish, I nipped over the quarry gate and ducked

75

down behind the hedge, where Pippa was already crouched, bright eyed and giggling. I made to speak, but shut up and squatted down to make myself as small as possible as I caught the growl of Mr Cudrow's Landrover beyond the hedge.

For one long, awful moment I waited for him to stop, with all the thoughts of what I could say to defend Pippa, and myself, running through my head. He drove on, and as the noise of his engine faded slowly a slow wave of relief spread over me, only to fade as I came to accept that I'd only delayed the inevitable. 'Pippa, really, that was not sensible,' I said when I was absolutely certain Mr Cudrow had gone. 'He'll come and complain, and what am I supposed to say?'

'No way,' she said, laughing, 'not his sort, 'cause now he knows if he sees me he might just get a flash of tit, but not if he gives me a hard time.'

'I only hope you're right,' I answered, far from convinced. 'Just don't do it again, please.'

'I won't,' she assured me. 'I don't need to, not more than once. That's how to deal with peepers, play them at their own game.'

I blew out my breath, less than happy about the situation but unable to be cross with her. If anything, I wished that I'd had the courage to do the same at her age. I'd done far, far worse things since, so had no right to lecture her either. We walked back to my new house along the upper field, keeping a careful watch for Mr Cudrow all the way. Pippa was plainly enjoying herself, full of energy and completely oblivious to the fact that we were supposed to be meeting up with the rest of her family at the Pot in Yatten.

The walk had sobered me up considerably, not to mention being chased by a farmer, and I decided to drive over. By the time we got there the others were in the garden, having tea and cake. I was wondering if I should admit to what had happened, as it seemed sure to come out anyway, but it was so much easier not to, and just take the line of least resistance. Pippa didn't seem to care, immediately pinching a spoonful of her sister's chocolate cake before running into the pub to order some for herself.

I drove them all back, by which time Jeremy was beginning to get flustered because there was something wrong with his mobile and he was expecting a crucial call from a work colleague. After just a few minutes back at the house he had persuaded Kate that they should leave, and all four of them piled into his Jaguar, Pippa after kissing me goodbye with every bit as much affection as her mother.

Suddenly I found myself alone with Elaine, and no reason I shouldn't be spanked. It was an abrupt change, and a stark contrast, from a happy family farewell at the end of a day together to sudden apprehension and an atmosphere of erotic charge. No question was even asked. No sooner had we watched Jeremy's car out of sight and closed the front door than Elaine had sat down on a convenient chair with a meaningful pat to her lap. I undid my fly and went straight over her knee, closing my eyes to savour my exposure as my jeans were taken down and my panties followed.

She began to spank me, very purposefully, still without a word spoken, laying firm pats across my bottom cheeks, gradually harder, until I'd begun to gasp and wriggle my feet. Her arm went around my waist and her spanking grew harder still, to set me kicking in my panties as she found her rhythm. I was warming quickly, my arousal already close to the surface after so much to keep erotic thoughts in my head.

There was no full-blown spanking tantrum, my pain giving way to a hot glow too quickly, just a few gentle tears at the thought of how much harder the next one would be once Mr Cudrow had made his complaint. Not that I tried to cut it short, staying meekly down across her knee with my bottom pushed up to the smacks until she felt I'd had enough and released me. I kissed her quickly, said thank you and ran upstairs still holding my lowered clothes. On the bed my top came up and my hands went to my pussy, face up for once as I began to masturbate.

My head was full of rude thoughts, and intense shame, building quickly as I realised what I wanted to come over . . . what I needed to come over . . . who I needed to come over – Pippa. I bit my lip, determined not to do it, to focus on something more acceptable instead, anything, maybe the spanking which had left my bottom so warm and my pussy so wet, or my lovely voluptuous girlfriend and going head to tail with her the night before, even being put through my paces by Colonel Aimsworth, or Mr Cudrow, or his monstrous bull, anything, but not my teenage cousin.

Jade was best, so naughty, so warm, so cuddly, her soft curves always good to turn me on, her uninhibited playfulness just what I needed to really let go, to be unashamedly dirty, side by side as some tough, hard-faced dyke beat us together, dunking my face in paint as Sophie spanked me, spreading her bottom in my face and demanding I lick her anus as she had the night before. It was all good. It was all wonderful, but her words came back to me, what she'd said when I'd told her Pippa was out of bounds – 'What about it? You've been to bed with Susan.'

It was true. I had been to bed with Susan. I'd done some extremely rude things with Susan. How old had she been the time we got drunk and I ended up with her New Age hippie boyfriend's cock up my bottom hole? A little older than Pippa, but not by much, only a little more than the difference between Susan and me. That did nothing to take the edge off my guilt, and for the second time I turned my thoughts away, now with my eyes tight shut and my finger working in my crease, teasing myself until I got it right and could come.

Colonel Aimsworth was better, and what he might have done to me had he been a little bolder. Maybe he'd have threatened to tell my mother I'd been bathing in the nude, or maybe he'd have managed to take some pictures of me being naughty with myself, as I had more than once down at the quarry, just like the other day, as I'd sat naked and masturbating, just yards from where Pippa was sitting. She'd seen me naked too, and when the weather was warmer perhaps she'd come in the water, without a stitch to cover her slender, pixie body.

I stopped, swallowed, and cursed softly. My muscles had already begun to contract, my orgasm just moments away, and it would have been so easy to just slip over the edge, imagining how Pippa would look in the nude as I came, with her lovely round bottom quite bare on top of her long, long legs and her little perky breasts too, so tempting, so alive.

Again I stopped at the edge, but it was no good. I had to do it, and hope that if I gave in to my feelings they would have less power afterwards. Sometimes it worked, with my very darkest desires, things it felt good to think about but which I could never do, dark, dangerous things, or in this case, making love to my beautiful young cousin. A fresh surge of guilt and shame caught me as I began to masturbate again, now abandoned to my own dirty needs.

She was just so lovely, so desirable, so full of life, so full of mischief and so cute. I could picture her on

Mr Cudrow's gate, vividly, the way she'd stood, her thighs pressed to the upper bars for balance, her little bottom pushed out, round and inviting in her jeans, her top pulled high to show her pert, braless breasts, her nipples stiff with excitement. They had been too, very stiff, and sticking up a little, like a pair of tiny cocks, and far more suckable.

I felt a shiver run through me, the prelude to an orgasm I knew would be rich with shame, and I made one final effort to turn my thoughts away from Pippa, and to concentrate on what a disgrace I was. It was true, beyond question, and it was a shame Elaine hadn't taken the hairbrush to me. I certainly deserved it, and hard, even the cane or a heavy strap, to leave me blubbering and penitent. No question, if a girl had ever deserved spanking, it was me, very hard, with an implement and preferably in public, to really punish me, to thrash me until I was a blubbering tear-stained, contrite mess.

That was what I deserved, perhaps to be made to strip naked and go outside, kneeling nude on the garden bench with a sheet of paper stuck to the wall above me proclaiming my crime. I'd wait, for ages, maybe until I'd peed down my legs to add to my awful shame. Elaine would come out, stern, silent, holding a school cane for my bottom, and see the wet on my skin, the puddle beneath the bench ...

My back had arched tight, my bottom cheeks had begun to squeeze, my pussy and anus were both in urgent spasm as I started to come, holding the image in my head of how I'd be, kneeling naked and contrite, my bottom pushed out for the cane, Elaine standing behind me, and Pippa too, to watch my punishment, to bring home my shame to me, cold and angry with me for daring to become aroused over her, maybe even to apply the cane to my bottom as I

80

writhed and squirmed in my own pee puddle, out of my mind with embarrassment and shame even before she slashed the cane down on my naked bottom.

I really screamed, too far gone to stop myself, bucking on the bed as I snatched and slapped at my pussy, bringing myself to peak after peak after peak with the image of my body prepared naked for Pippa's cane, my bottom stuck out, fat and pink and round, my cheeks spread to expose my anus and my sopping cunt, and her, fully dressed, so perfect, so delicate, so beautiful, and so wicked as she smacked the cane down again and again on my big, wobbling bum cheeks.

Four

I got all the guilt I'd expected for coming over Pippa, and more, so much that I was forced to try and rationalise my feelings. Again and again I told myself that my reaction was illogical, that she was old enough, and certainly wise enough, to do as she pleased, and that in any case I hadn't actually done anything, only imagined what I'd like to have done, or rather, to have done to me.

After a fashion it worked, at least in that I managed to deflect my bad feelings into a need for punishment, which, after all, was what I'd come over anyway. Not that she was likely to be caning me, as no doubt the idea would have horrified her. For all her sassy attitude, flashing Mr Cudrow was one thing, applying a cane to another woman's bare bottom quite another.

She was right about Mr Cudrow. He never did come round to complain, despite my qualms, with my apprehension fading only slowly as I came back each evening from work expecting to find a curt note from Aunt Elaine on my doormat. Nothing had been said about my Tuesday spanking, but I went over anyway, unsure if she'd want to do it again after the Sunday but also half-expecting her to have saved up Mr Cudrow's complaint so that she could take it out on me with a hairbrush.

Nothing happened, to my relief, although she dealt with me anyway, after supper, across her lap on the living-room sofa with my skirt up and my panties hanging off one ankle because she'd made me take them down in front of her. I felt a lot better for it, but afterwards, back in Colonel Aimsworth's house, I couldn't resist bending down over the bed in the nude and imagining another dose of Pippa's cane as I masturbated.

I was determined that nothing would prevent me from going down to Worthing the following weekend. That meant driving into the university first and leaving after an extra tutorial I'd promised to one of my third-year students, but I was away by half-past ten, with all the bits and pieces I'd salvaged from his attic in the boot of my car. I had just about everything, because I'd found it very difficult to dismiss any of it as out and out rubbish. After all, he'd had a reason for storing it in the first place, so even the old newspapers presumably had sentimental value.

A phone call to the residential home, called simply Beach View, had confirmed that he was still alive and fully able to receive visitors, although the tone of voice of the woman I'd spoken too had held a strong implication that I was being a nuisance. Remembering what she'd been like triggered an amusing if ridiculous little fantasy as I drove down through Wokingham, helping to pass the journey. It involved the place he was in being run by a crew of vindictive and bad-tempered viragos with a deep resentment of visitors.

I would walk in, entirely unsuspecting, and ask for Colonel Aimsworth. The woman I'd spoken to would conduct me into a large communal living room, with the entire population of the home seated either in front of the TV or entertaining themselves in one way or another. I'd be told I had five minutes, and not surprisingly I would protest, pointing out that I hadn't driven fifty-odd miles to leave almost as soon as I'd arrived.

Her answer would be anything but polite, making her opinion of me quite plain. I'd react with outrage, very much up on my high horse as I pointed out that she was to all intents and purposes a servant to an old friend of my family and should behave as such. She'd wait until I'd finished, her face growing increasingly red, and then deal with me the way I should be dealt with.

Over I'd go, tumbled across her lap in front of Colonel Aimsworth and a dozen or so other old gentlemen, ladies too, all delighted at the sudden and amusing break in the monotony of their existence as I was given a thorough spanking in front of them. Inevitably my jeans and panties would be pulled down and I'd be done bare, with my cheeky bottom bouncing and spreading to show off my pussy and anus as I begged and blubbered my way through punishment.

It was hardly going to happen, but it was nice to think about, and by the time I got to Farnham I was feeling distinctly naughty and wondering if my trip might not be worth at least a little mischief. I felt good about what I was doing, and generally friendly towards the Colonel, but it was impossible not to suffer at least some pique at his behaviour, simply at an instinctive level. Also, he was sure to realise that, if I'd taken all the ordinary papers down from the attic, then I would have seen the extraordinary ones too. Possibly it would be fun to tease him, not nastily, but in a way that would leave him wondering what I knew and what my reaction was. As Pippa had shown, although in rather different circumstances, one of the best reactions to a Peeping Tom is to make him think he's going to get what he so loves to look at, only to snatch it away at the last instant.

The feeling stayed with me for the rest of the journey, which was somewhat convoluted and far from fast. It was well after lunch before I reached the south coast, and another half-hour before I'd managed to identify Beach View, a process made harder by it being impossible to see the beach from it, while the road name Elaine had given me proved to be little more than a back alley. Otherwise, it was much as I'd imagined it, a big, white painted villa with a double bay window beside the front door looking in on a communal living room that might very well have been the one I'd been imagining myself being spanked in.

After I'd rung the bell three times, the woman who answered the door was much as I'd imagined her as well, except that she didn't immediately tip me over her knee and smack my bottom. Instead, she told me that the Colonel's room was number twelve on the first floor and that I could go up if I wanted to. I went, leaving his stuff in the car so that I could at least let him wonder if I was about to drop off a trunk containing several dozen semi-pornographic photographs.

Number twelve proved to be at the end of a corridor, and as I knocked he answered immediately, the same gruff voice I remembered from years before, only now asking me in instead of threatening to take a stick to me for pinching his plums. I pushed the door open, knowing that he had to be well into his eighties and probably wasn't in the best of health, only to be pleasantly surprised.

He was sitting in a chair, holding a copy of *Horse and Hound*, which he had looked up from as I came in. I recognised him immediately, the same short white hair and aggressively clipped moustache, the same no-nonsense bearing, possibly even the same expensive yet threadbare tweeds, deeper lines in his face, his skin slacker than I remembered, but with the same fire in his eyes. His mind hadn't gone either, with a lapse of only a second or two before he recognised me. 'Good heavens, if it isn't little Penny!'

I managed an awkward smile, already feeling as if I'd been taken back to when I was seventeen. 'Yes, didn't they say I was coming?'

'They said a woman was coming down to see me,' he replied, 'but I didn't expect you. You haven't changed a bit!'

'A little, I'm sure,' I managed, blushing as his eyes travelled down my body with no effort whatsoever to conceal his interest.

'Not in the least,' he insisted. 'So what brings you all the way here? Care for a spot?'

'Thank you, no. I'm driving – on second thoughts, I'm certainly going to stay and look round the town, at least, so I will.'

'Sensible girl,' he said, reaching for a cabinet beside his neatly made bed. 'Malt or Cognac?'

'Cognac, please.'

'Usually the ladies' choice. I'll have a malt myself.'

I waited as he poured spirit into a pair of small tumblers then began to explain after taking my first sip of the brandy. 'The thing is, I now live in your house – I mean to say, I bought the house you used to live in, opposite my aunt's.'

'Oh yes? Did that fellow Watts sell up then?'

'I think he had to. There was some scandal.'

'I remember, saw it in the paper. Dirty bugger.'

He chuckled as he spoke and I found myself colouring up again, a reaction very different to the easy control of the young woman over an old man I'd imagined. The Colonel gave a thoughtful nod and took a sip of his whisky as I went on.

'Anyway, I went up to your attic, and found a pile of boxes. I'm afraid I looked in them, not that I read anything, of course, but there were letters, and I wondered if you might like them? I've brought everything down, it's in my car.'

'In the attic?' he remarked, and seemed to reflect. 'Yes, I did leave one or two things in the attic, didn't I? There's not a great deal of space in a place like this.'

'Oh. I was going to burn them, but I thought –'

'No, absolutely, you did the right thing, very kind of you too. Old letters, you say?'

'Yes, from France and Germany, during the war, I think.'

'I have memories enough, I think,' he sighed, 'but yes, maybe – maybe it would be nice to glance over them, one last time as it were.'

His voice was so wistful that I found myself with a lump in throat, unable to speak, and could only spread my hands in a pathetic attempt at sympathy. He took another swallow of whisky, and turned to look out of the window, apparently lost in thought for a long while. I stayed as I was, imaging what he would be thinking, bitter-sweet memories of times long past, places now changed out of all recognition, comrades gone for fifty years or more, but when he turned to me he chuckled. 'Yes, I'm very grateful, my dear, very grateful indeed. Boxes of letters, you say? Nothing else?'

'All sorts of things,' I replied, caught off-guard and blushing again for the meaningful twinkle in his eyes. 'Documents, various books –'

'Photographs?'

There was no point in denying it, because as he said the word my cheeks had flared from warm to incandescent, and my face and neck must have been scarlet. He chuckled, openly amused at my discomfort, and I found myself letting out what resentment was left inside me. 'Yes there were, actually, quite rude photographs, of myself, and of Kate and Susan James, mostly.'

Again he chuckled. 'Yes, those photos, shame I had to leave them behind, really, but, as you can imagine, it would have been a bit tricky to ask anyone to bring the trunk down. Nosy buggers would be sure to look inside.'

'You don't seem very concerned now?'

'I'm not, frankly. You're not family, for one thing, and, for another, if you were going to be prissy about it, you'd hardly have come down to see me, would you? Or were you planning to give me a lecture on my behaviour?'

For a moment there was some of the steel I remembered so well in his voice, and I hastened to reassure him. 'No, absolutely not – I mean – that is –'

He'd got me completely tongue-tied, but before I could work out what I could possible say that wouldn't sound like an accusation and yet didn't actually approve what he'd done he went on. 'It's too late, anyway. There's no good lecturing a chap my age, is there?'

'Well, no,' I agreed, sensing that while he realised he could hardly expect my approval he would appreciate my forgiveness.

I wasn't quite ready to give it, but he was right. It would have been ridiculous to start haranguing him, especially after my two little sessions with my fingers between my thighs, the memory of which was now keeping the blush hot on my face as he went on reflectively. 'I suppose there are some vindictive sods who'd still want to try and prosecute. Worse than the bloody Nazis, some of them. I mean to say, what's wrong with taking a few photos of pretty girls, eh?'

'Nothing, I suppose,' I answered cautiously, 'although it is usually considered polite to ask.'

'And what would you have said, or Kate and Susan James?'

'No, of course.'

'There we are then. Don't begrudge an old man his hobby, any more than I begrudge you all that fruit you used to pinch when you were a tiddler.'

'You chased me with a stick!'

'Ah, but I didn't hit you with it, did I?'

'No, true.'

'Just good sport, that's all, no harm done.'

'You did haul me over to my aunt's by the ear.'

He chuckled. 'So I did, so I did, and what, are you saying you didn't deserve it? Besides, no real harm done, any more than by taking a few photos.'

'I suppose so, yes . . . I was thinking, as it goes, that after what you'd been through, in Normandy and so on, making a fuss over you taking a few pictures of me would have been rather petty.'

'That's true,' he replied, after a thoughtful pause, 'or at least, you'd like to think it would be. I don't suppose most people see it that way. Put yourself up as target practice for a load of bloodthirsty Huns and you get a pat on the back and a handful of gongs, that or your name carved up on some bloody monument. Pinch a pair of frillies off a washing line and suddenly none of that counts for anything any more.'

He chuckled and shook his head, leaving me wondering if he'd chosen his example at random or if there was more too it. If a Peeping Tom, why not a panty thief as well?

I could hardly ask, and he'd turned to stare out of the window again, doubtless thinking of daring raids, although whether on German positions or some unfortunate girl's washing line was a moot point. It seemed the ideal moment to fetch his things from the car, so I drained my glass and stood up. 'I'll get your things. Will they mind if I prop the door open while I bring them up?'

'Yes, but don't let that stop you.'

I smiled at his response and made my way quickly downstairs. My emotions felt a little raw, and a little muddled, happy enough, but with an underlying feeling that by not making more of a fuss about his dirty hobby I was betraying my fellow women. In comparison to what he'd done for his country it was trivial, and yet, as he so rightly said, a lot of people would have been ready to give far more weight to his bad behaviour than his good.

As I carried his boxes up the stairs I determined that I would not behave like that, and would forgive, if not forget, because I knew full well that later on, alone in my bed, I would bring myself to ecstasy one more time over what had happened, and what might have happened. Hopefully that would not only bring my long day to a satisfying conclusion, but also, having met him again, would allow me to make the house my own.

By the time all the boxes were stacked in his room I was puffing slightly and had twice had words with the irascible nurse, who seemed inclined to object to whatever I did. Not that I was too worried, thinking back to my earlier fantasy, and I was smiling to myself as I returned to the Colonel's room after going back down to shut the door. He was seated as before, a second tumbler of whisky in his hand.

'All done,' I announced.

'You didn't bring the trunk then?' he queried. 'The one with the photographs in it?'

'No,' I admitted. 'I didn't think it was a very good idea, and really –'

'You're probably right,' he broke in before I could point out that I could hardly hand him over sneakily taken photos of my cousins. 'Shame though, there were some rather good ones, as I recall. Look, may I take you out to dinner? It seems the least I can do.'

'I wouldn't want to impose on you –'

'Impose on me? Good heavens, how often do you think I get a chance to take a pretty girl out to dinner these days?'

'Well, I was planning on staying over in Worthing, so I don't mind if I eat here with you.'

'Here!? I tell you, I wouldn't inflict the muck they serve here on a pig. It's worse than school food, and that's saying something.'

'I'm sure it would be fine.'

'Oh no it wouldn't and, besides, it's no guests in the dining room except for family. I'm taking you out to dinner, and that's that. Seven o'clock sharp, and now if you don't mind, I'm a little late for my nap.'

I left, dismissed.

I had several hours to kill, and spent them booking myself in at a hotel and wandering along the sea front, watching the waves and thinking. It had been a strange experience, bringing my sexual needs sharply into contrast with my morals. Part of me still wanted to feel disgust for the Colonel, but that only served to provoke self-rebuke. How uncharitable, after all, to condemn a lonely old man who plainly saw what he had done as nothing more than a game. Not only that, but the urge to disapprove was definitely hypocrisy, because the idea of being peeped at, and worse, turned me on.

92

By the time I was ready to go back to Beach View I had made a decision. It was the right thing to do, not by society's standards, but by my own, the choice that I knew in my heart was right, although I was unlikely to be admitting it to anybody, perhaps not even to Jade. There was a spring in my step as I walked back, but I was also biting my lip.

I wasn't quite ready for what being taken out to dinner by the Colonel involved. For all his clear mind and brisk manner, he was a very old man, and I had to help him down the stairs and out to a waiting cab, with him leaning heavily on my shoulder. I kept expecting a hand to stray to my bottom, my tummy giving a little jump each time he moved his arm, but he was either disinclined or too busy staying upright.

He took me to a seafood bar in one of the big hotels on the front, very quiet and very respectable. Mentally, at least, he needed no help at all, and behaved in a way I suppose was typical of his generation, taking over completely. He even ordered for me, with considerable generosity, oysters with vintage Champagne and a delicious salad of lobster with big croutons washed down with a Grand Cru Chablis, the price of which made me blink.

By then I was feeling mellow and grateful, also a little drunk, too drunk to refuse the huge slice of Black Forest gateau he insisted on ordering for me, telling me I needed fattening up, which I found myself taking as a compliment. A glass of sweet white wine went with my cake, followed by black coffee with a double measure of cognac in it, drunk while he sipped a glass of malt whisky.

If getting him out of Beach View had been tricky, getting him back was ten times worse. I'd drunk most of the wine, but he was still tipsy, and far from steady, also a great deal heavier than me. His hands had also begun to wander, making it all the harder for him to stand up properly as he attempted to grope my bottom, for which he apologised, after a fashion, as soon as I'd got him back in his chair and sat down myself, more than a little out of breath.

'Sorry, my dear,' he began, 'I hope I haven't offended you, but – but, by God, I may as well say it, you're a fine girl, always were, and, well, I don't suppose I'll have the chance again, not in this life. There, I've done it, and I've said it. Now you can slap my face and tell me what you think of me.'

He looked up at me, completely forthright, and I could no more have slapped him than my own father. Instead I shrugged, smiling rather weakly, knowing what I had decided to do, but having real difficulty getting the words out. Yet they came, halting, little more than a broken whisper, my face flaring red as I said them. 'Do you – do you like my bottom? Because if – I mean, maybe – maybe I thought, perhaps you might like a – just before I go – a little peep?'

I didn't wait for a reply, because my nerve was close to breaking, but stood up, my hands trembling violently as I turned my back and began to undo my jeans. He made a little choking sound, no more, but my eyes were closed as the button of my fly came open under my fingers. I peeled down my zip, slowly, and pushed out my bottom, making it round and cheeky for him to enjoy as I told myself I was doing it as an act of generosity, of charity, and not just because behaving like a little tart turns me on so much.

With my fly wide open I stuck my thumbs into my waistband. One last moment of hesitation as I wondered what the hell I thought I was doing taking down my trousers to show an elderly Peeping Tom my bum, and they were coming down. I had to wriggle a bit to get them off my hips, drawing another little choking gasp from him, and I did it again, on purpose, as rude and insolent as any striptease artist.

'White,' he said softly as my panties began to come on show. 'You often used to wear white ones, that or pink.'

I nodded, unable to speak for my choking mix of arousal and shame as I slid my jeans lower, showing off my taut panty seat, my cheeks bulging in the tight white cotton. With my jeans held down I stayed as I was, showing off the full width of my bottom with just my panties to hide me as I managed to find my voice.

'Is that nice?' I asked. 'Is that what you like to see?'

'Don't move an inch,' he answered me, and I heard the soft rasp of his zip being pulled down.

Again I nodded, looking around as I held myself out for inspection, feeling more of a tart than ever, standing with my panties on show for him to get off over. He had his cock out, still limp in his hand, but quite big, and resting on a bulbous scrotum thickly grown with milk-white hair. I managed a little smile for him as he began to masturbate, his eyes fixed on my straining panty seat.

'Would – would you like me to pull them down?' I offered.

'No, no, not yet, in a while,' he croaked, 'just stay as you are, for now. D'you mind if I talk to you?'

'Whatever you like.'

'Good girl. Don't mind what I say then, it's not meant badly. How about another little wiggle?'

I nodded my understanding, sure I could cope with his fantasies, and wiggled my bottom for him, his little tart through and through. He began to stroke his balls and roll his cock over his thumb as he watched me, slowly bringing the blood into his shaft to make it thicken and extend as he spoke once more. 'I used to love watching you, Penny, and your cousins, brightened my life, you did. D'you know the best time, do you? You must have seen the pictures, when you and Katie undressed to swim down by the old quarry. I'll never forget for a moment how you looked, in your little pink knickers, and – and when you took them down I got the most perfect shot – the most perfect –'

'It – it's my favourite too,' I admitted.

He swallowed, tugging harder at his cock, which had begun to rise in his hand, the thick foreskin now peeling back from the glossy head within at every tug. 'God, I wish I'd known you were such – such a, game girl then –'

'A tart,' I sobbed, a bubble of shame breaking in my head as I said the word, 'Call me a tart. It's what I am – for you, anyway – now.'

'Tart,' he said with relish, 'as you like, you can be my tart, now stick that lovely fat bottom out a little more and wiggle it again, then it's down with your knickers.'

I swallowed hard as I obeyed, giving my bottom a little wiggle for him as I stuck it right out, resting my hands on my thighs. He continued to tug at his cock, now almost stiff, and licked his lips before speaking again. 'That was a fine day, one of my best, but yes, if I'd known you were game – that you'd play the tart for me, by God, I'd have been down there like a shot. I'd have had you both, side by side with your arses in the air, the way we used to fuck our trollops back in Paris, three or four in a row, skirts up and knickers down. How'd you like that, Penny?'

At the time I'd have run a mile, but that didn't matter. What did matter was my fantasy after I'd first found the picture. 'Yes,' I answered, 'I was naked, wasn't I, and Kate, but maybe another day you might have caught us, and made us do rude things for you, made us kneel like you said, lifted up our skirts to show our panties, pulled them down and smacked our bottoms. I like my bottom smacked, Colonel Aimsworth. Do you want to?'

I was already close enough for him to touch, and he didn't answer immediately, but put a hand to my bottom, stroking the seat of my panties as he tugged at his cock. 'Knickers down then,' he ordered, as he took hold of my waistband and pulled.

A gasp escaped my throat as my bottom was stripped, and I was sobbing and shivering as his hand touched my bare skin, knowing I was showing behind, the rear view of my pussy open to him, all wet and eager, my cheeks wide enough apart to show my bumhole. I'd said it, admitted it, that I wanted spanking, and as he began to pat my bottom, just hard enough to set my cheeks wobbling a little, I went on.

'Yes, please, that's nice . . . a little harder maybe, and do touch, touch me as you please. I wish you'd spanked me before, it would have been so good . . . in my school skirt maybe, down across your knee in your living room . . . my panties taken down, my bare bottom spanked, in front of Kate, and Susan . . . and you'd spank them, too, and make us all stand against the wall with our school skirts turned up and our panties pulled down to show our red bottoms, to let us know how naughty we were, three spanked schoolgirls all in a row – go on, smack harder – really spank me – punish me –'

He did his best, slapping at my bottom as he jerked his cock, now hard in his hand, a good-sized erection, thick and stubby, the head a glossy ball. I was lost, my head full of dirty thoughts, my pussy hot and urgent, but still my voice came out as a sob when I spoke. 'I'm going to do it – I can't help it!'

I moved back, feeling utterly ashamed of myself and utterly wonderful as I put my bottom in his lap and reached back to guide his cock inside me, deep up my pussy, until I was full, with my warm bottom thrust out into his lap. He took hold of my cheeks, spreading me behind to show off my anus as I began to wriggle and bounce on his erection. I was revelling in my own humiliation, and the image in my head, of Kate, Susan and I all lined up, our spanked bottoms showing to the room as he lectured us. Then we'd be fucked.

'That wouldn't be all,' I told him, now breathless with pleasure as his cock moved inside me. 'You'd fuck us, all three of us, side by side over your sofa, just like your French girls, skirts up and panties down, waiting bare bottomed . . . me watching as you fucked the others, first Kate, then Susan, to see their faces as your cock went in . . . then me, right up my pussy as you went on spanking me – go on, do it, smack my cheeks – I think I'm going to come.'

I was. I couldn't stop myself. My hand went to my pussy as I thrust my bottom out, presenting him with a full target as I began to rub. He grunted as he slid forwards a little and he was doing it, smacking my cheeks and calling me a little tart as I bounced on his cock, dirty words spilling from my mouth as I lost all control, all dignity. 'That's right, yes . . . spank me, Colonel, spank my naughty bottom . . . yes, please, and fuck me, fuck me hard, just like you should have done years ago . . . spanked me and fucked me, made me your little tart . . . down in the quarry and in your house, my bottom all rosy and bare . . . and Kate's, and Susan's, all rosy and bare, your three little tarts all in a row –'

My voice broke to a hoarse gasp and I was coming, squirming my bottom on his cock as shock after shock of ecstasy ran through me. He was rock hard, and he stayed that way, his erection a rigid pole inside my body, feeling so good as I let all my dirty feelings out, no longer fantasy, but reality.

It was only as I started to come down that I felt bad. I'd meant to give him a treat, and I'd got carried away completely, using him for my pleasure rather than the other way around. I'd also been very, very dirty, and when I finally realised he wasn't going to come inside me I stood up, turning to him with a sheepish grin. 'Sorry about that, I got a bit carried away.'

'Sorry?' He puffed. 'What the hell for? I haven't had one like you since – since, Paris, if not ever!'

'Thanks, but – but don't you want to come?'

'Couldn't make it, sorry –'

'Don't be, I understand. What would you like me to do?'

It was only fair, with his erection clearly in need of my attention, and I could hardly leave him to toss off on his own. Expecting to be asked to suck him, I'd already begun to get down to my knees when he spoke again. 'Take your knickers off, do it with them.'

'OK,' I answered, a little chagrined now that I'd come, but willing enough.

He took his cock back in hand as I quickly stepped out of my jeans and shoes. My knickers followed and I got down, kneeling between his open legs and folding them around his stiff shaft, still wet with my juices. It felt curious, holding an erect cock through the cotton of my panties, and also dirty, deliciously dirty.

Even as I began to tug I knew I wanted to come again for what I was doing, the whole situation was just too exquisitely rude to miss out. There I was, naked from the waist down but for a pair of socks, my bare bottom showing behind, flushed from spanking, a spanking dished out by the old man whose cock I was wanking with my discarded panties. It was so wonderfully submissive, his little tart, kneeling bare to pleasure him, about to get her panties all sticky.

I'd have to leave without them, or with his mess in them and smeared on to my skin as I walked to remind me what a dirty girl I was, what a dirty little tart. It looked good too, my hand clasped tight around his shaft among the folds of white cotton panty material, his cock head popping up and down through one leg hole, his balls protruding from the other. I leant forwards, to take him in my mouth, just the head, feeling dirtier than ever as he responded with a groan of ecstasy.

My knees came wide and my spare hand went to my pussy, to tease my wet, open hole and my puffy, excited sex lips before once more starting to stroke my clitoris. I was doing it, sucking Colonel Aimsworth's cock as I wanked him in my panties, my bottom bare and spanked, my pussy fucked. Soon he'd come, full in my mouth, in my face too, and in my panties.

His hand came down and he'd taken his cock, quickly adjusting my panties to encase the head, now bulging in the cotton. I took it back in my mouth as he began to grunt, sucking on his cock head encased in white cotton, and I knew I would come too, just as he did. It was perfect. He'd spanked my bottom, he'd fucked me, but he hadn't come in me, oh no, he'd made me take off my panties and toss him off in them, such a dirty thing for a girl to do, so, so dirty, something no respectable girl would ever do, only a filthy, dirty little tart – like me.

100

I felt the panty material in my mouth bulge, and he'd come in them. It was too much. I just came, then and there, my head jammed down to get as much cock as I could in my mouth, as much panty material and as much spunk. His hand was smacking on my mouth as he jerked at himself, but I didn't care, my own body locked tight in ecstasy as my mouth filled with the taste of the come squeezing through the white cotton wrapped so tight around his helmet, and even as he subsided I was still coming, rocked back on my heels with my spunk-stained panties held in my mouth as I came again and again.

Five

What I had intended to do with Colonel Aimsworth, or rather, *for* Colonel Aimsworth, was simply give him a peep show as a treat. I certainly hadn't meant to get so carried away that I begged to be spanked, fucked in his lap and helped him toss off in my panties. It had happened, though, and there was a rueful smile on my face as I drove north the next day. Not that I regretted what I'd done, far from it. I felt both the warm glow of a charitable act and the sense of satisfaction that comes only after good, dirty sex and sex that has involved having my bottom smacked.

I had also laid to rest the ghost of his presence in my house, as I discovered once I got back. Now I knew him, as a human being rather than a vague and at once enticing and slightly frightening memory. Billy Watts I could erase with plaster and paint, Colonel Aimsworth had needed his cock attended to, but it came to the same thing in the end. I even sent him a scan of the picture of me taking my panties down by the quarry, which was now something I knew I could never burn or throw away.

The one aspect of Billy Watts's tenure I couldn't get rid of was the football-shaped swimming pool. It was a fairly bizarre object, a perfect hemisphere six metres across and three metres deep at the centre, tiled in black and white rather than the usual aquamarine blue, with large polygons like those covering the surface of a leather ball. I couldn't afford to get rid of it anyway, and I wasn't sure I wanted to. Unlike with Colonel Aimsworth, I'd never met Billy Watts, or his wife, and so they didn't have the same effect on me. Jade, Sophie and my entire family, with the exception of Aunt Elaine and my mother, also wanted me to keep it.

In the end I gave in, as usual, and on a warm Saturday in late April took my first swim, with Jade and Sophie, who'd been coming up to stay with me most weekends. Between us we'd managed to get the house into at least reasonable condition, and without putting me all that much further in debt than I already was. That morning we'd got rid of the last of the pink, which I felt meant we deserved a rest and a glass of cool Sauvignon while propped up against the side of the pool.

Jade emerged from the house, in a bright-green bikini that barely managed to contain her ample curves, Sophie behind her, in minuscule yellow bottoms and no top. I was going to say something, but thought better of it as we were in my own back garden and only my mother could possibly have made a fuss anyway. Jade had brought a towel out and lay down on it, her chin propped in her hands, her wine within easy reach. Sophie slipped into the pool with me, splashing across to the far side and back before hooking one arm over the side and reaching for her glass.

'What shall we do this evening?' Jade asked after a moment. 'Whispers?'

'I'm not sure I'm in the mood for being abused by your butch friends,' I admitted. 'They're so rough.'

'Your auntie's going to have to know you get spanked by other people some time,' she answered me.

'She does, sort of,' I admitted. 'It's complicated, but it's very embarrassing to go to her with bruises. Anyway, you know what AJ's like. She might shave my head or something awful.'

'She's a fucking liability,' Sophie agreed. 'Why don't we go dogging instead?'

'Men,' Jade said simply.

'Who cares? They're only looking.'

'Not the way you do it, they're not!'

'We can keep the door locked if you like.'

'Oh yeah, and how long will that last, slut?'

Sophie stuck her tongue out. I wasn't too keen, not because I minded showing off for strangers, even having to suck cock through a rolled-down window, which was how it was likely to end up, but I was sure that one day the police would decide to have a clamp down, or one of the men who stayed back and masturbated in the shelter of the bushes would turn out to be a colleague.

'It's getting so risky,' I pointed out, 'what with all the sites being up on the net. For goodness sake, some bloke put up a review after that time near Bracknell!'

'I know, I saw it,' Sophie replied, 'I was a "pert, sophisticated blonde". You got called a butterball, Jade.'

'Bloody cheek! Who by?'

'The guy who fucked your tits, I think. It sounded like him anyway, from what he said.'

'The ungrateful bastard!' Jade retorted. 'Men!'

'You weren't exactly polite about him,' I added. 'What was it you said, "OK, you can put your little beetle cock between them if you insist", something like that.'

'I let him, didn't I!?' she retorted. 'And he came all over my top. Bastard!'

'Why don't you two just take me upstairs for a good spanking?' I suggested. 'Or you can spit roast me, or sit on my face, or pee on me –'

I broke off with a happy sigh, imagining an evening entirely devoted to humiliating me.

'You greedy little bitch!' Sophie laughed.

'Yeah, bad girl!' Jade added. 'Maybe we should make you drink a couple of bottles of wine and leave you tied up while we go out.'

'Yes,' Sophie added with relish, 'until you wet yourself, and when we got back we'd make you lick it up!'

'Better still,' Jade put in, 'we should order a fifteen-inch pizza and force her to eat it, then chain her to her bed and leave her until she shits in her knickers.'

'Excellent!' Sophie agreed. 'How would you like that, Miss Muffet?'

'If you insist,' I answered.

'What a disgrace!' Sophie laughed.

'Such a bad girl!' Jade agreed, and was going to get up when a movement caught my eye.

I put my finger to my lips, urging her to silence and wishing our conversation had been a bit less loud and a lot less dirty as Pippa appeared. She was smiling and waving cheerfully, so presumably hadn't heard anything, but I could still feel my cheeks starting to burn at the thought of what Jade had suggested doing to me, to say nothing of my response. I pushed off from the side, swimming out into the middle of the pool in the vain hope that the cool water would make my blushes a little less obvious, treading water as I turned again.

'Can I come in?' Pippa asked.

'Of course,' I told her.

'Great, thanks,' she answered, and with two casual motions popped the button on her hipsters and pushed them down.

I really thought she was just going to strip off and jump in, which made my throat go tight and filled me with guilt and embarrassment for my own reaction, because I shouldn't have cared, but I did. Fortunately she'd obviously realised I wasn't going to say no, and had put a bikini on under her clothes, a blue one considerable more decent than what either Jade or Sophie was wearing.

It still left her slender body near naked and, as she stepped out of her jeans and peeled her top up over her head and off, all the feelings I'd managed to push down since the last time I'd seen her came back. I couldn't help myself, just to see her with her tiny breasts and the gentle bulge of her pussy mound cupped in rich-blue fabric was more arousing than having Sophie topless and Jade bursting out at the seams. She turned her back to me to put her clothes on the wall, bending a little, and it got worse, her beautifully rounded little bottom perfectly held in the bikini pants, her legs so long, and so slender that the rear bulge of her pussy showed between her thighs.

Sophie caught my eye and licked her lips meaningfully. Jade had rolled over and was admiring Pippa openly. I shook a warning finger at them and tried to bite down my guilt, telling myself I was being ridiculous, that, if my girlfriends' bodies turned me on, then why not Pippa's? It didn't work.

'There's wine in the fridge, if you like,' Sophie offered casually.

Pippa padded indoors.

'That was close!' Jade laughed the instant the door had closed. 'We wouldn't want little Miss Legs finding out you get off on messing your panties, would we?'

'No, we would not!' I answered earnestly. 'So be quiet, please!'

'Sure,' Sophie answered, 'but, boy, I would love to have her out of that bikini!'

'Me, too,' Jade agreed. 'Do you think she'd skinny dip if we did?'

'Don't, please!' I answered her. 'I really couldn't handle that.'

Sophie laughed. 'I think Penny's got a crush on her cousin. What d'you reckon, Jade?'

'Looks like it,' Jade agreed. 'Come on, Penny, go for it. Who knows, if she's anything like you, bad girl —'

'Sh!' I urged as Pippa came back outdoors, now holding a glass of the Sauvignon.

'At last, real peace!' she sighed as she sat down at the edge of the pool, her legs dangling in the water.

'What's the matter?' Jade asked, rolling on to her side.

'What *isn't* the matter?' Pippa answered. 'Exams, coursework, sports. Mum and Dad seem to think I'm supposed to be Stephen Hawking and Kelly Holmes at the same time.'

'Get those qualifications,' Sophie advised. 'Relax later.'

'Easy for you to say,' Pippa answered, 'you've done it all already!'

'Done what?' Sophie queried. 'All I've got is a lousy diploma.'

'Aren't you at the university?'

'Sophie?' Jade laughed. 'You have to be joking!'

'Less cheek!' Sophie retorted, smacking her hand down on the water to splash Jade, who twisted away with a squeak.

'I thought you worked with Penny?' Pippa asked.

'No,' Sophie answered, 'I work as a promoter for clubs.'

'Clubs? Way cool! Which ones?'

'She works for a guy called Morris Rathwell,' Jade answered, her voice a snigger.

'Who's a property developer who also lets premises out as venues,' I added hastily before either of them could mention exactly what sort of clubs Morris ran.

'Oh, right,' Pippa replied, plainly disappointed, 'and what do you do, Jade?'

'Temp,' Jade responded. 'I went to art college, and a fat lot of good that did me. What are you going to do?'

'Law,' Pippa replied without hesitation. 'I want to be a barrister.'

I couldn't help but feel a touch of pride at her confidence and ambition, completely unlike me at the same age, although with the same certainty about her career.

'I wonder if you'll end up representing Morris?' Jade joked.

'I was thinking of criminal law,' Pippa responded.

Jade just laughed and rolled over again, away from the wet spot Sophie had made on the ground. I was beginning to get cold and hauled myself out, quickly nipping indoors for the bottle and a fresh towel. By the time I came out again Pippa was in the pool, swimming back and forth with a lazy athleticism. I filled our glasses and sat down on the wall.

'So what's it to be?' Jade asked quietly. 'Whispers, or the A4?'

'A4,' Sophie said firmly.

'Penny?' Jade asked.

'Neither really,' I responded, 'but, if we really have to, A4.'

'What's A4?' Pippa asked, twisting around in the water.

'Just some club,' I answered quickly, astonished how she'd managed to hear what I said.

'Are you going clubbing? Can I come?'

From the look in her eyes it was quite obvious she'd be hurt if we said no, and all I could do was suggest a softer alternative, the first one that came into my head. 'Maybe Sugar Babes?'

'The gay club?' Pippa asked, her voice full of both shock and delight. 'Yeah, cool!'

'You hate Sugar Babes, Penny,' Jade pointed out.

'Why?' Pippa asked. 'It's supposed to be really good!'

I couldn't think of what to say, making awkward motions with my hands as I tried to find a way out. Sugar Babes was better than Whispers, but there were still likely to be people there who were quite capable of wanting to snog me on sight, or would think nothing of smacking my bottom, calling me Miss Muffet, even suggesting they take me into the toilets to be licked.

Pippa spoke up before I could decide what to say. 'I do know you're a lesbian, Penny. I mean, how could I miss it?'

Jade and Sophie were laughing immediately as I went crimson, turning to face Pippa with my mouth wide open in shock.

She made a face. 'Oh come on, Auntie Penny, it's obvious. I've never once seen you with a man! Don't worry, I'm cool about it.'

'Thanks,' I managed, genuinely pleased for her acceptance, but completely unwilling to explain anything beyond what she'd already picked up for herself, 'I – I really appreciate your attitude, but – don't take this the wrong way, but what's your mum going to say if I start taking you to lesbian clubs?'

'What's Mum got to do with it?' she demanded, and for the first time I caught a note of aggression in her voice. 'I do as I like.'

'No, it's not that,' I said hastily. 'It's just that – that –'

'That I'm too young?'

'No, not at all!'

'You wouldn't be the youngest girl at Sugar Babes,' Jade put in, 'no way. It's always full of baby dykes. Come on, Penny, stop being such an old maid!'

I spread my hands in a helpless gesture, knowing they were perfectly right but certain Kate, and more importantly Elaine, wouldn't see it that way. Yet I was also desperate not to hurt Pippa's feelings. Sophie spoke up. 'It's perfectly easy. You tell Pippa's mum you're taking her out to a restaurant in central London, we go in, have a nice meal then go on to Whispers, or whatever. That way everyone's happy.'

'I'd be lying to Kate,' I pointed out.

'No, you wouldn't,' Jade answered, 'you just wouldn't be telling her the whole truth. After all, you're not going to give her a blow-by-blow account of what we eat for tea either, are you?'

'No, but –'

'And you can stay sober and drive us all back afterwards,' Sophie added. 'Perfect.'

'Yes, but –'

'Let's do it,' Pippa chimed in, hauling herself from the pool.

We ate at a fish restaurant in Charlotte Street, which was pleasantly civilised, although I was constantly on edge. Pippa had put on a silver mini dress when we'd stopped at Kate's house in Sonning Common to let her know what was going on, and looked more alluring than ever,

111

intensely feminine, cool and refined. Fortunately, she did not look like a baby dyke, but I was certain that somebody like Big Angie who did the door at Sugar Babes would make a pass at her and scare her silly.

I'd changed as well, into a plain black dress that could pass at Kate's, the restaurant and Sugar Babe's without drawing undue attention, while Sophie had simply smartened herself up and pulled on a different set of jeans and a new top. Jade had merely tugged on a clinging dress over her bikini, and looked better suited to pole dancing than anything, something I was praying was not going to be on the agenda at Sugar Babes.

Only when we'd finished did my feelings begin to get really bad, but the others were oblivious, the four of us linking arms as we walked down Rathbone Place and along Oxford Street. It was the first really warm night of the year, and London was buzzing, the crowds thick on the pavements, and a queue stretching for two blocks outside Sugar Babes, with Big Angie towering over everybody else beside the door.

'Sod that!' Sophie exclaimed. 'We'll never get in.'

'I'll have a word with Angie,' Jade offered, already stepping forwards.

'No, no,' I said quickly, with a vision of Pippa's face if Angie demanded her pussy licked in return for being let past the queue. 'Let's not bother.'

'What about the other place, Whispers?' Pippa suggested.

'I'm not sure –' I began, only to be cut off by Jade.

'Stop being such a mother hen, Penny. Pippa'll be all right in Whispers. She's with us, for fuck's sake!'

That was what I was worried about, but they were already starting down the street. I hurried to keep up, telling myself that whatever happened it could hardly be worse than having a twenty-stone female wrestler ask Pippa to come into the loos and lick her out. Unfortunately, I knew it could.

Whispers was crowded, but to my relief I hardly knew anyone there. Otherwise it seemed much as normal, with Gina behind the bar as ever and a mixed crowd of perfectly ordinary-looking women, obvious dykes with tattoos and piercings, a few girls in leather, others in frills and lace. Pippa was fascinated, her face full of nervous excitement as she looked around.

She was also the youngest and probably the prettiest girl in the place, a magnet for any butch girl on the prowl, while being with the three of us was only going to make it worse. I couldn't retreat to the back room either, not with the cross and the whipping stool set up and some girl or other almost certain to end up being punished before the evening was over. Instead, I chose a table as far away from it as possible, in a corner by the window, from which Pippa would be able to satisfy her curiosity and hopefully not attract any unwelcome attention.

Jade had got the drinks and joined us, casually answering Pippa's stream of thankfully impersonal questions. It was hard not to be drawn in, with the three of them laughing together, although I could picture the look of horror on Kate's face as Pippa took in each new piece of information. She was encouraging Jade, too, who was soon giving her personal definition of the difference between butch and diesel. 'A butch dyke is going to fuck you with a strap-on, a diesel dyke is going to smack you about a bit, piss on you, and *then* fuck you with a strap-on.'

Pippa replied with a nervous but uncomfortably excited giggle before her mouth opened to frame another question and I just had to step in. 'She's making it up, Pippa. A butch dyke is a masculine lesbian, a diesel dyke more so, and maybe into bikes and stuff as well.'

'Cool,' Pippa said and giggled, her eyes shining. 'And how about the girls at Sugar Babes? You called them baby dykes.'

'A baby dyke,' Sophie pointed out to her, 'is what people are going to think you are sitting here with us.'

Pippa giggled and smiled as if she'd been paid the highest of compliments, leaving me wondering what Kate would have to say if her elder daughter came out as a lesbian.

'So what does that make you, Penny?' Pippa asked.

'A slut?' Sophie suggested.

'She's not actually that fussy, your auntie –' Jade began but I managed to cut her off.

'I don't really like to define myself, but they'd call me femme, or maybe a lipstick lesbian, because I prefer other feminine women to masculine women.'

I was blushing furiously as I said it, but Jade and Sophie were drunk and might come out with anything, so I had no choice. Pippa nodded and bit her lower lip in a peculiar way as Jade cuddled up to me, speaking. 'So she goes out with me, like the little sweetie she is, but just occasionally we need something a little harder.'

'Like her?' Pippa asked, looking over my shoulder. 'She's a diesel dyke, I suppose?'

'Oh yes, and then some,' Sophie answered, and as I caught the sudden shock in her voice I twisted around.

It was AJ, and she looked more butch than ever, her head shaved, her lean, hard muscles showing beneath her skin, her khaki singlet barely covering her breasts, extra tattoos and piercings, a black iron chain around her neck with a huge female symbol hanging from the end. She was coming towards us.

'Hi, AJ,' I managed.

She gave me a friendly sneer and pinched my cheek, glancing around, with a nod to Pippa and Sophie and a look of raw, lust-filled aggression for Jade. 'Going to buy me a drink, Dumplings?' she demanded.

'I will,' I answered hastily. 'Come up to the bar, I want to talk to you.'

She looked surprised, but I took her arm and she came, speaking before we'd reached the bar. 'What's up, and who's the moppet?'

'She's not a moppet, AJ. She's my cousin,' I answered.

'That stops her being a moppet?'

'Yes, it does. She's just here out of curiosity, that's all, she not –'

'Oh yeah? Look's it.'

I turned around to where she was looking, and found to my horror that Jade had taken a miniature vibrator from her bag and was showing it to Pippa.

'They're just mucking about,' I said hastily.

She answered with a snort of disbelief and contempt. Gina had seen us and I spent a moment ordering drinks. AJ took a swallow from hers before she spoke again. 'I'm on my own tonight.'

'Oh?'

'Yeah, and I'm reckoning your little pet would warm my bed just nicely.'

I shook my head urgently. 'No, she wouldn't, AJ. She's not even a lesbian, and certainly not into your kind of thing.'

'You don't say? What's she doing with you three sluts then? Don't bullshit me, Penny.'

'She wanted to see what Whispers was like, that's all,' I insisted.

'Oh yeah, and I've never heard that one before?'

'Really, she –'

'Bollocks. Give me twenty minutes with her and I'll have her licking scat off my fingers, and loving it.'

That was too much, and I could feel my anger as I answer her back. 'Leave her alone, AJ, just leave her, OK? I am not joking.'

She looked at me in astonishment, and for one awful moment I thought she was going to slap me, or put me across her knee in front of everybody, Pippa included. Instead she gave a slightly forced laugh. 'Fuck me! Who rattled your cage, Miss Muffet?'

'You did,' I answered her, determined not to back down. 'You can do as you like, AJ, you know that, with me, with Jade, maybe even with Sophie, but you leave my cousin alone.'

'Oh I get it!' She laughed. 'Nobody's had her yet and you want to break her in. Yeah, great, no problem, I can handle that. Just let me know when she's ready for the real deal.'

'It is not like that!' I insisted, but she just laughed again and gently slapped my face as she spoke.

'Catch you later.'

She moved off towards a group of girls at the far corner of the bar and I went back to the others. Jade had put her vibrator away, but Pippa immediately turned to me. 'She's something, isn't she?'

'AJ?' I responded. 'Yes she is, she's trouble.'

'What's she into?'

'Nothing you want to know about.'

'Oh, come on, Penny, stop treating me like a little girl.'

'You tell her, Jade,' I answered, with a despairing gesture.

'She's great, really hard –' Jade began, only to be cut off by Sophie.

'She's a psycho bitch from Hell, full-on diesel. Making girls lick her boots is the least of it, she likes to piss on you –'

I held my peace, hoping that what Sophie was saying would be enough to destroy any glamour AJ might have had in Pippa's eyes. Sure enough, her expression was gradually changing from fascination to horror as Sophie want on. 'And all sorts of really nasty stuff, like sticking your head down a toilet and flushing it. She's well into CP too.'

'CP?' Pippa queried.

'Spanking,' Sophie answered, and there was no denying the relish in her voice.

'Corporal punishment,' I answered. 'Flagellation.'

'She likes to use a studded belt,' Jade added, and Pippa winced.

'Not somebody you want to know,' I said.

'She's not that bad,' Jade put in, 'just a bit rough, that's all.'

'A bit rough?' Pippa queried. 'Have you been with her?'

'Sure,' Jade answered blithely.

'Penny?' Pippa asked, her eyes wide.

'She's a bit much for me,' I admitted.

'Penny's just soft,' Jade went on, as casually as if she'd been talking about the weather, 'all she really likes is to have her botty smacked.'

I had gone beetroot, unable to speak, frozen with my glass of tomato juice halfway to my mouth. Pippa looked at me, and giggled. My mouth was open, wide, in a vain attempt to deny it, to make a joke of it, anything, but no sound came as Sophie began to talk, digging me deep into the hole Jade had created. 'Everyone has their own tastes, Pippa. Penny likes to be spanked, I like showing off, Jade's into being bullied by diesel dykes. AJ's just too rough for most of us, Penny especially.'

'You like being spanked on your bottom?' Pippa said, looking right at me and trying not to laugh.

She was waiting for me to say something. To confirm it or deny it, to explain myself. At last I managed to force myself to speak, babbling foolishly as I attempted to justify myself.

'It's – it's – I don't know, just something that's in my head. I don't know, like – like enjoying good food or something. I just like it.'

She smiled, one corner of her mouth twitching in amusement, and spoke to Jade and Sophie. 'Is that why you two always call her a bad girl, because she likes to be spanked?'

Just to hear her say it brought the blushes to my cheeks hotter than ever, and I could feel the tears starting in my eyes. I had to go, rising and making quickly for the loo, where I leant on a sink and closed my eyes, taking deep breaths and trying to calm the awful muddle of my thoughts. My secret was out, and Pippa thought it was funny, bringing me such powerful emotions of shame and arousal I could hardly bear it. When I'd come over Pippa caning me I'd imagined her cold and angry, not laughing. Laughing was a thousand times worse, a thousand times more exciting, more than I could possibly cope with.

I wanted to scream and I wanted to come, boiling with frustration and with arousal, while a tiny, wicked voice at the back of my head was telling me that all I had to do was ask, and I'd get it, in front of my lovely Pippa, panties down with my bottom bouncing, in an agony of shame beyond even what I'd felt sucking Colonel Aimsworth's spunk through my well-soiled panties. Sophie and Jade would do it, and laugh with her, but a dominant woman would be better, somebody I couldn't fight against once she had me held down. AJ just wasn't safe, but Gina would do it, maybe.

It was a really stupid idea, and I put it out of my head, forcing myself to think calmly and clearly. The situation was bad enough already without me making it any worse, while once I was alone I could play with myself to my heart's content, and have as many orgasms as it took to get the image of Pippa laughing at me while I was spanked out of my mind. I'd been crying, a little, and it took a touch of make-up to hide it before I came out of the loos.

The bar was getting quite crowded, with every table occupied and knots of girls standing together, just about shoulder to shoulder. AJ was still there, talking to a woman in a leather jacket who I didn't recognise. So was Gina, collecting glasses, with a half-full tumbler full of cigarette ends and some orange-coloured drink at an awkward angle in her hand. One touch, one jog, and it would be all over her shiny black army boots, and I . . .

'Oops! Sorry, Gina.'

She turned on me, drink and bits of cigarette ash dripping down her leather trousers on to the floor and all over her boots. 'Look, you stupid little bitch, if you want it, just fucking ask!' she snapped, putting her other glasses down.

'I – ow!'

She'd caught me by the ear, twisting hard, and as the girls near us heard my cry of pain they looked around, and quickly moved back. One stood, laughing, and pushed the chair she'd been sitting on out into the clear space, calling encouragement to Gina. 'Go for it, Gina, make her lick it up!'

'Hey, no!' I protested, but my head was being dragged down, my ear pinched hard between finger and thumb as she sat on the stool. 'Lick it up, all of it!' she spat.

'No, Gina, I –'

'Lick, bitch! You wanted this, so do as you're fucking told!'

'Gina, no – please –' I sobbed. 'I just wanted a spanking, that's all!'

I was already on my knees, pleading with my eyes, and Gina's grip had begun to loosen when AJ's voice sounded from above me. 'Don't take any shit from her, Gina, she loves it. Now do as you're fucking told, Miss Muffet, or you'll have me to deal with.'

'But –'

'Just fucking do it!' Gina screamed. Her open hand landed on my cheek, a stinging, open slap and I was gasping in pain, my mouth wide as I was pulled down to my knees. 'Lick my fucking boots!' she rasped. 'Then you get your arse done.'

I nodded feebly, already dizzy with pain and submission, knowing full well that Jade and Sophie had a clear view of me as I grovelled down at Gina's feet, and so did Pippa. Yet I'd done it, hoping for a spanking, and if I didn't do as I was told it was going to get a lot worse. Opening my mouth, I began to lick at the highly polished boots, sobbing bitterly and grimacing at the taste of polish, of whatever sickly drink had been in the glass, of fag ash.

The girls had formed a ring around me, looking down as I degraded myself with my emotions burning in my head, not for them, but for Pippa. I wondered if she'd laugh, or if it would be too much and she'd turn against me, and as my mouth began to fill with the horrible mess from Gina's boots I began to cry.

'What a baby!' somebody said, laughing. 'Go easy on her, Gina, she can't take it.'

'She can take more than you think,' AJ answered, 'even if she is a cry baby. Go on, slut, lick it all up!'

I already had, most of it, lapping at the ash and drink and using my lips to pick up bits of fag end. What was left was on her trousers and the floor, the rest already in my mouth. It tasted foul, gritty and horrible, making me gag as she took me by my hair. Some of the girls were laughing as Gina began to steer my head to the bits of filth on her leather trousers, making me take them in my mouth one by one, my tongue flicking out again and again, until my whole mouth was full of the vile mixture of ash and bits of cigarette wrapping and polish and dirt.

'Now the floor, down you go!' she ordered and my head was pushed low.

My face was pressed to the floor and rubbed in the mess, smearing it over my skin, my cheeks bulging with muck as I struggled not to be sick. They'd begun to close in, laughing and joking at the state I was in as my face was used to mop up the floor, until Gina had pulled my head up a little. My tongue had poked out and I was licking up fag ash and dirt, as much dribbling out as was going in, my head swimming with humiliation, agonisingly aware that Pippa's eyes would be on my lifted bottom and my filthy muck-smeared face.

'That'll do,' Gina said, 'now you get spanked.'

She still had me by the hair, and gave a sharp tug, making me cry out in pain as I was hauled up and cross her knee, between her open legs. A foot twisted around my ankle and I'd been spread behind, the seat of my dress stretched taut over my bottom, a silly, rude position, but not as silly and rude as it was going to get. I hung my head, mess dribbling from my mouth, my mind burning with humiliation as Gina tightened her grip, clamping me in my awful position as she began to pull up my skirt.

It felt so strong, twenty or more eager girls watching as my bottom was exposed for punishment, my smart black dress pulled up to show off my big white spanking panties, the sight of which drew hoots of derisive laughter and bitchy remarks about how I dressed. I began to cry again, really hard, blubbering in Gina's grip as I waited for that last, awful moment, as her hand clutched at the waistband of my panties, as they were hauled low, stripped off my bulging, open bottom to show me off, bare and ready, my hairy, flaunted cunt, my pinky-brown bumhole, all showing, all showing to Pippa.

As I came bare I screamed, unable to control my emotions any more. Somebody called me a baby again, and the spanking had begun, Gina's hand slapping down on my naked cheeks to make them bounce and wobble, to set my legs kicking and jerking in my lowered panties, to draw squeals and gasps of pain and consternation and self-pity from my lips, to show me off in front of my own young cousin, spanked bare.

The rest of them were laughing, jeering, calling me a cry baby and egging Gina on to spank me harder. I barely heard, lost in my pain and humiliation, so, so aware how I'd look from the rear, with my legs trapped and my fat red bum flaunted, my flesh squashing to the smacks, my pussy wet and puffy with helpless arousal, my bumhole winking lewdly between my cheeks. Pippa could see all of it, a ridiculous, pathetic sight, a full-grown, respectable woman punished with spanking, me, her own aunt, panties down across a barmaid's lap, howling and snivelling my way through punishment.

How I cried, how I writhed, how I kicked, without a shred of dignity, without a shred of modesty, in a full-blown spanking tantrum, so utterly pathetic, a fat-bottomed little brat spanked for punishment – smack, smack, smack – on my rosy red cheeks. I heard Jade, a crow of laughter as she saw what was to be done to me. I heard Sophie, a delighted giggle as my panties came down. I didn't hear Pippa until the very end, as Gina stopped and my body went limp across her legs, a single peal of girlish laughter, high and sweet.

I'd have come, at that point, with just the least touch to my aching pussy. Maybe I'd have even frigged off, I was so broken and so high. I wasn't given the chance, Gina once more taking a firm grip on my ear and pulling me to my feet as she herself stood up. The others stepped back, giving way to the one who'd made such an open display of her dominance, all except AJ, who took hold of my other ear.

'Right, you, in the shitter.'

'Ow! Girls, please –'

'Shut up,' Gina told me.

'Yes, but what are you going to do with me?'

'Make you lick our cunts, stupid!' AJ answered.

'Oh –'

We'd reached the door to the loos, and AJ kicked it open. Two girls were in there, and turned in surprise as I was dragged in, a fine sight with my dress still rucked up and my panties down to show my pussy at the front and my reddened bottom behind.

'You spanked her!?' one of the girls demanded, as I was led towards the cubicles.

'Yeah, want some?' AJ answered, and both of them fled.

'Who's first?' Gina asked.

'Whatever,' AJ answered, 'but I need a piss, come in here, Miss Muffet.'

'AJ, not that, please, my dress –' I babbled.

'Take it off then,' she told me.

I hesitated only a moment, wondering what Pippa would think if she came in to find me being made to lick cunt in the nude. It couldn't be worse than what she'd think if I had to drive all the way back soaked in AJ's piddle, which was what was likely to happen otherwise, and I quickly whipped it off, leaving myself feeling extremely vulnerable in nothing but panties and heels.

AJ had sat down, her combats and a plain black leather thong pushed to her ankles, her shaved pussy open to show her piercings and the stark black on white tangle of the barbed wire tattoo on her pussy mound. Gina folded her arms, leaning on the door jamb and smiling as I got down on my knees. AJ moved a little further back, letting me spit my filthy mouthful into the bowl before taking me by the hair to wedge my chin in over the edge of the toilet seat, my face pressed to her pussy.

I began to lick, my eyes shut, my tongue flicking over her piercings and the smooth folds of her pussy, waiting for the gush of piss in my mouth. She let go, with a dry chuckle as her urine exploded in my face, filling my mouth so quickly I was forced to swallow, gulping down mouthful after mouthful of hot, pungent pee. It wasn't fast enough and her piddle was soon running out of the sides of my mouth and splashing back over her thighs. Still I struggled to drink it, only to start to choke and have it explode from my nose as I went into a coughing fit, spattering her tattooed mound with a mixture of snot and piddle.

'You dirty fucking bitch!' she spat. 'You can lick that up, Miss Muffet, right now!'

She was still pissing, and her grip never slackened,

so that her stream was breaking on my chin and running down over my tits and belly, into my panties and on to the floor as my mouth was pressed to her mound for me to lick up my own snot. I was shaking, utterly broken to her, but with my own need too strong to be denied. My hand went down, into the now soggy crotch of my panties, my fingers pressing between my lips and I was masturbating as I cleaned up my own mess from AJ's sex, along with her piddle.

'You dirty, dirty little tart, Miss Muffet,' she sneered. 'OK, you can rub your little cunt, but you come when I say so, not before, got it?'

I nodded, all I could manage as my face was pressed to her sex once more. My tongue went to her clitoris, licking eagerly as I teased myself, on the edge of orgasm already, but not daring to tip myself over until I was given permission. Soon she'd begun to sigh, trying to hold back her emotions until the last second, but failing, and coming in my face with a long moan of ecstasy no harsher than any other woman's.

'Good girl,' she said when she finally let go of my hair. 'Now Gina, then you can do your own business.'

She took a handful of loo paper, dabbing at her pussy and dropping it into the bowl as I rocked back on my heels, my hand still down my panties, which were thoroughly wet. I was close, shivering, my head full of dirty thoughts, but as AJ stood up I expected Gina to take her place, not to have both of them grab me by the hair and pull me hard forwards, face down over the lavatory bowl. I cried out in shock, struggling in their grip as I realised what was going to happen to me as AJ laughed and Gina called out. 'In she goes!'

'Yeah,' AJ agreed, 'I reckon you need a wash, Miss Muffet!'

For one awful moment I was staring down at the mixture of AJ's piddle, slowly dissolving loo paper and the bits of cigarette butt and ash I'd spat out, before my head had been thrust down. My hair was in it, floating in the filthy water right in front of my eyes, and I was babbling for mercy and kicking my feet behind me in stupid, futile remonstrance. 'No, please, you two – not this – not my head –'

'Bollocks!' AJ laughed and I heard the grate of the lever.

'No! AJ! Gi –'

I never finished the word, my mouth filling with piss-flavoured water and bits of loo paper as it swirled up around my head, soaking my hair and filling my nose. I went into a frenzy, my feet drumming on the floor, my hands batting in the air. My eyes were tight shut, I couldn't see, I couldn't breathe, I could barely hear, my head completely immersed in water and piddle, thrust well down the lavatory, Gina and AJ crowing in delight for what they'd done to me.

They only pulled me up when the level had gone down again, leaving me kneeling in front of the lavatory bowl, spitting filthy water from my mouth, not daring to open my eyes, my hair a bedraggled mess around my face, soiled and dripping and full of bits of soggy loo paper.

'Do you really want *that* to lick you?' AJ laughed.

'Hang on,' Gina answered.

I was left, the mixture of piddle and water trickling slowly down my body and into my panties, trying to tell myself I didn't really want to masturbate over what had just been done to me. My knees were open though, my pussy urgent, the need to touch so strong, too strong, and my hand had slipped back into my panty crotch just as Gina upended a full bucket of cold water over me without the slightest warning.

'There, that's better,' she said and laughed as I gasped and spluttered underneath her, 'now you can lick.'

Before I could even catch my breath I'd been pulled into her, not her pussy, but her bottom, my face squashing against the softness of her cheeks. She was up against the wall, with it pushed out in my face, her leather trousers and the panties beneath well down, her hand twisted into my hair. I had no choice but to lick, my tongue finding the tight, rubbery knot of her anus, my mouth filling with the earthy taste of her bottom.

'Dirty, dirty Miss Muffet,' AJ drawled in satisfaction as Gina gave a pleased sigh.

My tongue was well in, wriggling in her bottom hole, and my hand was still down my panties. I'd given in, no longer fighting, but content with what they done to me. It was right, the only way to treat me, to use me for their amusement, to make me lick dirt off their boots and rub my face on the floor, to spank my bare bottom in front of my young cousin, to urinate in my mouth and make me lick pussy, to flush my head down a toilet, and last, to make me lick a bottom hole while I brought myself off under my own fingers.

As I started to come I jammed my tongue as far as it would go up Gina's anus. She was masturbating, her fingers jabbing at my chin, her bottom cheeks already squeezing in my face, her ring tightening on my tongue, but I was there first, violent shudders running through my body as I came over and over again, in blinding ecstasy for what they'd done to me.

* * *

Pippa knew I liked to be spanked. She thought it was funny. Pippa had seen me spanked. She'd laughed.

The agony of my embarrassment was matched only by the intensity of my arousal, but that did not mean one cancelled the other out. All the way back I was wracked with guilt and ill feeling, but I knew full well that once I was alone in my bed on the Sunday night I would have to come again over what had happened.

She'd also had several too many pineapple alcopops, adding to my guilt and sense of irresponsibility. I couldn't possibly return her to Kate in such a state, although I knew it wouldn't be a first. I was supposed to be looking after her. So I drove straight home instead, arriving at nearly three in the morning, by which time Pippa was asleep on Sophie's shoulder.

We put her on the couch, covered her in blankets and collapsed into my bed, by then too tired to care what she might think in the morning, while after what had happened it could hardly matter anyway. Sophie had woken up again, and wanted to play, but I was just too far gone, and sank into an immediate sleep to the sound of their excited giggling and wet tongues being applied to equally wet pussies.

In the morning I was the first up, or I thought I was, still trying to arrange my thoughts as I went downstairs to make coffee and found Pippa not only awake but in the swimming pool, floating on her back with her arms outstretched and dressed in nothing but Sophie's minute yellow bikini bottoms. I'd already decided that I was going to have to talk to her, in some detail, but possibly not while she was swimming topless in my pool. She saw me as I came out on to the patio and swam lazily to the edge, smiling at me. 'Coming in, bad girl?'

She giggled and I found myself blushing, completely unable to cope with what from Jade or Sophie would have been a friendly morning greeting after a good night out.

'OK,' I answered, not really sure what else to say, but certain that she could not possibly be as casual about what had happened the night before as she seemed. 'Just let me get some coffee on.'

I went back inside, my mind clearing slowly as I made coffee. One thing that was very clear was that she seemed determined to have us accept her as a mature woman. That doubtless meant she was putting on a bit of a front about what she'd learnt, and in particular about my spanking. She also seemed determined not to be fazed by my preference for other girls, although that might be simply a desire to fit in with the three of us. I had to face the fact that it might also be a genuine compulsion towards lesbianism, or perhaps bisexuality. Kate had often remarked on the number of boys who chased after her, with a mixture of pride and the same exasperation I recognised in my own mother, but that didn't necessarily mean anything.

What I didn't want to do was be condescending, but nor did I want Kate thinking I was corrupting her daughter. Making a secret of it was going to make me feel worse than ever, but then again, when I'd found my need for punishment getting out of control, it was my aunt I'd gone to and not my mother.

I was still thinking about it as I slipped into my bikini and brought the coffee outside, putting my tray down by the pool so that Pippa could make her own, and all I could think of to do was act as if nothing unusual had happened. Pippa was less reticent. 'That was a great night out,' she said happily as she poured her coffee out, 'the best.'

'It was good,' I admitted.

'Is Whispers always like that?'

'Um, more or less.'

'You'll take me again, yeah?'

'Again? Um –'

'Oh go on, please? I don't mind – you know, stuff, and –'

I pursed my lips, knowing exactly what Kate would expect me to say, but knowing exactly how Pippa would react to it. 'Maybe,' I replied.

'Cool, thanks!' she answered, and took a sip of coffee, looking thoughtful.

I wanted to qualify my remark, maybe make her promise not to go on her own, but was still trying to decide how to word it without sounding too much of the stuffy old aunt when she spoke again, her voice now deeply serious. 'What's it like, to be treated like that, like that barmaid treated you?'

There was an immediate lump in my throat. I swallowed, shrugged, trying to find the words even to begin to express myself. She was looking at me, expecting an honest answer. 'It's – it's wonderful,' I managed eventually, and suddenly my words were coming in a rush, 'but, the thing is, it has to be in your head and, if it's not, it wouldn't be wonderful at all, it would be horrible. I know that's hard to understand, and maybe it's hard to understand how somebody can feel good about pain and humiliation, but a lot of people do.'

'You included,' she said, not a question but a statement.

'Me included,' I agreed, 'and I suppose it is horrible, in a way, but not a nasty way, because it's what I want – what I need in fact. Don't think that means I like horrible things done to me in general, either, it's not like that at all. It's just that I enjoy certain, specific things that other people don't, like – like eating sprouts. Some people hate them, some people like them. If you hate them, the people who like them seem to be quite mad. In fact, the difference is genetic, because our sensitivity to the chemical allyl isothiocyanate varies. A quarter of people find it unbearably bitter, so they hate sprouts. Half find it fairly bitter, so sprouts taste unpleasant but not actually foul. The remaining quarter can't taste it at all, so they like sprouts.'

'Yeah, but you're saying getting a spanking is nasty and nice at the same time?'

'Um – OK, so it's not a perfect analogy, but you see my point? People who don't understand spanking might think I'm quite mad for enjoying it, because they're not wired the same way, so at best they can understand it in an intellectual sense, or somebody cruel might enjoy seeing it done to me, and all the more so because they don't understand my pleasure, but they can never share the experience. For me, it's something very, very important. It's in my head as often as – as the need to eat, maybe more so. I even dress for it.'

'How do you mean? You always seem to dress – well, sensibly.'

I hesitated before answering, flushed with embarrassment, but something within me wanted to say it, to make that embarrassment worse in front of her. 'Sensibly, yes, very sensibly. What would you say if I told you that almost every pair of knickers I own are ordinary white cotton briefs?'

She shrugged. 'That you believe in being practical? That you're not bothered about men's attention?'

'No,' I answered, 'it's because over the years I've come to associate white cotton panties with showing off my bottom, with being desirable, above all with being spanked. To you they're plain, practical, ordinary, but you haven't had partners making a fuss

131

over taking them down for years. To me they're special, my spanking panties.'

She giggled and I went on quickly, my face hot, but not as hot as between my legs. 'You see, it's a central part of my life. Please don't think of it as a problem, either, or – or something that needs to be cured. It's a delight to me, something that brings so much joy I find it hard to make a comparison. Put it this way, it's not something I need to see a therapist about, any more than I'd go to the dentist and ask to have all my teeth out because they hurt occasionally.'

She laughed, attentive, maybe doubtful or maybe not.

A thought came to me and I went on. 'What do you really like doing?'

'Swimming? Riding?'

'OK, let's take riding. Let's say, for example, that for some reason it became socially unacceptable to ride, not just to go hunting, but to ride a horse at all. Let's say that some radical group managed to outlaw it on the grounds of cruelty.'

'Cruelty?'

'Exactly, they'd be saying it was painful and undignified for Bell to have you on his back, maybe they'd say it was unnatural.'

'That's ridiculous!'

'Utterly ridiculous, but that's exactly how I feel about spanking. The general feeling in society derives from first-generation feminism, which says it's painful and undignified, and therefore that I shouldn't do it.'

'But it's your body and your choice, surely they'd have to accept that?'

'You'd hope so, wouldn't you, but it doesn't always work that way. You see, a lot of people like to think that their own concepts represent moral absolutes, and that if you don't agree it's either because there's something wrong with you, or you're somehow immoral. They therefore present arguments to make you change your behaviour, but as often as not what they're really doing is finding reasons to confirm their own prejudices and thus impose them on you. I prefer to make my own moral choices.'

'So you're saying you want the right to be spanked?'

'Yes.'

'But couldn't people argue that you're trying to make them accept your morals.'

'Not at all. I'm not saying that anybody else ought to be spanked. All I want is the right to enjoy my sexuality without interference. Not too long ago people used to be locked up for being gay.'

'Yes, I know. You're right, I suppose. I just thought it was fun. Sorry I laughed at you.'

'It is fun, and so much more! And don't be sorry you laughed at me, again it's hard to explain, but that – that made it nicer.' I was blushing again, and moved back to sexual politics, taking a swallow of coffee before I went on. 'As you know, I don't believe in God, much to your granny's disgust, and part of being an atheist is that, because you have no religious code to guide you, you have to establish your own framework of morals, according to your conscience.'

She nodded, this time both understanding and eager.

'I base my morals on a number of considerations,' I continued, 'some drawn from religious principles, some not. One of those is the principle of sexual consent, which means that no sexual act can possibly be immoral unless it harms or endangers another person. I believe that, sincerely, but unfortunately not everybody else does. A significant proportion of society would consider my moral choices to be wrong, so much so that if I insisted on being open about them life would be very difficult. Therefore, I have to make a choice: to fight my corner, to do as I please but keep quiet about it, or to try and suppress my needs.'

I paused to take another sip of coffee, wondering if I might have lost her attention or be starting to bore her, but her face was set in an expression so studious it was hard not to smile.

'I really admire people who're out and proud,' I went on, 'like AJ for instance, but I prefer a quiet life. On the other hand I'm not prepared to sacrifice something that's so important to me, and I consider my moral choice as valid – no, *more* valid than those whose moral principles derive from values I consider outdated, or divine edict from a non-existent supreme being. I know that sounds really arrogant but, when you have no god, you have no choice but to take responsibility for yourself. So, that's my choice, to do what I like, at least within the bounds of safety and consent, but to keep it to myself and close friends with the same tastes. Now you know.'

Pippa pursed her lips, clearly thinking deeply. I wasn't sure what to expect, hopefully acceptance and understanding, as she was so clearly intelligent, perhaps some remark based on the viewpoints of her own generation, not condemnation, after the way she'd laughed at me while I was being punished, and certainly not what she came out with.

'I enjoyed seeing Gina do it to you. Does that make me cruel?'

'No,' I answered immediately, and paused, because obviously it did but the last thing I wanted to do was make her feel bad about her own reactions. 'Well, yes, in a sense, but not in a nasty way, more like as if you laughed because I fell in the swimming pool or something.'

She still looked a little doubtful, so I went on, doing my best to reassure her.

'The thing is that you already knew I enjoyed it. Let's say Mr Cudrow had caught me the other day and spanked me. You wouldn't have laughed then, would you?'

'No.'

'There you are then. Now AJ *would* have laughed, because AJ really is cruel. She'd probably have intervened as well, to stop it, but she'd have laughed even if I hated it.'

'Would you? Have hated it?'

Again I paused, analysing my own reaction to what she was asking, Mr Cudrow, with me over his knee in front of her. Just the thought sent a shock right through me, but that was fantasy. The reality was less straightforward. 'Yes and no,' I answered. 'The important thing is that he doesn't know I like it, so if he'd done it to me he'd obviously have been prepared to do it to another woman, maybe even you. That would make him an abuser, so I wouldn't actually want that to happen. On the other hand, the idea appeals, yes, as a fantasy.'

She giggled and looked up at me with her most implike expression. 'So, what does it actually *feel* like?'

'Physically? It hurts. I mean, I'm having my bottom smacked –'

'Do you actually like the pain?'

'Not really, no, but the pain is essential for two reasons. Physically, it causes the release of chemicals called endorphins, which effectively provoke pleasure as a reaction, and it brings the blood to the surface of my skin across an erogenous zone, so I grow aroused. At first I sometimes wonder what I'm doing, when it's really hard, but there's a sort of barrier,

135

when it stops hurting and becomes nice, and it can be quite hard to get over that. But, as I said, it's mainly in my head, and the mental aspect of the pain is equally important, because a lot of the pleasure comes from the knowledge that I'm being punished, and a punishment is supposed to hurt.'

'So it has to be a punishment, for something you've done wrong?'

'Usually, yes, but not always. You probably won't understand this at all, but your gran and your great-aunt belong to a generation that still thought of sex as sinful.'

'Yes, I know all that. You don't believe it, do you?'

'No, of course not. It's nonsense, but enough of that rubbed off on me to make sex feel naughty, and what better punishment for a naughty girl than a spanking?'

'But you like it?'

'Exactly. I've turned something bad into something good.'

'I understand, I think.'

It was becoming easy to talk to her, my words no longer forced, and in my enthusiasm for my pet subject I'd forgotten who I was talking to or, if not forgotten, I was no longer concerned. With her acceptance and understanding, it was impossible to think of her as Kate's little girl. As she hauled herself out of the water I went on. 'What Gina gave me was definitely a punishment spanking. Once I'd given my initial consent by making her spill that glass I had no say in what happened at all, which is the way it ought to be, although we do have what's called a stop word. That's an unusual word which the girl who's getting it can say if she really does want it to stop. So however much I'd begged and pleaded, Gina would have taken no notice, but if I'd said the word red, she'd have stopped immediately. We have another word too. If I'd said amber, she'd have slowed down and asked me what was the matter.'

'That's sensible,' she replied. 'So even though you're being punished you have the final say?'

'To an extent, yes. It's very important for the girl being punished to retain the ultimate control, at however deep a level, otherwise the situation risks becoming abusive. On the other hand, once I'd spilt the drink I would have needed a pretty good reason to back out.'

'What if you had?'

'Without good reason? It would reduce her respect for me, which is why I let her make me clean her boots. That's more the sort of thing she's into, but she knows I like to be spanked, so she did that too.'

'Right. Did you like what she did to you?'

'It was revolting, but it was also deeply humiliating, and that turns me on. I'd have done it anyway though, for her sake.'

'You play hard, Penny.'

'Sometimes, yes. It doesn't have to be that way though. I prefer to feel I'm being punished, but a playful spanking needn't hurt at all, if you have a really kind and skilled partner, like Jade or Sophie, who knows how it feels and what's going on in your head. They would take their time getting me ready. There's a little ritual to it, telling me my panties are coming down, that sort of thing, to humiliate me and make it more exciting.'

'I think I understand.'

'Then, when I was bare, they'd start, just pats at first, only getting harder very slowly as my ability to take it rose, and – and touching me. A spanking like that might last twenty minutes, even half-an-hour, and we'd take turns.'

I felt a little embarrassed and more than a little aroused by what I was saying, and by saying it to Pippa. She had wrapped a towel around herself when she got out, but let it come open, taut across her back as she stretched in the morning sunlight. It was impossible not to admire her slender, pale body, her long legs still wet and glistening, the wet bikini pants loose around her hips and moulded to the form of her pussy, the gentle curves of her midriff, her little upturned breasts topped by erect nipples, her neck so pale and elegant, her pixie face so sweet and pretty beneath her unruly mop of wet black curls. As I realised just how badly I wanted her, my sense of guilt came flooding back and she spoke. 'I think I might like that.'

It was nearly eight o'clock before the girls left, Pippa included. We'd spent a pleasantly lazy day, messing about around the swimming pool and walking down to Pangbourne for lunch. Because I'd been the one who got it the night before, both Jade and Sophie were inclined to tease me, with Pippa joining in either for the fun of it or to make herself feel one of the gang, perhaps both. Inevitably the constant reminders that I'd been punished in front of her had their effect, and had Jade and Sophie not been hungover from the night before I might very well have got it again.

I didn't, and was left feeling aroused and guilty as I watched Sophie's car disappear down the lane on their way to drop Pippa home. For a long time I stayed at the gate, but I knew where I was going and what I needed. Rationally, I'd done the right thing by giving Pippa an honest explanation of my feelings, even if I had got a little carried away. Unfortunately, rationality had no bearing whatsoever on my raging emotions, of guilt and in response to what she'd said.

The idea of giving Pippa an erotic spanking was enough to make me weak at the knees and impossible to get out of my head. Every quiet moment of the day had been crowded with impressions of how it would have felt to take her gently across my knee, peel down the little yellow bikini pants and very gently, very tenderly, spank her all the way to orgasm. More intense still, once I had done it to her she might have accepted an offer to do it to me in return, a prospect at once so guilt inducing and so exciting it was physically painful. I badly needed discipline, harsh discipline.

Yet to face what I needed was another matter, and I was still leaning on the gate when Aunt Elaine came out of the house, wiping her fingers on an apron in a fastidious manner as she spoke to me. 'Are you coming in, Penny dear?'

'Yes,' I answered. 'Sorry, I was miles away.'

'You always were inclined to daydream,' she replied as I reached her, to be greeted with a gentle peck on the cheek. 'You'll have dinner with me, won't you?'

I could smell the roast lamb as I came into the house, that hot fat scent when the joint has only been in the oven a little while. It was very late for her to eat and I wondered if she'd timed it deliberately. She also seemed a little drunk, which was very unusual for her.

'Yes, thank you,' I replied, following her into the living room.

'Did you have a nice day with your friends?' she asked. 'Sherry? I've just opened a rather pleasant dry oloroso.'

'Just a little please, Auntie, thank you. Pippa stayed over.'

'So I noticed. I do think she might have come over and said hello to her granny.'

I swallowed at a sudden image of Pippa being put across Elaine's knee and spanked for thoughtlessness, but hastily pushed it away as I took my sherry glass. It was full almost to the brim, and to judge by the level in the bottle she'd already had several glasses.

'That was really my fault,' I said, 'for keeping her chatting all day.'

'You're much more of an age, of course. I see you're putting that vulgar swimming pool to good use.'

'Yes. It's rather nice to have, actually.'

'I'm sure it is, although I do wish you'd ask your friends to keep their tops on. It was bad enough with that Billy Watts and his wife, without my own niece behaving like a tart at the seaside.'

My response was automatic, a hot blush and an instant denial. 'But, Auntie, I didn't take my top off!'

'Well, your friends did, which is the same thing, and in front of Pippa.'

I swallowed again, hard, wondering what she'd have made of Pippa that morning, trotting happily about the house and garden with nothing on but Sophie's yellow bikini pants. Evidently Elaine hadn't seen, but that didn't make me feel any less guilty.

'Sorry, Auntie,' I answered her. 'Do you think, maybe, you should be – be a little harder with me today?'

'Do you feel I should be?'

Her answer was cool, matter-of-fact, in no way betraying that I'd just brought my punishment routine into the conversation.

'A little, perhaps,' I managed. 'I – I just feel it would be right for me.'

'Then no doubt it is. I shall use a hairbrush, so I think you'd better come upstairs.'

She put her sherry glass down on the sideboard and offered a hand. I took it, and was led from the room and up the stairs in silence, my body shivering, my head hung down, thinking of my coming pain. In her bedroom she let go my hand and went to her chest of drawers on top of which rested a big old-fashioned hairbrush of dark, polished wood. My stomach went tight at the sight of it, and I very nearly backed out, but held my peace, waiting meekly at the end of her bed as she picked it up.

'Are you quite certain?' she asked.

I nodded but she went on.

'I appreciate that you need to be smacked from time to time, Penny dear, but I have no wish to hurt you.'

'I – I know it's going to hurt, Auntie, but – but today I think it should hurt – more than usual.'

'Very well, but first, tell me what the matter is. Have you done something?'

I just shrugged, desperately in need of punishment but unable to confess.

She gave her familiar sigh. 'There's no need to be obstinate, Penny. If you feel you need to be punished more severely than usual, I am prepared to do so, but only if I know why.'

'Couldn't – couldn't you just beat me?'

'Absolutely not. Now what is it?'

I couldn't answer, my emotions simply too tangled, for all that in many ways her situation with me mirrored mine with Pippa, but there was one other thing. 'OK,' I said weakly, 'when I went – I went down to take Colonel Aimsworth his things, I let him take me out to dinner, and afterwards he – he managed to persuade me to – to pull his cock . . . in my knickers. I – I suppose I just felt sorry for him. There, I've said it.'

To my surprise her response was to step forwards and hug me, kissing my cheek and smiling as she drew back. 'Then I quite understand,' she said, her voice as soothing as I had ever heard, 'of course you need to have your bottom smacked properly, if you need to have it smacked at all.'

'I do.'

'I know, dear, and I completely understand. Come along then, I think we had better have you kneeling on the bed.'

'I – I'd much rather be over your knee, please, Auntie.'

'If you prefer. I know you like to be held.' She sat down on the bed, still holding the hairbrush, her lap ready for me. 'Would you like to be naked?'

'Perhaps with my dress off. I prefer – would rather –'

'Yes, you like me to take your knickers down, I know.'

Her voice held that so familiar note of exasperation, and I smiled in response. I'd put a summer dress on to walk down to Pangbourne, and quickly pulled it up over my head. With no bra underneath I was left in nothing more than panties, shoes and socks. Elaine gave a reproving tut. 'I do wish you'd wear a bra, Penny. Sometimes you do look like a seaside tart.'

'That's how I felt,' I managed as I climbed on to the bed, kneeling, 'with the Colonel.'

'No doubt that's how he saw you,' she told me, tucking her arm around my waist as I crawled into position across her lap, 'as a common little tart. It's no surprise he made a pass at you. Any man would, but then you always were very naïve, going about with your books and your head in the clouds.'

She'd taken hold of my panties, pulling the waistband up. I shut my eyes tight as they were peeled down off my bottom, baring me for the hairbrush. With that I had already surrendered myself completely to her will, laid bare bottom across her knees, about to be punished the way a naughty girl should, with nothing to cover her most intimate secrets, panties down, always panties down.

'Lift your hips a little,' she instructed and I pushed up my bottom to let her get me fully exposed, feeling my cheeks part to show my anus as I did it.

A single, sharp tug, and my panties had been pulled out from under my pussy, leaving my flesh against the material of her dress. One final adjustment and they were around my thighs, neatly inverted to leave me bare behind, the air cool on the rear lips of my pussy where they showed between my legs. I was shaking badly, and biting my lip, one muscle already twitching in anticipation of what was about to be done to me, of what I'd asked for, and was now going to get, only for the wrong reason.

'Now,' she said, tightening her grip on my waist, 'this will hurt a great deal, so I won't mind if you make a bit of a fuss.'

'No, Auntie – ow!'

I'd squeaked as the hairbrush touched my bottom, just a pat to get her aim, but the wood so hard it still stung. She kept it there, resting on my cheeks as she spoke again, now stern. 'Well then, shall we see what happens to little girls who play the tart at the seaside?'

'Yes, Auntie.'

'Who go without their bras?'

'Yes, Auntie.'

'They have their bottoms smacked, that's what.'

'Yes, Auntie – ow!'

She'd begun to do it, bringing the brush hard down across my cheeks. It stung like mad, making me kick my legs in my panties, and again with the second stroke, and the third as she began to beat me, slow but firm, the smack of the hairbrush on my bottom flesh punctuated by my cries, then by her words as well. 'Yes, Penny, they have their knickers taken down and their bare bottoms smacked.'

I was wriggling and gasping, my bottom already on fire, at the stage I'd described to Pippa, where you wonder how you could ever be so stupid as to want all that pain and indignity. Elaine's words were cutting into me, too, bringing out my humiliation, until I'd begun to sob and snivel in between the slaps of the hairbrush on my bum flesh and my shrieks of pain.

'Their knickers taken down and their bare bottoms smacked,' she repeated, and began to beat me faster, to a firm, even rhythm, a word to each slap of the hairbrush on my flesh, and saying the word too. 'Their – smack – knickers – smack – taken – smack – down – smack – and – smack – their – smack – bare – smack – bottoms – smack – smack – smack – smacked!'

I was crazy with pain, my legs cocked wide, not caring for the rude show I was making of my pussy and my bumhole, yet still hearing every word she said as the spanking grew more frenzied still, the hairbrush rising and falling on the rounded, bouncing balls of my bottom.

'Yes, Penny, their knickers taken down, just like yours are and their bare bottoms spanked, just like I'm spanking your bare bottom, you bad girl – you little – you little tart – Well, now you've got your comeuppance, haven't you? Smack! Smack! Smack! Haven't you, Penny?'

I couldn't answer, the spanking hurt too much, my body no longer even remotely under control as my legs pumped frantically in my lowered panties, howling my head off as that awful brush smacked into the meat of my bottom again and again, every blow sending a jolt right through me. The bed was spattered with tears, a streamer of snot waving wildly from my nose, one shoe off and my sock waving like a little white flag from my toes, a truly pathetic gesture of surrender of which she took no notice whatsoever, spanking and chiding me with a vicious enthusiasm far beyond her normal calm routine.

'Yes, my little tart, knickers down and smack, smack, smack on your bare bottom, that's what you need, Penny, my girl – knickers down and smack, smack, smack on your bare bottom, only not here, not where nobody can see what you're getting, but out in the open, so everybody can see – so everybody can see you get your knickers pulled down – so everybody can see you get your bare bottom spanked. In public, Penny, that's where you need it, you need your knickers taken down and your bare bottom spanked in public – smack, smack, smack on your bare bottom in public – on Bray Beach, perhaps, from your big sister! How would you like that? Spanked for dressing like a little tart, your knickers taken down and your bare bottom spanked by your big sister, at twenty-two years old!'

Her voice was nearly hysterical, but I barely heard, out of my mind with pain as the hairbrush smacked down on my bottom to a frenzied rhythm. I'd gone wild, writhing across her lap, completely out of control, my legs kicking in all directions, my fists beating a tattoo on the bed covers, snot and spittle running from my nose and mouth, blubbering my

145

way through a spanking tantrum beyond anything she'd taken me to before.

A smack caught my thighs and my legs kicked up from the knees, quite involuntarily, catching her. I heard her cry out in pain and suddenly it had stopped, but it was a moment before I could speak, my breath knocked out of my body and trying to snuffle up the snot hanging from my nose before it went on her bed covers.

'Do be careful, Penny!' she chided.

'Sorry,' I managed, still panting, but with the blazing heat in my bottom now bringing me feelings too strong to be denied. 'Carry on . . . please.'

'Very well, but if you don't keep still I'll have to hold your leg under mine, and you know what will happen then.'

'I – I can't help it! Sorry –'

I was going to tell her I felt punished, which was true, but as I spoke she had wrapped her leg around mine, pinning me helpless with my bottom well spread out. A little sob of humiliation escaped me as I realised she was going to bring me off, and this time it would be no accident. I was showing everything too, my cheeks well spread, hot and red and fat, with my bumhole winking between them in my rising excitement and my pussy on full show, a rude, wet tart, just like me.

'Not on my dress, I think,' she stated, and began to tug the material out from under my body.

My eyes were shut, my head shaking in utter mortification as she prepared me for my orgasm. Her pinny and dress came up, to leave my pussy spread on her stocking top, wide open, my aching clitoris pressed to the nylon. I could feel both my holes squeezing in excitement and knew that she could see, that she was going to enjoy what she was about to do to me.

'Such a little tart,' she said happily, and began to spank me again.

I couldn't help myself, already well past the barrier and unable to resist her anyway. The hairbrush was now being applied across the tuck of my bottom, painful, but now hot and desirable, every smack bringing me that little bit nearer to orgasm, but slowly, unhurried. She was still calling me a tart as she beat me, but no longer stern, merely amused by my helpless erotic reaction to punishment.

'Should I do it, do you think?' she asked suddenly. 'Should I take down your knickers and give you your weekly spanking in front of everyone else?'

'No, please, Elaine!'

'Sh, Penny, I'm only playing with you. I won't, but I really think I should. How Jeremy would stare! How angry Geraldine would be, to see her precious daughter get a bare-bottom spanking –'

'Aunt Elaine, please!'

'Oh do shut up, Penny! Must you whine so?'

'Yes, but – ow!'

She'd smacked my pussy, not hard, but enough to sting, and I shut up, frantically trying to keep my thoughts away from the appalling things she was saying as she began to spank me properly again. Each smack was pressing my open pussy to her leg, my clitoris rubbing on her stocking, to an even rhythm, too, and there was simply no way I could prevent it from happening to me. Still she spoke, her voice full of a wistful delight. 'Yes, I would love to spank you in front of Geraldine! She thinks you are so wonderful, so clever ... and I suppose you are, really, but that doesn't stop you being a naughty little tart who needs her knickers taken down by her auntie, does it, Penny dear?'

'No, but, Auntie –'

'Shut up, Penny,' she warned and again tapped the hairbrush on to my pussy. 'Oh yes, I really should, shouldn't I? How she'd stare, to see your dress lifted up and those big white cotton knickers you always wear pulled well down!'

She laughed, and tightened her grip on my waist as she began to spank harder, also bringing her leg up to press her thigh more firmly still to my pussy. I heard my own gasp of ecstasy and despair and I was right on the edge, unable to stop myself as I imagined the picture, my own mother staring wide-eyed with shock as her sister took my panties down to spank me.

It was too awful, too much, but I was coming, wriggling my pussy on my aunt's leg as she spanked my bare bottom, in an agony of humiliation but in ecstasy too as she spoke again. 'That's right, Penny, just let yourself go. Wouldn't it be funny, with Geraldine looking on, and Jeremy, and Kate, and Susan, and little Pippa too –'

The orgasm just hit me, like a dam breaking at the sound of Pippa's name, and I was screaming and thrusting my bottom up and begging Elaine to beat me harder, with that awful image in my head, of the moment my panties were pulled down in front my family, my mother ... and Kate ... and Susan ... and Pippa ... and Pippa, watching her grandmother take down her auntie's panties for a spanking ... and Pippa, watching her grandmother spank my naughty bottom for me ... and Pippa, watching her grand-mother spank me ... and Pippa, watching me spanked ... and Pippa, taking her turn to spank me herself.

I screamed the house down, my whole body jerking and bucking in Elaine's grip, in a frenzied orgasm that lasted until my vision had gone red and the blood was singing in my ears, until I was grinding my pussy on Aunt Elaine's leg in the most shameless display of wanton behaviour imaginable, until my shoe had fallen off and my legs were cocked so wide my straining panties had given in, and all the while with Elaine's hairbrush smacking down over and over again on my naked bottom and her high, mocking voice searing into my brain.

It only stopped when the spanking did, otherwise I'm sure I'd have fainted. As it was she let go and I rolled off her lap, to sit down heavily on my aching bottom, gasping for breath, my face a tear-stained, snotty mess, my vision blurred as I looked up into her eyes. They were glittering, so full of pleasure, so full of delight for what she'd done to me, mischievous to the point of evil, and uncannily like Pippa's. It was also very far indeed from her normal calm response to punishing me.

Her dress and pinny were still up too, showing her stocking tops and the sticky smear where I'd rubbed off on her leg, also a hint of frilly white material between her thighs. I held my gaze, knowing she only had to say the word, or not even that. Before I could stop myself I was leaning eagerly forwards, burying my head between my own aunt's legs, to press my face to her panty crotch. She gave a gasp of shock and spoke the word no, just once, before I'd pulled her knickers aside and my mouth was on her pussy, licking.

Fresh tears were streaming down my face as I did it, something so intimate, something I had imagined so often before, but never dared suggest, and a well-deserved reward from a spanked girl to the one who has done the spanking. For a moment she was trying to resist, her thighs tense around my head, her hand in my hair, trying to pull me away as she found her voice one last time. 'No, Penny, you mustn't – oh –'

She gasped, her grip tightened in my hair, but not to pull me away, and her thighs had come wide as she fell back on her bed. I busied myself with her pussy, now under control as my skill at the familiar task took over. Behind me my bottom felt big and rosy, well spanked, my cheeks bruised and open, my cunt and anus showing behind, as I licked the woman who'd punished me.

My fingers went back and I was rubbing myself once more, teasing my pussy and stroking my spanking marks, fingering my sopping hole and tickling my anus, and all the while lapping urgently at Elaine's ready sex. After a moment, I paused to pull down her knickers and bury my face again, now licking more freely still. As I set my knees wider apart one touched something hard, the hairbrush she'd used to spank me.

It went straight up my pussy, my excitement too high to think twice about such rude behaviour. Her thighs began to tighten around my head and I was fucking myself, deep in, as I used a finger to tickle the mouth of my slippery little bumhole. She was going to come, and I paused, the hairbrush still up me as I took hold of her thighs, opening them, my hands cupping her bottom cheeks, my little finger in her anus, my tongue applied to her clitoris. I heard her groan of ecstasy, felt her muscles start to spasm, and she was there, open under my mouth, coming right in my face, my own aunt.

The thought of what I'd done stayed in my head as I rocked back, too high to think of anything but my own pleasure, despite my burning sense of shame, *because* of my burning sense of shame. I spread myself open on the floor, my legs rolled up and wide apart, knowing she could see every rude detail, my smacked bottom, my spread anal star, my gaping pussy with her hairbrush thrust well up my hole. Again I began to fuck myself, pulling the hairbrush handle in and out of my hole, rubbing it on my clitoris, smacking it to my hot cheeks, pressing the rounded head to my bumhole, and up.

I cried out as the long hard shaft pushed in me, and I left it there, my anus penetrated with the same brush she'd used to spank me as my fingers went back to my pussy. It was perfect, my bottom spread wide to her as she sat up, the bottom she'd spanked so hard, with the brush she'd used to spank me deep up my bum, utterly submissive to her, well punished, my mouth wet with her pussy juice, rubbing my pussy . . . no, wanking my cunt like the dirty little tart I am.

Six

The aftermath of my session under Aunt Elaine's hairbrush was embarrassing to say the least. I'd let myself go in front of her in a way I never had before, first bringing myself off on her leg as she laughed over the thought of spanking me in front of my own mother, then licking her to orgasm and finally rolled on my back with my penetrated bottom flaunted for her and my fingers working on my open pussy, my ruined panties flapping from one ankle. It was intense, but no more so than the way she'd let herself go in front of me, providing me with a far more intimate experience than any of my previous spankings, which was what had allowed me to be so rude with myself at the end.

I'd been giggling as I ran from the room with the hairbrush wobbling between my well-reddened rear cheeks, but, as I washed, the reality of what I'd done slowly began to sink in. The spanking was bad enough, and masturbating so rudely, but to have licked my aunt's pussy really took the biscuit. I still wanted to talk, but she didn't and after a dinner spent making completely inconsequential small talk I ended up going home extremely puzzled.

For four years we had followed more or less the same routine. I would arrive, be prepared for punishment in one way or another, have my bottom spanked and go upstairs to soothe my feelings under my fingers. Sometimes I'd wondered if she did the same, but there had always been an unspoken agreement that we talk about it as little as possible. True, we had slowly been growing more familiar in our approach, especially with me asking for exactly what I needed, but now all that had changed.

It had changed with a vengeance, and almost from the first. In fact, it was not easy to decide at what point out normal routine had been broken. Certainly it was well before the point she'd begun to tell me what a little tart I was, because that was hardly normal. Almost from my arrival she had tormented me in a way she never had before, deliberately playing with my emotions and with my body and there had to be a reason.

Perhaps it was simply the amount of oloroso she'd drunk before I came over? Or my wanting a harder spanking? Something to do with the Colonel? Something to do with Pippa or somebody else in the family?

I pondered each option. She had drunk more than usual, and it had made a difference, but that could only account for so much, maybe the way she'd let go, but not the details. Me needing a proper beating had also contributed, perhaps, but she'd given me the hairbrush before, once or twice, and aside from a few more tears on my part there had been no difference. My admission of sex with the Colonel had also triggered something, initially her calling me a tart, just as he had done. Possibly she had some history with the Colonel?

That seemed to fit the facts, except for her sudden desire to punish me in front of my mother. Thinking back, that had come at more or less the same time as

154

my spanking had ceased to be purely disciplinary and had become sexual. Then there was something she'd said during the crescendo of my spanking – how I'd feel to be given a bare-bottom spanking on Bray Beach by my big sister at the age of twenty-two.

It was highly specific, and a distinctly odd thing to say to me. I knew Bray Beach, in the Channel Isles where we'd always been on holiday, my mother and Elaine since before I was born. Curiously, the last time I'd visited there I had actually been twenty-two, but I quite definitely had not been spanked, or even threatened with spanking. I didn't even have an older sister, but Elaine did, which opened up a shocking possibility.

As I lay face down on my bed with my nightie turned up and my bottom liberally coated with soothing cream I was trying to work it out. Aunt Elaine had been born in 1943, was now sixty-two and so would have had her twenty-second birthday in 1965. That was before she'd been married, and I wasn't even sure if they'd been going to the Channel Isles that long ago. Presumably they had, but would my mother really have dished out a public spanking to her younger sister, let alone taken her knickers down for her?

It was hard to imagine, but then it always is hard to imagine one's parents doing anything other than being staid and sensible, at least in my case. Yet the idea fitted the facts, even the way Elaine's mind had run on from me dressing, as she'd said, like a seaside tart, to what might have been a reflection of her own spanking. If it was true, I wasn't even sure I wanted to think about it, and yet one thing was clear, if that was what had happened, it went a long way to explaining the particular satisfaction Elaine took in spanking me, both at Kate's wedding and afterwards.

155

She had confessed to wanting to do it, the very first time, because of my supposed superiority about my academic success and the way my mother always compared Kate so unfavourably. It had never occurred to me at the time, but looking back it made sense. So did the idea of Elaine enjoying a vicarious revenge by punishing her niece for a long past session across her big sister's knee on Bray Beach. Maybe there had been more than one session? Maybe . . .

I did eventually manage to get to sleep, by about three o'clock in the morning, and was feeling tired and somewhat ill at ease all the next day, the exact opposite of my usual reaction to a spanking from Elaine. As usual my feelings were distinctly ambivalent, the situation at once uncomfortable and providing a broad scope for the erotic humiliation I am so helpless to resist. I am also intensely inquisitive and, one way or another, I was determined to find out the truth.

Elaine herself quite clearly did not want to tell me, and I had no intention of risking the relationship I'd built up for so long and which did so much to fulfil my needs. Asking my mother was an absurdity, impossible, and also pointless. She would not have told me, while the question was sure to make her ask questions in return. The possibility of her finding out that her sister spanked me on a regular basis made me feel physically weak, or even that I liked to be spanked at all. Two years previously it had very nearly happened for real, with the dreadful Marjorie Burgess, an incident that had taken a great deal of explaining. I had no intention of going there again.

Yet I had to ask myself who would know, and be prepared to tell me. Specifically, I had no idea, but in general terms there had to be people who'd witnessed the event, and would remember. Nobody had ever mentioned it to me, despite all my time on the island, but that was hardly surprising. None of my contemporaries would even have been born.

Going to the island and trying to seek out some old boy who'd witnessed the event was tempting, but simply not a practical proposition. I could just see myself going up to old Mr Allen who'd run the pub overlooking Bray Beach and asking him if he could remember seeing one girl spanked by another on the beach in 1965. Knowing me I'd end up with his cock in my mouth. Besides, it was the middle of term and therefore impractical.

My thoughts turned back to Elaine. Perhaps after a few sherries, with me over her lap in a lather of spanking pain and humiliation, she might be persuaded to revisit the fantasy. She'd certainly enjoyed it, and just possibly I would be able to steer things my way. Very possibly it would work, while no alternative suggested itself. For the time being, there was nothing I could do.

For the rest of the week I kept my mind firmly on work, determined not to be distracted. It was far from easy, with the thought of the weekend to come, and made a great deal less so on the Thursday evening when I got home. There was a letter on my mat, along with a gas bill, a bank statement and a square cream-coloured envelope containing a stiff card and postmarked Worthing.

It was obviously an invitation, and could only be from Colonel Aimsworth. Sure enough, I was invited to celebrate his birthday, at the same hotel he'd taken me to before, only for lunch. There was no hint of impropriety, or even any suggestion that we'd be alone, just the letters RSVP neatly written in one corner, which I understood, and WWK in the other, which I could guess at.

I may be naïve sometimes, but not that naïve. Colonel Aimsworth was going to expect something, probably in the way of a birthday treat, and if I went at all it would have to be on the understanding that I would give it to him. At the least I'd have to pose, maybe let him spank me, perhaps toss him off the way I had before.

The prospect was as embarrassing as it was alluring, and all that evening my mind kept flicking back to how I'd felt, sucking spunk through my panties with my bottom hot behind me, in a glorious blend of humiliation and ecstasy. In the end it was simply too much.

I was in front of the TV, a glass of wine in one hand, the control in the other, and simply turned the sound off, swallowed my wine at a gulp, rolled my legs up to pull off my panties, stuck them in my mouth and brought myself to ecstasy as I imagined being put through my paces by him in a variety of rude and intimate ways. By the time I'd come, I was sure I would accept.

Inevitably I felt a little guilty, but the invitation was also an excellent opportunity to bring up the conversation of my behaving like a seaside tart with Aunt Elaine. Not that I was even quite sure what a seaside tart was, unless it was simply a girl who behaved the way I had with Colonel Aimsworth.

Yet it was some time away, so there was no rush, and I decided that to have moved too soon might make her clam up completely. That Sunday I got my regular punishment, to my relief, but Aunt Elaine was definitely reserved, taking me across her knee in the dining room and pulling down my panties for a session of purely domestic discipline that left me tingling pleasantly. Afterwards, I felt my usual sense of wellbeing, making me realise that, whatever her motives, there was something very special about the way she handled me.

The following week was entirely mundane, with plenty of rather routine work, until by the end I was in the peculiar state of feeling that the secret side of my life was almost a dream, something embarrassing that lived in my imagination, while reality existed only within the boundaries of the department and my existence as Dr P. Birch, Senior Lecturer/Genetics, which was what it said on my door. The feeling was by no means unfamiliar, and I determined to make up for it at the weekend by being thoroughly naughty.

Jade and Sophie had argued, mildly, during the week. Sophie was fed up with being the plaything of hardcore dykes and wanted to indulge her exhibitionist streak at the weekend, while Jade, never keen on men, wanted to go to Whispers. Inevitably I was called on to adjudicate, which meant going into London on the Saturday morning and boxing their ears for them. With luck we'd end up playing together and stay clear of both Jade's sadistic bull dykes and Sophie's voyeurs and dirty old men.

What I didn't expect was Pippa, never mind at just after nine in the morning, wandering casually in at my patio door. She was in jodhpurs, riding boots and a cream-coloured roll-necked jumper, also wearing a hard hat, so she'd obviously been riding. There was no sign of her pony, but she was carrying a bag.

'Hi, Pippa. Where's Bell?'

'Being shoed,' she answered. 'Mum and Jem are going to pick her up. Do you mind if I shower and change?'

'No, of course not. Coffee?'

'Yes please.'

As I went to put on fresh coffee she leant over the kitchen table, turning the pages of my paper in a somewhat distracted manner. Something was obviously on her mind, immediately making me worried I'd said too much when I spoke to her before, something to unsettle her or make her feel bad about herself. Whatever it was, I determined to do my best for her, and not to think about the rounded cheekiness of her bottom in her jodhpurs, because in reading the papers she'd accidentally put herself in a prime spanking position.

'What's up?' I asked, as casually as I could manage. 'Is everything all right?'

'Great,' she answered, turning around to take her mug. 'I just wondered, are you going to Whispers tonight? You promised you'd take me again, remember?'

'Did I?' I answered, trying to remember what I'd actually said.

'Yes,' she said. 'You did. You haven't changed your mind, have you?'

'No, no, not at all, um – I am going into London, but I was thinking more of a quiet night in with the girls.'

'That's OK, I don't mind just the four of us. I mean, if that's OK?'

I took a sip of my coffee as I tried to work out what to say. For all her outward confidence I could detect something fragile in her voice and I didn't want to hurt her feelings. Nor could I very well ask her to come with me when I was hoping for a night of naughty behaviour with Jade and Sophie. She spoke again before I could decide on a reply, now sounding more vulnerable than ever.

'Do you think – no, never mind.'

'Tell me.'

'No. You'll just think I'm being silly, or give me a lecture or something.'

'I won't, I promise.'

She pursed her lips, an odd half-smile, then looked down as she spoke, her voice a whisper. 'I just wondered if you – you –'

'Say it, anything,' I urged, delight and alarm milling together in my head at what she might be about to suggest.

'If – if you – if you might like to spank me?'

'Pippa!'

It came out as an exclamation, before I could stop myself, and immediately regretted it, wishing I'd taken time with my reply. She turned away, blushing red and looking as if she was about to cry, and would have run if I hadn't caught her by the arm.

'Pippa, no, come back – I'm sorry,' I stammered. 'It didn't mean it to sound like that, but, look, you have to understand. I can't do that!'

She turned on me, her eyes large and moist, one corner of her mouth twitching. 'Why not? I knew you'd be like this, I –'

'Sh! Pippa, please! It's not that – it's not that I don't want to –'

'Well, do it then!'

'I can't! Please try and see it from my point of view. What would your mother say?'

'Much the same as Great-Aunt Geraldine would if she knew you go over to Granny's for it every weekend!'

I let go of her arm, struck dumb, my mouth falling wide, the blood coming up to my face in a great, burning rush.

Pippa looked right into my eyes. 'You do, don't you?'

'How – how do you know?' I managed.

'Jade told me,' she said. 'Sort of, when they drove me back. She was joking with Sophie, saying you'd be getting it right at that moment. I asked who from.'

'And she told you!?'

'No, she wouldn't, but I guessed, and I'm right, aren't I?'

I nodded, then forced myself to speak. 'Yes, but – but that's something very private, and very complicated –'

'I understand,' she interrupted, 'or maybe I don't, but I think I want the same.'

'The same? I'm not sure you do, Pippa. It's – between Elaine and myself, it's a – it's domestic discipline, really, something that fulfils a very deep need in me –'

'Maybe not exactly the same,' she cut in, 'but something like that. Ever since I saw you getting it at Whispers, and we talked, I can't get it out of my head. It's just so much more – so much more alive!'

'Alive?'

'Yes, alive, like it means so much to you, like it's so edgy, and not – not boring, like my life. You have to let me try it, Penny, just once at least –'

'I don't know, Pippa, I would like to – I really –'

'No, you wouldn't, you think I'm just some messed-up –'

'That's not true, Pippa. I think you're very intelligent and also very attractive.'

'Why won't you do it, then? Don't you think I could cope?'

'Well, to be honest –'

'Did I freak in Whispers?'

'No, but, you were only watching, and –'

'Yeah, and now I've thought about it and I want to try it. Oh come on, Auntie Penny! When you were spanked by Gina you could have used your stop word, couldn't you?'

'Yes, I suppose so.'

'And you knew I'd see, so you must have wanted it in front of me? You said it turned you on when I was laughing.'

'Yes, but there's still a big difference –'

'And I can handle it. AJ and Gina, what did they do with you in the Ladies?'

I hesitated, trying to find an acceptable answer, but she spoke again before I could decide on one.

'Like I don't know. You went down on them, didn't you? What, do you think I've never been down on another woman?'

'I – I don't know,' I stammered, completely taken aback, 'there's no reason why not, I suppose, but spanking is different –'

'Well, I have, and yes, I know spanking is different, which is why I'm coming to you, because most people are just going to think I'm weird.'

'That's part of the problem, Pippa. I don't want people to think you're weird.'

'I'm me!' she snapped back, angry and pleading all at once. 'Now please, I want it!'

'Pippa, I'm not sure –'

'Penny, I am a grown woman, and I have a right not to be treated like a child! I would very much like you to do it, but I'm going to have it done with or without you, so if you won't help I suppose I'll just have to ask Jade or Sophie.'

'They won't either, Pippa.'

'AJ then. She will.'

'Pippa, no! Believe me, please, you have no idea what you are letting yourself in for!'

'Penny, I mean it.'

'I'm sure you do, Pippa, but, look, let's talk about this another time, OK? For now, come into London with me and we'll get a pizza or something and have a girls' night in at Jade's flat. You can ask us anything you like, and maybe – I don't know, but maybe, only promise me you will not go to AJ, please?'

She hesitated, then spoke again. 'OK, that's a deal, but I want a little, now, so I know you mean it. Maybe even if you just get me ready, the way you described. That sounded so horny.'

I hesitated, wrestling with my conscience and my desire to see how she looked with her jodhpurs down, maybe even her panties. Seeing her bare wasn't a problem, that meant nothing, but this was sexual, and it meant a lot. It was just too tempting. 'Maybe,' I said, 'maybe if you just pop your jodhpurs and panties down for a moment, and maybe bend over, as if you were getting ready? If you don't like that, you won't like spanking.'

'Oh I'd like that, I love to show off, but I want *you* to take my jodhpurs down.'

'Oh, Pippa, no. Can I at least think about it?'

'I want it now, Penny, just to make me feel right. I don't think I could ask again, so do it, please. Here I am, so do it.'

She turned as she spoke, to lean over the table again, looking back at me over her shoulder, her little round bottom stuck out, pert and inviting beneath the smooth tan corduroy of her jodhpurs, so spank-able, so tempting. Her eyes were on mine, wide and moist with unshed tears, her lower lip trembling badly. All I had to do was step forwards, take down her jodhpurs and the panties beneath, and spank her bottom for her, what she wanted . . . what I wanted.

There was a huge lump in my throat, making it impossible to speak, but I nodded and stepped forwards. Her expression changed immediately, her face softening, her mouth coming a little open, her eyes closing in bliss, to squeeze a single, heavy tear from beneath each lid. As I touched her she gave a sigh, expressing a need every bit as powerful as my own.

164

She hung her head low, her breathing deep and even as she waited for her exposure. I kissed her cheek, hoping to give a reassuring touch as my hands circled her waist, to unfasten her belt. My guilt was raging in my head as her buckle came loose in my fingers, a voice screaming at me to stop, but I was lost, unable to hold back if I'd wanted to. She was too lovely, too beautiful, too urgent, her slender body so vital, irresistible.

With her buckle loose I pushed my thumbs into the waistband of her jodhpurs, still hardly able to accept what I was doing. She gave another little sob as I began to push them down, the elastic stretching over her slender hips, her jumper pulling free, her pale smooth flesh showing at one thigh, and her panties, plain white briefs pulled taut over the neatly turned ball of her bottom.

'Plain and white,' she said. 'I'm in spanking panties, especially for you.'

I shook myself, again trying to keep my feelings under control, but it was really no good, not when her beautiful bottom was just inches in front of my face, not when I could catch the scent of her excitement, not when she'd put on white cotton panties to tempt me into spanking her. 'Thank you,' I said, and kissed her bottom, just gently, on the seat of her panties and wondering if she'd like it licked.

A new pang of guilt hit me at the thought of poking my tongue up Pippa's bottom. I swallowed, wondering what in hell I thought I was doing, holding my own cousin's jodhpurs down around her thighs with her panty-covered bottom almost in my face. Yet she looked so perfectly spankable, with it stuck out for exactly that purpose, her cheeks bulging in the thin cotton, spilling out, soft and full around her leg holes, tucked under to where the neatly split fig of her pussy showed, encased in white cloth, moist white cloth, with the scent of her excitement teasing my senses.

'You will take my knickers down, won't you?' she asked suddenly. 'I think I want my knickers down.'

'Of course,' I promised, although it had never occurred to me for a moment to leave them up.

When a girl is to be spanked her knickers come down, as surely as you peel an orange, and Pippa would be no exception. I paused a moment to roll up her jumper, and the tail of her blouse beneath, and again to admire the full view of her panty seat, fresh and white over her lovely bottom, looking so sweet, and about to be pulled down. My tongue poked out to wet suddenly dry lips and I squatted low, right behind her.

She gave a little whimpering noise in her throat as I took hold of her waistband, and I was doing it, pulling Pippa's panties down, a thrill so exquisite my eyes stayed riveted to her flesh as it all came on show; the twin dimples in the small of her back, the first low swell of her beautiful cheeks, the tiny V where her crease began, and slowly, the full, feminine swell of her pale smooth cheeks, deeply cleft, deeply tucked under, and open, to show the tiny pink star of her anus and the sweetly turned lips of her sex.

'Is that better?' I asked softly. 'Now you're bare?'

Her answer was a sob, given as I settled her panties around her thighs, a tangle of white cotton, moist where they'd pulled free of her pussy. No detail was hidden from me, my own Pippa, bare and ready, her panties well down, her pussy so sweet, so neatly formed, a purse of silky smooth pink flesh with moist, richer pink folds just showing between, her anus a little dimple of pale flesh, so tight, so tiny, with just a little colour to mark the bumps and bulges around the secret little hole up which my tongue would have fitted very nicely indeed, or my nose, stimulating her and humiliating myself as I licked her to orgasm.

I shook myself again, trying to focus on the task in hand. My throat was dry with desire as I stood up and stepped back a little, eager to remember her as she looked, prepared for her first ever spanking, with her jodhpurs and panties pulled down, her upper clothes rolled up to show her completely, her riding boots strangely severe, incongruous for a girl about to be punished, her black curls peeping out from under the rim of her riding helmet, her freckled, pixie face looking back at me, flushed with arousal, her bottom bare.

'Well?' she demanded. 'Are you going to spank me, or just stare at my bum?'

There was a hint of laughter in her voice, and the last of my qualms dissolved.

'You said you just wanted me to get you ready,' I answered her, 'but OK, if you're going to behave like a brat, I'll treat you like a brat. I'm going to punish you, Pippa. I'm going to take you across my knee and I'm going to spank your bottom for you. Come here!'

I'd stepped forwards as I spoke, and grabbed her wrist, pulling her with me as I sat down on one of the kitchen chairs. She came, giggling in excitement as I put her across my knee, her bottom well up, the little round cheeks parted to show her bumhole and pussy, the same rude position I've been made to adopt so many times, only now it was my Pippa, my beautiful cheeky pixie cousin, my Pippa, ready for the spanking she genuinely seemed to crave.

For one brief instant I looked up, my attention off the darling little bottom I was about to smack for less than a second, intent on pushing the table away so she wouldn't catch it when she began to kick. In that one brief instant all my excitement, all my arousal simply vanished. Aunt Elaine was walking across the patio, right towards us, and in maybe five more paces was going to see in, at her granddaughter laid bare bottom across my legs, a pose that would be all too familiar to her.

'It's your gran, Pippa, hide!'

Pippa swore, and dived under the table, wrenching at her panties and jodhpurs as she struggled to get them up in time. I stood up, jerking my thumb frantically towards the shelter of the kitchen units as I walked to the door with what I sincerely hoped was a calm, welcoming smile. As I reached it, Pippa was still on her back, struggling to pull her jodhpurs up over her bottom.

I stepped outside – it was all I could do – to greet Elaine with a peck on her cheek and a completely inane comment about the progress of her delphin-iums. A single curious glance and she responded, allowing me to steer her away from the house with my heart hammering in my chest. By the time we got back, Pippa was seated at the kitchen table, on the very chair I'd been about to spank her over, innocent-ly sipping coffee from her mug.

Seven

Elaine had only come over to borrow some of my decorating things, but by the time she left the moment was gone for Pippa and me, while neither of us felt safe. Yet I'd made it plain I was willing to do it, and there was no doubt in my mind that she was going to expect it in the future. We were both quite shaken because, while, rationally, it was quite hard to see how Elaine could have justified her objections to me giving Pippa the same treatment I received myself, neither of us wanted to risk it. My reaction was shock, Pippa's nervous excitement, and she was laughing about it as we drove down to the station.

'Imagine Gran's face! Wouldn't it have been a picture!?'

'Yes, but I'd rather not if you don't mind.'

'She'd have roasted you, really roasted you!'

'It's not funny, Pippa. I think she'd just have been cross.'

I wasn't going to mention the way Elaine had tormented me by suggesting I be spanked in front of Pippa, because I knew it had only been done to tease me, but it made for a disturbing picture. Possibly, just possibly, she'd have done it, my dress up and my panties taken down there and then, my bottom spanked hard as I was told off, and left blubbering on the floor. I also knew exactly what effect it would have had on me, which was making me distinctly uncomfortable between my legs as we waited for our train.

The platform was too crowded to let us talk about anything other than mundane subjects, and so was the slow train into Reading. Pippa had changed, into black hipster jeans with a pattern of flowers and butterflies picked out on each leg, along with a pink top that left her midriff bare. It was hardly country wear, confirming my suspicion that she'd had everything planned from the start, just as I would have done in her position.

Not that I intended to say anything, but I did want to talk to her before we met up with Jade and Sophie. My chance came at Reading, where we just missed one fast train into Paddington from the West Country, so that when a second arrived a few minutes later there were plenty of spare seats. Pippa was chatting happily about their Christmas skiing holiday, and I waited until she'd drawn breath before asking my question. 'Did it feel the way you expected it to, at my house?

For an instant she looked indecisive and I was telling myself I wanted her to have disliked the sensation, or been indifferent, but knowing it was a lie. 'The best,' she said suddenly, 'just the very best, even better than I thought it would be, and I've been thinking about it every single minute since we spoke that time by your pool.'

'Oh, good – great,' I answered, smiling despite myself.

'Really yummy,' she went on happily, 'and you're right, it's all in the head or mostly, that feeling of – of doing something I shouldn't, something that's just way inappropriate. I mean, I just get all this stuff all the time, how I'm supposed to look, how I'm supposed to behave, who I'm supposed to fancy, and it's all such crap. I don't want to yearn for some pop idol or football player I'm never going to meet, or to go out on dates with some guy who comes in his pants just because he's got his hand up my top! I want to be a baby dyke, I want to take a spanking, I want to be made to lick AJ's pussy –'

I'd been going gradually pinker as she spoke, but that was the limit. 'Uh, uh! Pippa, not AJ, you promised.'

'OK, but you're as bad as my mum, sometimes. What's the big deal with AJ anyway?'

'She's hard, really hard. Believe me, being made to lick her is the least of it.'

'So what's the most? Come on, tell me.'

'I really don't think you want to know.'

'Yes I do, or I wouldn't have asked.'

I hesitated, keen to put her off but not too keen on admitting what had been done to me personally, until a picture came to my mind of Pippa turning up at her house on the back of AJ's bike, dressed as I'd seen Jade dressed sometimes, her hair spiked and dyed, her crop top so short the undersides of her breasts showed, no knickers under a leather mini skirt barely long enough to cover her bottom, knee-length boots with block heels. AJ liked to have her playthings pierced too, and tattooed. There was really no choice. 'Last time, at Whispers,' I said, keeping my voice completely matter-of-fact, 'she and Gina urinated on me, then put my head down the toilet and flushed it. For AJ that's just a bit of casual fun. Is that what you want?'

For a moment Pippa was staring in horror, but there was still a giggle in her voice as she replied. 'She gave you a swirly? Gross!'

'That's AJ for you.'

She nodded earnestly, then spoke again, in astonishment. 'And you let her?'

I'd been expecting the question, but the blood still rushed to my cheeks as I answered. 'Yes, which is one reason I wasn't too keen on going to Whispers in the first place. As I explained before, if I want my thing, I have to be prepared to give in return. You saw what Gina made me do, and she's soft next to AJ. There's another thing too, which I suppose you deserve to be told. When you've been spanked – or when I've been spanked anyway – you get into a sort of submissive high, when you want to be made to do that sort of thing, yes, even what AJ did to me. That's one very good reason only to play with people you can trust, because you know they'll respect you, unlike Alice Jemima Croft.'

'Who?'

'AJ, but don't ever call her that, or you'll get what I did and worse.'

Pippa made a face, and would have said more, but a trio of businessmen sat down in the seats across from us and she returned to her earlier conversation, describing her efforts to learn to snowboard. A moment later the train had begun to move, and there was no more opportunity to talk openly until we'd got out at Turnpike Lane. I had at least managed to ask her not to discuss our interrupted spanking session, because I knew Jade and Sophie wouldn't be satisfied until they'd done the same. If she really had to be spanked, and it seemed that she did, I wanted her first time to be intimate, and, to be honest, mine alone.

What with one thing and another I hadn't bothered to ring Jade and discuss the evening, so I was expecting to have to adjudicate between them. What

172

I was not expecting was the sleek black motorbike parking directly outside Jade's flat, an all-too-familiar motorbike.

'Cool,' Pippa said, as I stopped in hesitation. 'Mum won't even let me ride pillion.'

'You wouldn't want to ride pillion on that one,' I told her, 'it's AJ's.'

'Oh, I don't know. I mean, she can't do anything to me if I'm on the back of her bike, can she?'

'It's where she might take you to I'm worried about. Um –' I was going to suggest going to a nearby café until it was safe, although I knew that might not be for hours, until I glanced up at Jade's windows to see AJ herself looking down at us. With her shaved head and her leather jacket half open at the front she looked positively vicious, which her smile did nothing to alleviate. She made a curt gesture and moved her lips, an obvious command. Pippa had been stroking the petrol tank of the bike with something close to adoration and I pulled her hastily back. 'Don't touch her bike, she gets funny about that.'

'Moody cow, isn't she?'

'Yes. Oh, and above all, don't touch her boots.'

'Her boots.'

'Yes, it's a dyke thing. To her it's a privilege for Jade to polish them, nuts I know, but –'

'I thought you were into all that?'

'I'm not – let's just say that because I enjoy what they can do for me doesn't mean I buy in to the whole package. I'm more like Sophie.'

'A slut?'

'Thanks, Pippa!'

'That's how she describes herself.'

'OK, fair enough, I suppose, but I'm not quite as bad as she is. I suppose we'd better go up.'

Jade had opened the window, and threw her keys down along with a cheerful greeting for both of us. I let myself in and climbed quickly up the stairs, telling myself I was going to have to be firm with AJ and make very sure she didn't get any ideas about Pippa. All three of them were in Jade's tiny sitting room, AJ lounging in the most comfortable chair in her leathers, underneath which she appeared to be top-less, Jade in baggy, fashionably cut combats that still managed to look indecent on her figure, Sophie in a plain red floaty summer dress that went with her blonde hair and sweet face to make her look as if butter wouldn't melt in her mouth. In practice, it was just the sort of dress she liked to go dogging in, easily lifted.

'Never touch the bike,' AJ growled, as Pippa followed me in.

'Sorry,' Pippa replied, 'I was just admiring it.'

'Look but don't touch, unless you want a ride.'

'I don't think she's allowed to,' I said hastily.

'Penny!' Pippa hissed.

'Not allowed to?' AJ queried, her voice rich with scorn. 'Says who?'

'Says nobody!' Pippa snapped, throwing me a dark look.

'She – she doesn't have a crash helmet,' I pointed out.

AJ reached down beside her chair to lift up a battered gold motorbike helmet as she spoke. 'I was going to take Dumplings up the Pumps. Come on, Pippa.'

'You are not taking Pippa to the Pumps, and that's final!' I stated.

'What's the Pumps?' Pippa asked.

'A place all her dyke friends hang out,' Sophie answered.

'A garage on the old A1,' Jade added.

AJ had got up, and rounded on me in amazement, shaking her head. 'You are getting well up yourself, Miss Muffet. Need another lesson, do you, like last time?'

I put my hands out, forcing myself to speak calmly. 'AJ, you are not taking Pippa to the Pumps.'

'Did I say I was?' she demanded. 'I was just going to give her a spin up to the North Circ, that's all. Jesus, Penny, what's with you recently?'

'Nothing,' I lied. 'OK, I'm sorry. Go for a ride, Pippa, but do be careful, AJ, please?'

'I'll be fine,' Pippa insisted. 'I can look after myself, Penny.'

'OK, go,' I sighed, 'but you're not going to take her to the pumps, are you, AJ?'

AJ merely shook her head and made for the door, Pippa following. They were talking about motorbikes as their voices faded, and I went to the window. Jade came to stand beside me, putting her arm around my waist. 'Relax, Penny. She'll be fine. AJ's a good driver.'

'She's psychotic! Anyway, that's not what I'm worried about.'

'What's the problem? Are you scared AJ'll get into her knickers? You've got to let her make her own choices, Penny.'

I drew in my breath but didn't reply, knowing it was exactly the same argument I would have employed in different circumstances, and applied to myself. Pippa had to make her own moral choices, just as I'd had to make mine, and she was every bit as intelligent. Down in the street Pippa had put her helmet on, and I watched as she swung one long leg over the back of AJ's bike. The position left her bottom stuck out, beautifully rounded in her tight

175

black jeans, with the waistband so low the top of her panties showed, those same white cotton panties I'd pulled down just a few hours earlier.

A strong pang of jealousy caught me at the thought, but I bit it down. It was bad enough that I fancied Pippa, without the suspicion that I was beginning to fall in love with her. I was just going to have to control my emotions, or at least try. Sophie spoke up from behind me. 'Are we going out or what?'

'I don't know what we're doing,' I answered. 'I just want to wait for Pippa and AJ to come back.'

'They won't be back, Penny,' Sophie responded. 'After the way you spoke to AJ, she's bound to go to the Pumps. I reckon your Pippa fancies her and all.'

'If AJ was going to the Pumps she'd have said so,' Jade put in. 'AJ doesn't do sneaky.'

'That's true,' I admitted.

The prospect of an evening in was no longer so enticing, not with AJ there, and Pippa did seem to have a fascination for her, a horrified fascination, but still a fascination. I bit my lip, considering my options as Sophie went on.

'I want to go to Barn Hill. There's this mixed-race guy who goes there, and he is huge, and I mean huge.'

She made a gesture with her hands, like an angler boasting about the size of a fish, only less believable.

Jade laughed. 'What is he, Sophie, a donkey?'

'He's hung like one!' Sophie insisted. 'And all smooth and silky, I could suck him for hours . . .'

She trailed off, closing her eyes in bliss as her tongue flicked out to moisten her lips.

'And what are we supposed to do while you're entertaining Mr Donkey Dick?' Jade demanded.

'Watch?' Sophie suggested. 'Play with each other? Suck on his balls?'

'I don't do men,' Jade pointed out.

'Liar,' Sophie answered her. 'Come on, Penny, we haven't been out dogging together for months, and it's not close to home for you either.'

'What about Pippa?' I asked.

'She can come too.'

'She doesn't even know I'm bi!'

'Yes she does, we told her.'

'Sophie! And, oh, yes, that's another thing, Jade, when I told you about me and my aunt it was supposed to stay a secret!'

'She guessed!' Jade protested.

'Yes,' I pointed out, 'she guessed because you said I'd be getting it while you were driving back to drop her off!'

'Sorry,' she answered, making a mock contrite face. 'Do you want me over?'

'I should,' I told her. 'In fact, yes, why not? It'll make me feel better.'

She giggled as I stepped back from the window, and came over my knee without protest, up on her toes to make it easier for me to get her combats down. Her bottom looked as delectable as ever, straining out the patterned khaki and green fabric, but she was enjoying herself altogether too much for my liking. I was determined to get her bare anyway, and curled my arms around her to open her fly before jerking her trousers down over her bulging cheeks.

All she had on underneath was a bright-green thong, pulled deep into the crease of her big, meaty bottom and offering no protection whatsoever. I took it down anyway, and spread her cheeks in a vain effort to humiliate her by showing off her anus and between her legs. She'd waxed, her fat little pussy quite bare and slightly red, also moist. I begun to spank her, making her big cheeks wobble and bounce, but only provoking sighs and gentle purring noises. Sophie laughed, and probably more for the expression on my face than the state Jade was in. I spanked harder, until my hand had begun to sting and Jade was gasping a little, only not with pain.

'It's no good, Penny,' Sophie said, getting up, 'you can't match AJ.'

'I aim to try,' I answered, tightening my grip on Jade's waist and laying in with all my force.

Jade's whole body was shaking, her bottom wobbling and squashing like a fat pink jelly, her huge boobs bouncing against my legs, but she hadn't even began to kick and my hand was getting extremely sore. It was far from satisfying, more frustrating, until Sophie came back from the kitchen with the biggest of Jade's wooden spoons. I responded in silence, with a smile and a nod of approval, took the spoon and just laid in without the slightest warning.

The way Jade squealed as the heavy spoon smacked down on her bottom flesh must have made people down in the street think we were torturing a piglet, which I was, in a sense. She gave a frantic jerk too, almost tumbling off my lap, but I clung on, belabouring her bottom with the spoon as fast and as hard as I could, the smacks of wood on meaty, girlish flesh blending with her high-pitched piping and Sophie's hysterical laughter.

I was grinning as I beat her, letting all my bad feelings out on her fat bottom, yet secure in the knowledge that it was exactly what she wanted, the treatment she needed to take to fully turn her on. Sure enough, when I'd finally satisfied my need to punish her and let go, she went straight to her knees, cuddling on to me with her whole body shivering in submissive ecstasy. I began to stroke her hair, soothing her, and wondering if I should have her lick me, which I badly needed.

There was time, probably, and I pushed her down as I set my knees apart and lifted my dress. She gave a little sigh as she realised she was to be made to lick pussy and eagerly burrowed her face into my panty crotch. I'd been going to take them down, but it felt too nice, with her lips and nose nuzzling at my flesh through the cotton, to send a sharp jolt of ecstasy through me each time she jogged my clitoris.

She was playing with herself too, her hands back to stroke the fat, reddened cheeks of her bottom and tease in between. I watched, pleased to have a spanked girl attending to me for a change and enjoying the sheer opulence of her body. After a moment she paused to pull up her top, spilling her huge breasts out of her bra and into her hands. I slid forwards on the seat, spreading my thighs wider still.

Jade looked up, her eyes bright, her smiling mouth stained with my pussy cream. I pointed down and she giggled, shuffling forwards on her knees with her breasts cupped in her hands, to press one fat globe to my pussy. My mouth came wide as she began to rub herself on me, the smooth, plump curve of her boob spreading out my pussy lips with her erect nipples bumping on my clitoris. It was too good to resist, a delightful sensation and so naughty too, bringing me up towards orgasm in moments, and over the edge as I came with a long sigh.

The moment I was finished, her face was back between my thighs, her tongue licking me as she masturbated, only no longer for my pleasure, but her own. I knew what she'd want and came right to the edge of the chair, allowing her to push her tongue between my bottom cheeks up into the little hole between. She was coming almost immediately, with her tongue burrowed well in up my bottom hole in a gesture of apology and submission.

I felt a great deal better for my climax, but we'd barely sorted ourselves out when AJ came back. Pippa was glowing, so full of nervous energy she couldn't keep still, going straight to the window to stare down at where they'd parked the bike. Even AJ looked well pleased with herself, speaking as soon as she'd removed her helmet. 'One ten on the Pinkham Way, and it would have been more if it wasn't for that fucking speed camera. Hang about, I smell cunt. You three dirty bitches been at it already?'

'Penny spanked me,' Jade announced casually, as Pippa turned to me with a pleased look.

'You're turning into a right little top, aren't you, Miss Muffet?' AJ responded. 'So which one of you is coming to the Pumps?'

'We're going dogging at Barn Hill,' Sophie answered her.

'Not me, I'm not!' AJ laughed. 'What, you think I want to watch you suck some dirty old bastard's cock?'

'No,' Sophie admitted, silently chagrined but doing her best to hold her own, 'but that's where we're planning to go. Wasn't it, Penny?'

'Yes,' I answered, trying not to sound too doubtful.

'It's no big deal,' AJ insisted. 'I need somebody at the Pumps, that's all, nothing heavy. You can come, Pippa, leave these three sluts to their dirty old men.'

Pippa threw me a doubtful look and I quickly stepped in. 'Why can't you take Naomi or Sam or somebody?' I asked.

'That's no fucking use,' AJ objected. 'I need somebody cute and femmy, as a birthday treat for Xiang, she'd fucking love you, Pippa. You lick cunt, don't you?'

I could just imagine the mixed doubt and desire in Pippa's mind, but for all my warnings she clearly had

180

no idea what she was letting herself in for. Xiang was a big, beefy Chinese dyke, who was going to expect a lot more than Pippa would be bargaining for.

'I'll go,' I said hastily, 'as long as you promise to bring me back, OK?'

AJ shrugged. 'Yeah, that's good. She's well into you, thinks you're a stuck-up little bitch who needs a hiding. I'll bring you back and all, if you still want to come.'

'Yes, but not here,' Sophie demanded, 'because I'm not sitting around half the night waiting for you. Come back to Barn Hill. It's a lot nearer anyway. Do you want to come to Barn Hill, Pippa? It's fun.'

'What's at Barn Hill, a club?' Pippa asked, all wide-eyed innocence.

'It's a dogging site,' Sophie explained as I hid my face in my hands.

'What's a dogging site?'

'A dogging site,' AJ answered her, 'is where dirty bitches like Sophie go to tart around so that dirty old men can jack off over them –'

'That's not really fair,' Sophie interrupted. 'OK, there are some pretty gross guys, but there are some cute guys too, like this one I was with last week. He's half-black, half-Greek, or something like that, and he is well horny!'

'What did you do?' Pippa asked doubtfully.

'I sucked him off,' Sophie said with open relish. 'I'd have gone further, only I was on my own and I didn't want to open the door. There were a lot of wankers around and I wasn't up to getting gang-banged.'

'I think I'd be scared,' Pippa admitted. 'Maybe – maybe not with you four –'

Again I could see her doubt, intrigued and yet scared.

Sophie hastened to reassure her. 'It's all right, Pippa. Most of the guys stay right back in the bushes

and just watch the show. Nobody gets anything they
don't want to.'

'I – I really don't think I could,' Pippa responded.
'But maybe just to watch?'

'That's good with me,' Sophie answered, 'you take
it easy.'

I was not happy, and feeling guiltier than ever, but
I really didn't see I had much choice. Pippa was
obviously determined to push her own limits and I
couldn't stop her without risking a blazing row, after
which she would no doubt do just as she pleased
anyway. Sophie and Jade might have backed me up,
but not AJ, while if she went to Barn Hill there was
a good chance she'd be disgusted by the whole
process and decide she'd been daring enough.

'Let's go, Muffet,' AJ announced.

She made for the door and I followed, taking the
spare helmet from Pippa. 'Be careful, please?' I asked,
and she nodded, leaving me with visions of Kate's
face as I left her daughter to go out dogging.

At the door I very nearly turned back, and would have
done if AJ hadn't taken me firmly by the arm, leading me
downstairs as she spoke. 'She's not a fucking baby,
Penny, and, anyway, Sophie and Jade will look after her.'

'That's what I'm worried about.'

'Give it a rest. They're in a car, they've got mobiles
– what's the worst that's going to happen?'

'She'll get into it?'

'You're weird, Muffet, or do you want her all to
yourself?'

I just shrugged, on the edge of tears and yet telling
myself it was only right to let Pippa make her own
choices. Yet maybe AJ was right, because the thought
of letting Pippa go to Xiang provoked a pain that had
nothing to do with my desire to protect her. So did
the thought of her with Jade and Sophie, but nothing

like as bad, even if she was watching Sophie suck the man with the giant cock, maybe even if she got talked into taking him in her own mouth.

Somehow the men didn't really seem to matter, and as I mounted up on the back of AJ's bike I was soon more worried about my own problems. For a start I had to hitch my dress up, which left my legs bare and vulnerable and my bottom sticking out behind, but even my awkward position was soon forgotten, out of sheer terror. She drove as if her life depended on getting there quickly, dodging between lines of traffic, out-accelerating the cars at every traffic light, and taking corners as if she was on a racetrack.

Getting up over Muswell Hill was bad enough, but once she was on the North Circular all I could do was close my eyes, cling on and wish I believed in God so I'd have somebody to pray to. She'd said she'd done a hundred and ten earlier, and I was sure she was going faster still as she opened the bike out beyond the last of the lights. Twice she had to brake hard, setting my stomach tight with fear and my bladder so weak that if I'd been drinking I'd have wet myself.

By the time we got there I was shaking so badly I had to sit down by the side of the road, unable to stand up. AJ ignored me, speaking to two girls who'd come out from the main building of the garage, her friends Naomi and Sam.

'Got her?' Sam asked.

'Not Dumplings, no, Miss Muffet,' AJ responded.

'She hasn't got much tit,' Naomi said doubtfully.

'Use her arse,' AJ suggested. 'Which bike?'

'Mac's old Goldwing.'

'She'll freak.'

'No she won't, she's in Oz.'

'Sounds good, let's do it. Will you get up off the fucking road, Penny?'

I didn't know what they were talking about, or care, sure that after that ride anything they could do to me would be a relief. My legs were still shaking as I hauled myself to my feet, but I followed the girls into the garage, where an enormous motorbike in dark-red livery was resting on a stand. Various other girls were standing or sitting around, most of whom I recognised by sight and there were a few claps and jeers as I came in, now with my helmet off.

'Strip off, and climb on,' AJ ordered casually.

'You don't expect me to ride it, do you?'

'Don't be stupid.'

I began to undress, still feeling distinctly shaky. With court shoes and just panties under my dress I was soon naked, the girls watching me with casual but somewhat predatory interest, both the tough mainly leather-clad bulls and their marginally softer more feminine girlfriends.

'How do you want me?' I asked as I approached the huge bike. 'In that thing like a baby-seat?'

'On your back along the tank,' AJ instructed, 'arms and legs well spread.'

'I tell you, she hasn't got enough tit,' Sam objected. 'Straddle the seat, Penny, and stick your bum up.'

I climbed on, very aware of my rear view as I went forwards, my chest on the cool metal of the petrol tank, my arms outstretched. My bottom was well spread, my anus showing, and I was wondering what might have been done to Jade's chest. Taking hold of the handle bars, I turned my head for AJ's approval, but she was looking doubtful. 'Maybe,' she said. 'Turn over.'

The bike didn't feel too stable, despite being propped up, and I rather gingerly changed my position, lying on my back along the petrol tank as she had first suggested, with my pussy spread to the audience.

'Got it,' AJ said. 'Give us some tape.'

Somebody threw her a roll of black masking tape and she stepped forwards to take hold of one of my wrists and quickly tape it to the handle bars. My other wrist followed and I was spread-eagled helpless on the bike, unable to protect myself. With my arms fixed, AJ went to my ankles, binding each with tape before rolling me up, legs well spread, using more tape to force each ankle towards my bound wrists until I cried out. 'Careful, AJ! I think I'm going to fall off –'

Her answer was to pull a strip of tape across my belly and pass it down under the bike, again, and I was firmly lashed to the seat. My other leg was pulled up like the first, and I was done, in a lewd and extremely undignified position, rolled up on my back, legs akimbo, my bottom and breasts flaunted, my pussy and bumhole on show, like some ridiculous sex doll with no purpose other than fucking.

'Looking good,' AJ stated. 'Candles?'

'Candles?' I queried as Naomi passed her a handful of assorted candles.

'Yeah, it's her birthday.'

'Yes, but what are you going to do with them – AJ!'

I broke off with a gasp as she pushed the longest, fattest candle in my pussy, my wet hole taking it with embarrassing ease. She was chuckling to herself as she fucked me with it, to make me gasp and shiver in my bonds, but eventually stopped. 'One,' she stated. 'How old is Xiang anyway?'

Naomi shrugged.

'Thirty?' Sam suggested.

'No way,' another girl chipped in, 'more like twenty-five.'

'I've known her eight years, she has to be thirty, maybe more.'

'She'll be pissed off if we do too many.'

'She probably won't even count them, let's go for thirty anyway.'

'How am I supposed to fit thirty?' I protested.

'That's why we wanted Dumplings,' Naomi told me, and lit a candle.

'What – Ow! Naomi! Ow!'

'Keep still, will you!'

She'd moved the candle over my chest, dripping hot wax directly on to one nipple. It stung, enough to make me gasp and jerk in my bonds, but she took no notice, bringing it closer and aiming the drips carefully to coat my aching nipple in wax, into which she quickly pushed a second candle. I was left panting, the stubby red candle quivering slightly where it stuck up from my nipple.

'Two,' AJ said.

'Slowly, please,' I begged, my muscles still twitching as the wax congealed slowly around my nipple. 'I can take it, but slowly.'

'Don't make such a fuss,' Naomi told me. 'We have to coat your skin properly, in case a candle falls over and you got burnt.'

'Yes, but –'

'But nothing,' she said, still dripping wax down between my breasts. 'Safety first.'

'We'd better hurry, as it goes,' Sam said, glancing at her watch. 'Xiang'll be here in a minute.'

'It won't take a moment if we all do it. Hold still, Penny.'

'Hey, hang on, you lot – look – ow! AJ! Ow! Not up my bum, no – ow, you might have used some lubri– Ow, ow, ow! Stop!'

'Will you shut up, Penny?' AJ demanded.

'I can't, it hurts!'

She shook her head and turned away, leaving me to the mercy of Sam, Naomi and another girl I barely recognised, who'd begun to drip molten wax on to my breasts and belly. Somebody else had also stuck a candle up my bottom, only using the juice dripping down from my already penetrated pussy hole to open me up. I could feel them inside me, that odd sensation, not touch, not like having something rammed in and out, but like having an extra bone. My breasts ached too, my nipples stiff with excitement, making the candle Naomi had stuck on lean out at a drunken angle.

I never even realised what AJ was doing until she pinched my cheeks and thrust something dry and yielding into my mouth, my panties. My mouth had been stopped before I could even begin to protest, as they were fed right in, until my cheeks were bulging with material, and taped off. Well and truly gagged, I could only wriggle pathetically in my bonds as they went back to work with the candles, fixing one after another to my squirming flesh until there was a great forest of the things sticking up over my tits and belly, my pussy mound too, with my hair clogged with wax and my whole body trembling violently.

Whenever one had fallen over, they'd just stuck it back up, and I tried my very best to keep still as Naomi and Sam began to light them. Soon more wax had begun to drip down on to my skin, leaving me fighting for control and not a little scared despite my intense arousal at being made into Xiang's birthday cake. She was sure to use me properly, bound and gagged as I was, to touch me as she pleased, exploring my helpless body, penetrating my pussy and bottom hole with her fingers, her tongue, her fists, dildoes, or worse.

I heard the bike before Naomi had lit the last candle, and AJ hurried to the door to delay her. A moment more and the full thirty candle flames were dancing over my chest, with Xiang looming above me, grinning and thanking the girls. I tensed up as she blew, but one massive puff and twenty-eight had been put out, two more and the ones in my pussy and bottom had followed. I relaxed a little, still trembling, but looking forward to the fucking I was so obviously going to get as AJ passed Xiang a fat, black strap-on dildo.

'Thanks, girls, I've wanted to fuck this one for ages!' Xiang said as she unzipped to feed the big dildo into a metal ring sewn on beneath her fly. 'How's it feel, bitch?'

I managed a weak nod as AJ replied. 'I stuck her knickers in her mouth to shut her up. Do you want them out?'

'No, leave them.'

Her hand had gone to the candle in my pussy, pulling it free to leave me gaping and ready. She climbed on, awkwardly, cursed, took hold of the candle in my bottom hole and pushed it deeper, right up, and in, inserting one thick finger behind to leave the whole thick waxy shaft inside me. As her dildo touched my pussy hole, she laughed, and it was in, filling me so full I was arching my back immediately, only wishing I could get enough friction to my clitoris to come off as she fucked me.

'That's good,' she said, 'nice to see the stuck-up little bitch with eight inches of rubber up her. Not so high and mighty now, are you, Miss Muffet, not so fucking perfect?'

I wriggled on the dildo, hoping she'd take pity on me and make me come while I was so helpless, bound and gagged, covering in wax, a fat candle wedged well up my rectum and my pussy full of dildo. She took no notice, fucking me with short, irregular jerks as she rubbed herself on the base of the dildo, then speaking again. 'Who's got the keys?'

'You're not going to ride?'

'Yeah, why not, I can reach.'

She leant forwards as she spoke, crushing me down on to the bike and driving the dildo deeper up my hole. Her hands did reach the controls, and she was laughing as one of the girls tossed her the keys. I was desperately shaking my head, but not one of them took any notice, least of all Xiang, who was still moving the dildo in and out of my hole as she turned the key in the ignition. I felt the bike come to life beneath me, a deep, throbbing vibration, and at that first instant I knew I was going to come. My pussy was spread on her leathers, a fold of her fly right on my clit, rubbing, and as she revved the engine my whole body went tight with ecstasy.

I almost forgot to be frightened, so high as she bumped the bike down off its stand and began to trundle across the floor, every bump jarring me that little bit closer to orgasm, which hit me in a great blinding rush as she suddenly twisted hard on the throttle, to hurl the bike forwards and bring the vibration up to an unbearable pitch. My body was jerking on her dildo as I came, deliberately fucking myself as she accelerated across the concrete apron behind the old garage, laughing with pleasure.

For one awful moment I though she was going to take me out on the road, but she wheeled the bike and came back, only not into the garage, but the deep shadow of a clump of sycamore. There she began to grind herself on the base of the dildo, the engine still running, her eyes glaring down at my spread, helpless body. I was still on the edge of orgasm, wriggling myself on the thick rubber shaft in my sex and squeezing my bum on the candle stuck so deep inside my gut.

It felt so good, utterly helpless as she used me, with the vibration of the engine running through my body, spread-eagled in that ludicrous position, naked and smeared with wax, my mouth taped shut and stuffed with my own panties, a fat, heavy candle stuffed deep up my rectum, my pussy full of rubber dildo shaft as Xiang used me, no longer an aloof little bitch to her, but just a fuck toy.

I came as she did, wriggling in ecstasy on the dildo, completely abandoned and hers to use as she pleased. Only as I began to come down did I think of Pippa in the same awful, wonderful condition, and of Kate. I'd done the right thing, sacrificing myself to spare her, although a little mocking voice deep in my head was laughing at me for considering my experience a sacrifice.

It took quite a while to get me off the bike, and longer for me to clean up. I'd come twice, and I couldn't deny it had been good, but it had also been painful and frightening. My panties were sodden, and I had to abandon them, meaning I'd be naked under my dress until I could get to my bag and a spare pair. I was going to have to shave too, or depilate, or something, because my pussy hair was matted with wax. Then there was the candle up my bottom, which might have felt nice but was a major nuisance to get out.

I was on what passed for a loo, stark naked, my bottom pushed out and my mouth wide open because I had three fingers up my well-lubricated bottom hole, trying to get a purchase on the base of the candle when AJ came in. She gave a snort of laughter. 'You dirty pig! What, didn't Xiang get you off?'

'I'm not trying to get off!' I protested. 'She stuck a candle up my bum and I can't get it out.'

'Let me,' she said, laughing, 'if there's one thing I'm good at, it's fisting girls' arseholes.'

I nodded and pulled my fingers out, quickly washing them before AJ could make me suck them clean. The sneer on her face told me she knew exactly what I'd been thinking, and I got over the loo feeling more than a little worried, my thighs spread over the bowl. She took off her jacket as I pushed out my bottom to make my anus available to her, and as I'd suspected she was naked underneath, looking as hard as ever with her pierced nipples and tattoos.

'Gently, please, AJ,' I asked as she put her fingers together in a cone for insertion up my bottom.

'Take it easy, Muffet, some girls beg for this. You're well lubed up, yeah?'

'Yes, Sam lent me some . . .' I answered, trailing off with a gasp as her bunched fingers touched my anus.

I leant down on the cistern, my head hung low, my mouth open as she slowly opened me, my bumhole stretching to the gentle pressure, and more, until it began to hurt. 'Ow! Stop, AJ, that's too much!'

'Sh!' she answered. 'Nearly there. I can feel the candle, but it's well up. Hang on.'

Her other hand touched my pussy, opening me, stretching me wide and I was gasping in reaction, the bulk of both her fists in my body, both my holes trying to contract as she began to stroke the candle through the fleshy barrier between pussy and rectum.

'Push,' she instructed, 'like you're trying to have a shit.'

I nodded, sobbing with embarrassment as I squeezed. Her hand pushed once more, and I gasped as my bumhole took her knuckles, her fist now right in me. I could feel my heart pounding, and my breathing was deep and hard, the bloated feeling in my pussy and rectum and the humiliation it brought too strong to be denied.

'Got it,' AJ announced.

'Thank you,' I managed, 'could – could you make me come?'

'You're a slut, Miss Muffet,' she answered, and her hand twisted in my pussy.

Her thumb came out, slid up between the lips of my spread sex to find my clitoris and I was being rubbed, whimpering with pleasure and with self-pity as my orgasm began to rise with astonishing speed. AJ started to move her fist in my rectum, twisting and easing it deeper to make me feel so helpless, so full, well and truly sodomised, her fist bloating me out and the candle a hard bar in my gut.

I screamed out as my climax hit me and I felt my twin holes go into spasm, shudder after shudder running through my body until I could bear it no more. She didn't give me a choice, holding me on her fists, her thumb still rubbing on my clit, her hands twisting inside me, and I was screaming repeatedly as I slumped down on the loo pan, my legs gone beneath me. One last, shivering peak ran through me and it was done, AJ's hands and the candle easing gently from my body to leave me gaping behind and clutching the loo seat in blissful exhaustion.

'Now I get mine,' AJ said, 'suck on this, Muffet.'

Her words barely registered before I'd been taken by my hair and the candle thrust into my open mouth, the candle which she'd just extracted from my bumhole. My eyes popped at the taste of my own bottom, and AJ was laughing at me as she twisted the tap on to wash her hands. With that cruel, derisive laughter in my ears I just gave in, and as she stepped close again I was sucking on the candle, an obedient little slut completely broken to her will.

'Head down the bowl, Muffet,' she ordered as her hands went to her trousers. 'I like to see you that way, suits you.'

I waited until she'd pushed down her leather trousers before putting my head in the toilet bowl, right down, with my hair dangling in the mixture of water and my own piddle and pieces of pink loo paper. She laughed to see how willing I was as my hand went back to my pussy, stroking the waxy mess of my pubic mound, and between my lips. My clitoris was a sore, aching point, but I had to come again, as the water and mess swirled around my head.

'Slut,' AJ repeated as she saw what I was doing, her voice rich with derision.

My answer was to spread my knees, showing off my cunt as I masturbated, my bottom pushed right up, my anus dribbling lubricant. She kicked me, planting the sole of her boot firmly on my bottom, and again on the other cheek, no doubt leaving big, dirty prints on my skin and forcing my head deeper down the loo. I was going to come, at any moment, only holding myself back with difficulty as I revelled in my degradation.

Again she kicked me, only this time her foot was bare and inside my thigh, to make me spread further. I did it, as her foot went to my back, forcing me to pull my spine in and spread my bottom wider still. One more push, to shove my head as deep into the lavatory bowl as it would go, and she had mounted me, straddling my back, her pussy spread across my spine, wet and open, her piercings hard on my skin.

She began to ride me, rubbing herself on my back with her hand twisted into my hair to keep my head well down the loo. I had to come, it was simply too much, used so badly, so well, soiled and humiliated, treated as her little fuck toy, with her riding my back, sucking on a candle she'd had up my bottom, my head down a toilet where it belonged, my head flushed down a toilet.

I heard her laughter turn to a blissful groan. I heard the gurgle of water in the cistern. I heard the cry of despair and of ecstasy in my own throat, and my head was under, water and piddle and loo paper swirling around my face and in my hair, in my mouth and up my nose as AJ began to come on my back.

Every awful sensation was stark in my head at that instant, as I jerked and shook in orgasm; the slippery, raw feel of my messy, lube-smeared pussy, my gaping bumhole pulsing and oozing fluid between my dirty cheeks, AJ's weight on my back and the wet of her sex as she rubbed off, the lukewarm mixture of lavatory water and my own piddle against my face, the thick, waxy candle in my mouth and, best of all, the acrid taste of my own bumhole.

I very nearly blacked out, it was just so intense, so good, so completely and comprehensively filthy, the behaviour of a dirty, depraved, lewd little slut, a girl whose behaviour is an outrage to everything decent and proper and prissy and dull. To be used so badly, as a butch dyke's sex toy, and to delight in every single instant of my ordeal. It was me, through and through, and I would never want to be any other way.

With that, it was over. I washed as best I could and came back to the others. Having had me, they were mostly very friendly, despite an underlying feeling that I wasn't really one of them. When a girl I'd never met before complemented me on how well I'd taken it and offered a beer, I accepted it gratefully. I was desperately thirsty, after having my panties wadded in my mouth for so long, and had finished it in no time. A second was enough to calm my shaking, and I was halfway through my third when AJ sauntered over to me. 'So what, Muffet, you staying for some more or do I dump you at Barn Hill?'

'I really have to get to Barn Hill,' I told her. 'Sorry.'

'I'll catch up with you,' she promised. 'Serious, do you reckon your Pippa's up for fun? I would love to have her.'

It was one of those rare moments I could talk to her as an equal, after I'd given myself completely, and I gave the honest answer. 'I'm not sure what she wants, AJ, and I'm not sure she does either, but I do know she couldn't possibly handle you. I'm not being funny, and I know she seems really full of enthusiasm, but she's just not ready for the sort of thing you like, and I don't suppose she ever will be.'

'Yeah?' she asked, and for once there was genuine emotion in her voice.

'Sorry, AJ,' I went on, spreading my hands. 'Pippa hasn't even been spanked, and she thought what you and Gina did with me in the loos at Whispers was just unpleasant. She's curious, yes, but she's not into any of the things we like to do, especially golden showers. Leave her alone, and I promise I'll make it up to you, OK?'

She nodded, far from happy about it, but accepting what I'd said, then spoke again. 'Yeah, OK, but if you're bullshitting me, Penny –'

'I'm not, I promise,' I said quickly.

AJ shrugged. Like me, she was clearly deeply affected by Pippa, and for a moment I wondered if I was being a hypocrite, only to put the thought aside. With me the worst Pippa would get was a rosy bottom, with AJ she could confidently expect a dozen piercings and another dozen tattoos, things she might regret a lot more than a gentle and private spanking over my knee.

AJ was silent as we walked out to her bike, and kicked it into life immediately, leaving me to scramble on as best I could. Wheeled around to face the road, she just let go, accelerating so hard the front wheel

195

came off the ground. I clung on to her, certain we would crash, my eyes tight shut, my head full of horrible visions as we tore down the old road and on to the new, back into London.

I didn't even open my eyes until we stopped at a traffic light, with AJ waiting in the right-hand lane to turn towards Edgware. We were off the fast roads, and I let myself relax a little, sure the worst was over. Our light turned green, AJ took off at her usual break-neck speed and I realised a black BMW was coming right at us, through the light that had just turned red. I screamed in terror as the bike shot forwards, missing him by what must have been inches as he slammed his brakes on, and I'd wet myself, piss dribbling down my legs and soaking into my dress as AJ drove on as if nothing out of the ordinary had happened. She stopped at the next light, in response to my urgent tugs at her shoulder, and turned to me the moment we'd both dismounted, speaking as she pulled off her helmet. 'What's the matter?'

'I've had a little accident,' I managed. 'I've peed in my dress, when you nearly hit that car.'

'What car?'

'The black BMW, just now.'

'Oh that prat. I was well clear. Oh for fuck's sake, you've pissed all over my seat!'

'I'm sorry!' I answered her, almost in tears. 'I couldn't help it –'

She shook her head. 'Don't get in a state, just wipe it up. Penny, when you ride pillion you have to move with the bike, it's like riding with a sack of fucking spuds tied on behind me! You don't have to cling on quite so tightly either. Now come on, wipe the seat and get back on.'

'Have you got a rag or something?'

'Use your dress, it's wet already.'

196

I made a face, but bunched up the hem of my dress and began to wipe the seat dry. Several people were looking at us, and I was sure they knew I'd wet myself and was being made to clean up my piddle with my own dress, adding fresh humiliation to my already powerful emotions. I really did not want to get on the bike again either, but it was that or use public transport, or a cab, with no knickers and my wet dress clinging to the contours of my bottom and legs. Even AJ's driving was better.

A few more minutes of terror and we were at Barn Hill, where AJ simply dropped me off and sped away. I immediately felt apprehensive, in a way I hadn't even when bound to the motorbike in a ring of grinning dykes. Well-spaced-out street lights cast a wan illumination over a number of cars, while as soon as the noise of the bike engine had died I could hear the quiet conversations, the rustling of foliage, the occasional moan or giggle, and the meaty slapping sound of some man trying to get his cock hard among the bushes, uncomfortably close. My guilt came back with a great rush at the thought of leaving Pippa in such a place, but she was at least with Sophie and Jade, while I knew she would have been entirely incapable of coping with what had been done to me.

Four orgasms, and I knew that once I'd calmed down I'd take another over the way I'd wet myself on the bike, and perhaps again for the way AJ had fisted me and flushed me. For me it had been ecstasy, for Pippa, an impossible ordeal. Yes, I had a least spared Pippa – who was in the back seat of the car, the interior light on, her top up to show off her perky little breasts, cuddled up to Jade and giggling in delight as she watched Sophie suck a large dark cock through the open window. The man was nearly there, masturbating into her mouth with his eyes fixed on the two girls in the back, and I paused, glancing quickly around me. An instant later and he'd come, Sophie's cheeks bulging as she struggled to swallow what he'd done in her mouth.

They saw me as I stepped forwards into an area of pale light between the dark shadows of the cars, first Jade, who waved and bounced her bare tits at me, then Pippa, who was smiling happily as she spoke. 'Hi, Penny. Hey, you're all wet, and you've got loo paper in your hair! What, did AJ give you another swirly?' She laughed.

Eight

Pippa was due to be spanked. In fact, she was overdue. She was *long* overdue.

It was no longer a question of if, but when. She needed it, perhaps not quite in the sense that I need it, a craving that grows and grows until I get it and will never go away, but in the sense that she wanted it, and agreed that it was an appropriate thing to do to her, that she deserved it.

She did deserve it, no question, the whole works, with her panties taken down and her little bottom smacked until she was feeling thoroughly sorry for herself. If she was also in ecstasy, that would be all well and good, but she was going to get it anyway, both to give her the experience she wanted, and to punish her.

I still had my qualms, but had managed to push them aside after our night out in London. While AJ and her dyke friends had been using me as their plaything and scaring me silly into the bargain, she had been having a great time, drinking alcopops from the bottle and letting Jade play with her tits while they watched Sophie indulge both her exhibitionist streak and her penchant for cock sucking.

That was bad enough, but her real offence was finding the state I was in funny, in my wet dress with the little bits of pink loo paper I'd missed after my bog washing still in my hair. Even that I could have forgiven, but to point the fact out in front of a complete stranger was simply too much, even if he had just come in Sophie's mouth.

I'd told her she was going to get it, and she had agreed it was fair, so it was just a question of choosing my place and time. Both had to be perfect, because for all my righteous indignation a girl's first spanking is something very important. If it was to be done, I wanted it done properly, to be special for her, something she would remember for the rest of her life and could revisit in moments of idle pleasure, just as I had so often over what Aunt Elaine had done to me at Kate's wedding.

That had been sudden, if not entirely spontaneous, and fairly well deserved considering she'd caught me getting a mouthful of spunk from her son-in-law of just a few hours. Not that Toby had given me all that much say in sucking his cock. With Pippa it came with a warning, allowing her to build up her apprehension, but my task was far harder than Elaine's, who'd simply had to punish me. With Pippa I had to punish her and make sure she liked it.

I felt nervous all week, alternating between guilt and the same sort of methodical, detached calculation I apply to my research. The consequence of the guilt was that I needed my own bottom attended to more than ever. The consequence of the calculation was that by the Thursday evening I knew exactly what I was going to do. I'd given her apprehension, which is always good, but I could also give her that wonderful shock which comes with the realisation that you're going to be spanked, and now.

On the Friday I had a two o'clock lecture to give, on predator/prey dynamics. The moment it was over

I went straight to the station, and half-an-hour later I was in Pangbourne, sipping coffee in a convenient pub. The Bradfield bus arrived before I'd even finished my drink and I went out to greet Pippa as she said goodbye to two of her friends. She looked really quite demure in her school uniform, jacket and knee-length navy-blue skirt, white blouse fastened by her scholar's tie, long white socks, very different from the bubbly young woman I was used to, but there was the same glint in her eye as she saw me. 'Hi, Penny, what are you doing here?'

'I stopped in for coffee on my way back from the university,' I told her. 'Are you in a rush?'

'Me? No, not really.'

'I was going to walk up beside the river, as it's such a lovely day. Do you want to come? We could have dinner in the Swan.'

'I'd love to,' she answered without hesitation. 'Just let me make a call.'

I waited as casually as I could while she told Kate she was with me and might be back late or not at all. It was a real effort to keep my guilt down, so much so that had it not been for the smile of pure mischief Pippa turned on me as she cut the connection I think I would have backed away.

'It is great to see you. It's like – like, I don't know, getting out of jail!'

She kissed me and took my arm as we crossed the street, waving to her friends as they made for the station. I began to feel better, drawn in by her fresh, unreserved joy, in life, in my company, in what was about to happen to her. For a good way out of town we had to walk alongside the road, in single file with noisy traffic to our left, making it impossible to talk. Only where the river and road split apart could we go side by side again, following the bank along the edge

201

of a field to where the reeds and ponds of the wildfowl trust began.

Just as we'd left the busy town and its people behind, it was as if we'd also left the mundane world behind, moving instead to my own, more private existence, where I didn't have to be respectable, and naughty girls got spanked. There were still people around, other walkers enjoying the mild air and spring sunshine, the occasional boat moving gently past on the river. Pippa was at her best, so full of life, talking of everything at once and never still, so enticing that had I had only a guarantee of a moment's peace I'd have done it then and there, seated on the bank with her school skirt lifted and her panties pulled well down, her pretty bottom bare to the woods, and to me.

Beyond the sanctuary we moved out on to open fields, with a steep wooded bank rising on the far side of the river. In among the trees she'd have been bare in seconds, or I might have taken her into the pretty old church at Lower Hampton and punished her across the very altar at which Kate had been married just hours before Aunt Elaine had taken my knickers down for my own virgin session. Unfortunately, the vicar knew us and was unlikely to approve.

If Pippa had guessed, she was oblivious, laughing and carefree as we walked, not even questioning me when the footpath turned back from the bank but I insisted on following the river. The Brunel Bridge was ahead, the huge arches towering up from the water and, beside it, the little red brick and concrete pillbox presumably built to defend it.

'Do you know, I used to run across that bridge,' I told her. 'I'd wait until a train went past on the nearest track and then run like anything.'

'Me too,' she said, laughing. 'Shall we?'

202

'In a minute, maybe. I just want to look around. This place used to be a bit special for me, somewhere I'd go when I wanted to be alone. I used to come down here with a book and sit in that little pillbox. I don't think I ever saw another person.'

We'd reached the fence, and climbed over, in among the elders and brambles at the base of the towering embankment. The pillbox looked as lonely as ever, the door choked with nettles, which I beat down with a stick. Inside, the air was warm and still, the bright sunlight streaming in through the slits making patterns on the floor and the low gunstep running around the walls. 'Isn't it lovely here, so tranquil?'

'I agree. Some people think it's weird, but I love places like this, hidden away from everything.'

'I'm glad, because it's somewhere you're going to remember for ever.'

'Why?'

'Because I'm going to spank you.'

Her eyes and mouth came open, surprised and shocked and delighted all at the same time. I'd sat down on the gunstep, and looked up at her, determined that my every gesture, my every word, would be just so. 'Put your bag down,' I instructed, 'and take off your jacket.'

She met my gaze, her large, dark eyes looking right into mine, her lips still slightly parted as she shrugged off the bag and jacket, letting them tumble to the floor.

'Hang them up,' I told her, 'just because you're about to be spanked is no reason to be a sloven.'

Her teeth met her lip in a brief, nervous bite as she bent to retrieve her things, hanging both on a twig of elder pushing in at one of the window slits. I waited until she'd turned back to me before speaking again.

Her blouse was crisp, lightweight fabric, and didn't quite succeed in hiding the outlines of her small, upturned breasts, quite clearly not confined by a bra, her stiff nipples showing as tiny bumps.

'Yes, why not?' I said. 'A little something extra for being so slovenly. Your breasts will be bare while you're spanked. Take off your tie and open your blouse.'

'Completely?' she answered, with a quick glance to the door.

'Just do as you are told, Pippa. Nobody will come, but if somebody did I'd keep them occupied while you covered up.'

'What would they think?'

'Probably that you'd been caught short and I was guarding you while you had a pee, certainly not that you'd been having your bottom attended to. That sort of thing isn't supposed to happen to modern young women. Now take off your tie and open your blouse, or there'll be extra.'

She began to do it, her fingers shaking badly as she pulled open the knot of her black ribbon scholar's tie. I waited, feigning patience but enjoying every instant, and every detail, her delicate, freckled face with her eyes full of doubt and expectation, the very tip of her nose twitching ever so slightly, the gentle quivering of her lower lip, the faint pink flush of embarrassment and arousal on her neck.

With the tie loose, she began to work on her buttons, popping each one open, from top to bottom, so that her blouse came a trifle further apart with every one, showing first the delicate shape of her collarbone, the smooth skin of what little cleavage she had, the gentle curve of one firm little breast.

'Good,' I told her. 'Now I'm going to punish you, Pippa, and while it's done I want you to remember that your breasts are showing, and why. That's not all that will be showing either, because I'm going to take your panties down and spank you on your bare bottom. You need that, don't you?'

She nodded briefly, showing a touch of confusion.

'Say it,' I ordered.

'I – I need to have my bottom bare.'

'Properly, a little more.'

She took in a breath, making her tummy tighten before she answered. 'I need to have my bottom bare, to be spanked. I – I need to have my panties taken down, and – and be spanked on my bare bottom.'

'That's right, Pippa, you do. Now come across my knee.'

I patted my lap, and she gave a little tense nod. As I pushed my knees out a little more she began to get down, my heart absolutely hammering but outwardly calm and composed. Just to feel her body against my legs was enough to set my pussy tight, the softness of her belly and the firm muscle of her thighs, the gentle curve of her waist as I circled it with an arm to hold her steady.

She braced herself on the floor and on the gunstep, her feet a little way apart with the toes of her smart black shoes turned down, her fingers splayed on the concrete. Her blouse had fallen open, leaving her little breasts dangling down. She was mine, and I took a moment to touch her, stroking the hard buds of her nipples and her creamy smooth skin. After a moment she gave a sigh, from deep in her throat, and I stopped. 'Now, now,' I chided, 'let's remember why you are over my knee, to be punished, and I do mean to punish you, Pippa, because you certainly deserve it. Anyway, you've wanted this for months, haven't you? Tell me.'

'Yes,' she admitted, 'since – since I saw the picture of Suzie over Gran's knee.'

'When was that!?'

'That first day – when I met you at the pool. It was in the drawer –'

'I know where it was, in the drawer of the telephone table. What were you doing looking in there?'

'Just – just having a look around –'

'You nosy little cow! You do deserve this, don't you!? Right, let's have your skirt up.'

I renewed my grip on her waist, holding on tight as my hand went to the hem of her school skirt. Her long legs bent knock-knee as I began to pull it up, showing the tops of her long white socks and the backs of her knees, her thighs, long and smooth and rounded. I paused, holding her skirt well up, at the level of the cheekiest miniskirt any girl ever wore, with just the tiniest hint of panty material showing, plain white cotton bulging with cheeky teenage bottom – spanking panties.

'Now feel it,' I told her, 'feel the shame as your spanking panties come on show, the little white panties you put on especially in the hope that I would take them down, and not just because you're desirable, but so that I can spank your bottom. How shameful, to feel like that, to want another woman to take down your panties and spank your bare bottom. How shameful is that, Pippa?'

I'd lifted her skirt as I spoke, slowly, exposing her as if raising the curtain at a theatre, with her bottom the focus of attention and her coming spanking the show. Her answer was a choking sob, and she'd begun to wriggle a little, her rounded cheeks squirming beneath the seat of her tight white panties. My desire was already at fever pitch, but I forced myself to take it slowly, laying my hand on her panty seat and stroking gently. 'You, Pippa, are an invitation to spanking,' I told her, 'an invitation to having your panties taken down and your bottom smacked, which is just what I'm going to do. Yes, Pippa, I'm going to take them, nice and slowly, and I'm going to tell you what I can see before you're spanked. How will that make you feel?'

A fresh sob escaped her throat, full of emotion. I spent a moment more caressing her through her knickers and took hold of her waistband, pulling it open so that I could see down the back of them as far as where the gentle V of her bottom crease began to open out. She lifted her hips slightly, making my task easier, and I began to peel her panties down. 'You have a pretty bottom,' I told her, 'and I do like to see it, but that's not why your panties have to come down. Do you know why your panties have to come down?'

'You said – to humiliate me.'

'And do you feel humiliated?'

'A little.'

'Only a little?' I asked, pausing with her panties held halfway down, to show the top of her crease and the first swell of her cheeks.

'A lot,' she answered, 'and I want to come – go on, bare me – spank me – touch me.'

'Patience, darling. Panties down first, then your spanking, and if you've been a good girl I'll let you come. Yes, you do have a pretty bottom, don't you, Pippa? Usually I like a plump bottom, like Jade's, but you manage to be meaty and slim at the same time, ideal spanking material in fact. OK, down they come, Pippa – oh now you're showing, so pretty, and so rude! It must be embarrassing to be so slim and leggy your bottom hole shows behind, not to mention the way your pussy peeps out between your thighs, so sweet – and so wet, you bad girl!'

I'd turned her panties down around her thighs, completing her exposure, and as her pussy came on show I'd realised just how excited she was, the mouth of her sex a wet, fleshy tart, oozing juice down between her lips. Her scent had grown suddenly strong too, rich and feminine and enticing, making me want to lick her from behind. She'd begun to push her bum up, and I contented myself with teasing her, running my fingers up the smooth, pouted lips of her pussy and tickling the tiny, pale pink bud of her anus. She winced, her cheeks tightening.

'Sh!' I chided. 'If you're to be spanked, you must expect attention to your bottom hole. No modesty, remember?'

'But –'

'Sh!' I repeated.

I put my hands to her cheeks and pulled them wide, stretching out the little pink star between and wishing I could stick my tongue right up it. Her body tightened and another sob escaped her throat, but I held her wide, allowing the thought of having her anus inspected sink in, letting go only when she'd begun to shake her head and whimper.

'There's no need to make a fuss, Pippa,' I told her. 'You have a pretty bottom, you even have a pretty bottom hole, and, if you are to be spanked regularly, you'd better get used to showing it off. And yes, you should be spanked regularly, very regularly.'

'Please,' she sobbed, 'do me now, Penny – spank me – punish me!'

'If you insist,' I answered her, and raised my hand over the soft pink globe of her perfect, virgin bottom.

She was lifted, ready and waiting, her cheeks quivering a little, the mouth of her bottom hole loosening and squeezing, her pussy oozing juice, as ripe for spanking as any bottom ever was, even my own. My hand came down, one smack, and she was virgin no more, now a spanked girl, just as I was. Her little cry of pain and of release sent a jolt of pleasure through me, and again as I brought my hand down a second time, a third, a fourth, and more. I'd found my rhythm and my mouth had curved up into a delighted grin as I watched my darling Pippa's bottom bounce to the first spanking of her life.

Just ten or so and she was gasping, with her legs kicked up and open, her panties stretched taut between her thighs. I spanked harder and she was shaking her head and wriggling on my lap, her tummy in contraction against my legs. Harder still, and her gasps had turned to cries of pain and her kicking into a frantic pumping motion, her thighs spreading and closing, her feet waving wildly as she began to babble. 'It hurts, Penny – it hurts – ow! Ow! Ow! Ow! Oh, my poor bottom – that's awful – no don't stop, punish me – I know it hurts but punish me – hold me and spank me, take me there – get me over that barrier –'

Her voice broke to a long whimper and more cries as I spanked harder still, putting all my attention into her bottom. She was rosy, her pale skin flushed and prickly with goosepimples, her thighs showing the first prickle of sweat from her now frantic struggles. Now was her punishment, and I clung on, determined not to let her go, spanking away at her wobbling bottom.

Soon she was in a fine little tantrum, gasping and sobbing, without a shred of dignity or reserve, just the way it should be. My palm was stinging like anything, but I didn't care, just too delighted by what she was showing and the way she was reacting, crazy with the stinging of my slaps and her consternation, showing everything, yet determined to see it through.

She'd had a hundred, maybe more, when the bitter note in her cries began to change, growing softer, and I knew the pain was gone.

'Panties off, Pippa, time I attended to your pussy,' I told her, pausing just long enough to snatch her panties down and off one leg.

They stuck on her other shoe, waving in the air as I went back to spanking her, now with her thighs well parted, her sex spread to my hand. I pushed a leg between hers, opening her out further still, and jerked up my own skirt, to leave her sex splayed naked on my thigh, flesh to flesh.

'What – what are you doing?' she gasped. 'Oh that feels so open – so shameful –'

'Be ashamed, if you want,' I told her, 'shame can be nice, but just let yourself go. It doesn't matter what you do in front of me, not when I'm punishing you.'

I'd never once stopped spanking her, applying my hand over and over to her bottom as I got her into position. Now she was wiggling urgently, her cheeks squirming under the slaps, red and open, her bum-hole in spasm, her wet pussy squashed out on my leg, but she was still resisting, in a fine state but unable to give that final surrender.

'Let yourself go,' I repeated, 'be a bad girl, Pippa – show me you need it, Pippa, show me you how badly you need your bottom spanked! Show me how ashamed of yourself you are, having your bottom spanked across Auntie's knee!'

One, final, despairing gasp, and she was there, tipped over the edge, her bottom bucking frantically up and down as she rubbed herself on my leg, her cheeks spreading and closing to her movements and still bouncing and wobbling to the smacks as I beat her as hard as I could. Her dignity was gone, completely, her nude bottom spread wide, her anus in contraction, her cunt in contraction, coming in front of me, so intimate and so lovely, my Pippa brought to spanking ecstasy across my knee, and as she began to go slowly limp I knew beyond doubt that I was in love with her.

She came up with a sheepish, sleepy smile, satisfaction blended with acute embarrassment. I took her straight into my arms, cuddling her and stroking her hair, to let her come slowly down from her experience. Her whole body was trembling violently, near naked and so vital in my arms that it took all my willpower not to put her straight down on her knees. I cupped her bottom instead, gently stroking her hot skin, hard from spanking and wet with sweat. She gave a little sob at my touch, holding me tighter still, melting into my arms as I soothed her and stroked her smacked bottom. At last she found her voice. 'That was – that was, amazing – so good. I never knew it could be that strong, Penny.'

'Well now you do,' I told her. 'You see why I like it?'

She nodded, pulling back a little, her smile no longer sheepish but bright and happy. I could wait no longer.

'How about me?' I asked. 'Don't you think you should say thank you nicely, perhaps give me a little reward for taking the trouble to discipline you?'

'Yes, of course,' she answered, her eyes suddenly full of mischief.

'Down you go then,' I told her, giving her bottom a last squeeze before letting her climb off my lap.

I tugged my skirt high as she got to her knees, her beautiful impish face turned up to me in expectation. My panties were soaking, and tight against the smooth flesh where I'd had to shave after the dykes

211

had had me. I took them right off and sat forwards on the gunstep, my thighs well parted. Pippa licked her lips as her eyes fixed on my bare pussy, then spoke. 'I have wanted to do this for so long, Penny, so badly –'

She leant forwards as she spoke, and trailed off, mumbling, as she buried her face in my pussy, kissing with clumsy urgency, and licking. One touch and a jolt of pleasure shot through me, close to orgasm, and I made myself comfortable, leaning back to watch, her eyes locked to mine as she worked on my sex, my own darling Pippa, spanked and licking pussy.

It was right for her, all my qualms so much nonsense, because it was what she wanted to do, and what I wanted to do. I'd given her her virgin spanking. I'd made her come, and now she was on her knees to me, her blouse hanging open to show her little breasts, with her perky nipples sticking up on top of each gently sculpted mound, her knickers off and her skirt tucked up, her bottom bare behind and rosy with spanking.

Her eyes closed and she buried her face in my pussy, licking full on my clitoris to set off the first tremors of orgasm in my head. I took one last look, fixing the image of her in my head, my Pippa as a spanked schoolgirl, the perfect English spanked schoolgirl, in her dishevelled uniform, her panties off, her bottom all rosy, and I closed my eyes. I could still see her as I started to come, back across my lap, her school skirt turned up, her plain white panties pulled down and her bottom wriggling to her virgin spanking. My thighs tightened around her head, my fingers locked hard in her hair, my back arched tight and I was there, crying out her name as what I'd done to her ran over and over in my head – taken her over my knee and pulled down her panties and spanked her bare bottom – I'd pulled down her panties and spanked her bare bottom – I'd spanked her bare bottom.

Of course, what I really wanted was for her to spank my bare bottom, but after what had happened we were both too emotionally drained for any further misbehaviour. We did at least run across the railway bridge, and walked into Streatley holding hands, also without any panties under our skirts. By the time we'd finished, both hers and mine had been soggy, cold and dirty from the floor. We'd left them there, and were laughing and joking over what whoever eventually found them was going to think.

We were still a little early for dinner at the Swan, so I bought a bottle of Champagne to toast her first spanking and we went to sit at a table beside the river, where we could watch the boats and the ducks. There were too many people around to speak freely, but that only added to the wonderful sense of secrecy as we clinked our glasses together in appreciation of what we'd done. No doubt they thought we were simply celebrating some social triumph, a promotion or good exam results, something essentially mundane, never that we had just become lovers, and in such a way.

I still had my guilt, but it was very easy to push it down, my sense of euphoria simply too strong to let anything else get in the way. Once the restaurant was open we ate, and shared a second bottle of wine, leaving me feeling pleasantly tipsy as we left, hand in hand once more. No choice of how to get back was made, we simply began to walk, talking as we went, now safe from being overheard. I knew she was happy about what we'd done, but I wanted to hear her say it, for the sake of affirmation, and to help her to resolve any last qualms she might have.

'Now you're done it, how do you feel about it?'

'Great, the best,' she answered, with no trace of doubt in her voice, 'but I knew I would.'

'You're a lot more confident than I was at your age! I wanted it, but I'd never have dared ask. Not that I had anyone to go to anyway, not until Elaine decided to take matters into her own hands. So you saw the picture Colonel Aimsworth took of Susan being spanked? Did that spark the desire in you, or was it there anyway?'

'It's been there since the moment I saw you across another woman's lap, and not Gina's.'

'Marjorie Burgess?'

'Is that her name?'

'Yes. That was so embarrassing – beyond embarrassing, and not in a nice way. Not at the time anyway.'

'I can imagine! But yeah, it triggered something inside me. I was really shocked, at first, although I admit I thought it was funny too, but then – I don't know, I just couldn't stop thinking about it, and wondering how it must have felt, to be held like that, and smacked.'

'I understand, exactly.'

'I wanted to know more, but it's hard to get below the surface. Everything on the web seems to have its own agenda, and I didn't even know you liked it, so I could hardly ask you. Then there's all the psychobabble stuff about birching in schools leading to fixation but, true or not, that doesn't relate to me.'

'Nor to me. So you already knew, before the girls let on that night at Whispers?'

'I knew you'd had it done to you, but I didn't know you liked it, just that I did. Maybe it runs in the family?'

'It could well be genetic or, at least, have a genetic basis. There's no reason why not, if getting a warm bum turns girls on, then in the long run there'll be more girls who like warm bums running around.'

'As long as men like to warm them.'

'That's true, speaking of which, I suppose it's confession time. You know from Jade and Sophie that I'm bisexual, and that goes for spanking too.'

'I don't think I could let a man spank me. I'd feel – I don't know, as if he would think I was a lesser person because I'd allowed him to punish me.'

'Some people are like that, both men and women, but mainly men. But it's your choice, so you do as you like and be proud of yourself.'

'I am proud of myself. Like you said, it's harder to make your own choices than just follow along like a sheep.'

'That's true. So no regrets?'

Her answer was just a touch uneasy. 'No, although there is this nagging doubt right at the back of my mind telling me I've done wrong.'

'That's just the echo of social disapproval, I get it all the time. You've done nothing wrong, believe me.'

'Why were you so reluctant to let me join in then? You must think it's immoral, at least a bit?'

'No, but I'm aware that it's something society disapproves of, and especially as you're my cousin. I didn't want to – not to corrupt you, because I believe in the choices I've made, but to be seen as corrupting you, or to take your somewhere you didn't really want to go.'

'Oh I wanted to go, badly.'

'I accept that now.'

'So is it immoral?'

'No, not for me, or for you. Another person might consider it immoral, and so for them it would be, but I dispute their right to impose their views on us. As I mentioned before, some people like to think their personal views represent moral absolutes, but that's never true. In fact, there's no such thing as a moral absolute, only the consensus of society, which may be framed as law or as custom. Each individual must choose to go with those, or against them, according to the dictates of her own conscience.'

'How about murder? Thou shalt not kill seems pretty basic to me.'

'How about war? We make heroes of people for killing each other.'

'That's true, but there must be something. Cannibalism?'

'In some societies it was considered an honour to eat the flesh of defeated warriors.'

'Incest, bestiality?'

'Now there you may be partially right, in that in both cases there is a biological disadvantage to the act and therefore our taboos may be seen as the consequence of negative evolutionary pressure. Nevertheless, there are exceptions. At various eras the Ancient Egyptian royalty would only marry close relatives, as to do otherwise was seen as diluting the divine principle in the pharaohs. It seems to have cost them though, just as less extreme inbreeding cost European royalty in the nineteenth and twentieth centuries. As for bestiality, the Romans used to paint and sculpt bestial scenes as a form of low humour, much in the same way as we have mugs fashioned as a pair of breasts or a bum.'

'So how do you cope?' she asked. 'Not with being punished, but with wanting to do it to other people. Don't you feel cruel?'

'Not really, no, especially as I'm usually on the receiving end. Did you ever read *The Waterbabies*?'

'Yes, Gran's got it. It's about a chimney sweep, isn't it?'

'Mainly, yes, but there's a strong sub-text of Victorian morality, including a character called Mrs Do-as-you-would-be-done-by. It's pretty mawkish stuff, but the moral principle makes a lot more sense than many. When in doubt, just ask yourself how you would want somebody to treat you if the roles were reversed.'

'Have you been doing that with me?'

'Not entirely, no. If I'd treated you the way I wanted to be treated at your age I'd have put you across my knee when you flashed Mr Cudrow.'

'You should have done.'

'Maybe I should. You certainly deserved it, but I could never have done it.'

'Because you didn't know I'd like it?'

'Exactly, but do it again and over you go, young lady, as soon as we're home.'

She laughed and squeezed my hand. 'I bet old Cudrow would like to have seen that!'

'I'm sure he would, but I would never do it in front of him.'

'Yeah, I suppose it would give him ideas – not that I want to be spanked in front of him.'

'I wouldn't mind, maybe, but it's always best not to involve people unless you're sure of them. We don't really know Mr Cudrow after all, not that well, and who knows how he might react? Maybe he'd report us for indecency or something, you can never tell.'

'No way. He didn't tell Gran I flashed him.'

'That's true, and you're probably right. After all, imagine if he did, and we denied it. It would be our word against his, and can you imagine the police's reaction with a middle-aged man complaining a teenage girl flashed her tits at him? They'd lock him up, once they'd finished laughing. Odd, isn't it, the way things change so quickly? When Kate and I used to go and pinch Colonel Aimsworth's fruit, it never occurred to us for a moment that he might be in the wrong threatening us with his stick. Not that he ever hit us, but if he had we'd never have dared tell anyone. After all, we were thieves! It's the same with spanking. Back in the fifties, the sixties even, it was considered perfectly reasonable for a man to spank his wife, even humorous. I've seen cartoons, from mainstream papers and magazines, not pornographic ones, showing wives being spanked by their husbands, secretaries over their bosses' knees, all sorts. There's one with a young man who's put his girlfriend across his lap in a crowded restaurant, to punish her for ordering all the most expensive items, I think. He's turned her skirt up, although she's been left with her knickers, and the other guests are all either laughing or looking on with approval, men and women. There's no question of consent, her face shows consternation and shock. She's being punished, pure and simple. Can you imagine that nowadays?'

'No way!' She laughed. 'But they wouldn't really have done things like that, would they?'

'Not generally, no,' I admitted, 'or at least, I don't suppose so. If it wasn't considered important it wouldn't get reported, would it? Any more than nowadays somebody eating a meat pie is newsworthy, but what if vegetarianism became the social norm?'

'It would still have been shameful for the girl.'

'I don't suppose it's much fun for the meat pie.'

She laughed, no longer uneasy, but carefree. I took her hand again as we walked on, swinging our arms together, both silent with our own thoughts until we reached the stile from the river path on to the road. Pippa immediately climbed halfway up, balancing on

218

a rung exactly as she'd done the day Cudrow chased us, with her thighs pressed to the top bar and her body a little forwards for balance so that her bottom stuck out. Then I'd thought how ripe she was for spanking, in a purely physical way. Now I'd done it, but my desire was stronger still. I had to ask. 'You do want to again, don't you? And to –'

'After what you did to me!' she broke in, laughing. 'Oh I want it. I want it regularly!'

She jumped down, and I opened my arms for her, cuddling her to me just as I had after her punishment, only no longer as a spanked girl seeking comfort, but as equals. Our lips had touched too, just a brief, friendly peck, a second, more hesitant but firmer, a third, and our mouths were open together, our tongues touching, kissing in open, unashamed passion and held tight in each other's arms.

I wanted it to go on for ever, but it couldn't, not possibly, where we were so likely to be seen. We quickly broke apart and climbed the stile, then crossed the road to where a footpath sign pointed up a narrow lane. As we turned down it, I picked up more or less from where I'd left off. 'Attitudes are changing, spanking is becoming more acceptable again, as an aspect of sex play and generally with men on the receiving end, but it is changing. Who knows, in ten years it may be considered perfectly reasonable to bend a girlfriend over and apply a few firm swats to her bottom in the street. You wouldn't get arrested for it now, probably. Or the pendulum may have swung the other way, but that's not the point. I don't want to be spanked in ten years when society says I can be. I want to be spanked now!'

'No problem.'

She smacked my bottom, not hard, but it still sent a thrill right through me. I'd spanked her, and enjoyed every instant of it, but my original desire had always been for her to punish me, and to enjoy the exquisite humiliation of being under discipline from my teenage cousin. Had we been somewhere private I'd have stuck my bottom out and begged for it. The time for inhibition was past, and I was sure I knew her answer, but my voice sounded pathetically hopeful as I spoke. 'What I was going to ask earlier, Pippa, you will do that, won't you? Punish me?'

'I might,' she responded archly, 'if you deserve it, or maybe I'll take you over to Gran's and have her do it. That would be fun, as it goes, to watch Granny punish you.'

'Pippa! You're a disgrace – you're as bad as me, worse maybe!'

'Shouldn't I be?'

I answered with a shrug. Maybe it was true, certainly she wasn't far off, but what mattered was that she was an adult human being, capable of making her own choices. Her choice had been me, right from the moment Marjorie Burgess had taken down my knickers in front of her, which was a wonderful irony.

We walked on, Pippa taking my hand again as she spoke. 'There are so many cool things we can do, more if people would only be a bit less stiff. Seriously, do you think Granny would mind if I was to watch?'

'Yes,' I answered hastily, 'or, at least, I'm pretty sure she would. She doesn't see it as sex play or, at least, I don't think so. She's hard to read and she won't really talk about it.'

'Weird. I mean, she likes to do it, doesn't she?'

'Not weird, just old-fashioned. Yes, she does like to do it, mainly because she knows it's something I need, but it goes deeper than that, I think –' I paused, because I'd just had something of an epiphany, so clear that I was astonished I hadn't realised before. How many times had Elaine told me that spanking was just something some women needed? I kept my thoughts to myself and went on. 'Anyway, she feels it's better she gives it than – than I go around making a slut of myself.'

'A bit late for that!'

'Cheek!'

I let go of her hand to give her a playful swat across her bottom, making her squeak and jump, then abruptly retaliate, catching my wrist to try and pull me around and into range. We'd come to the end of the little lane, with a big 4X4 sheltering us from sight, and I let her, her palm smacking down on my bottom a good dozen times before she stopped, to leave me with a lovely tingly glow. We were laughing together as we continued, now on a narrow footpath between ivy-covered walls.

'I'd quite like to be spanked once a week,' Pippa said thoughtfully, 'the way Granny does you, so I can look forward to it and feel that lovely sensation I had between you telling me it was going to happen and actually being given it.'

'It is nice that way,' I agreed. 'We can make it every weekend, if you want?'

'Yeah! I can ride over, stop in, and go home with a smacked bum. It feels so nice afterwards, doesn't it?'

'Yes, which is how I'm feeling right now. You have to attend to me too, Pippa.'

She laughed, no doubt at the need in my voice. A brief flash of her impish smile and she'd reached out to pull a stick from the bank.

'You wait until you get home!' she chided, her voice mocking but so like her grandmother's I flinched, and again as she applied the stick to my bottom, goading me up the hill.

I'd have let her beat me then and there, but we'd heard voices ahead and stopped, walking sedately on and bidding a polite good evening to the trio of elderly women who passed us coming the other way. It was beginning to get gloomy, and still nearly a mile to my house, so we hurried on, taking to the road through the village and arriving just as the last of the colour faded from the trees.

Indoors felt cosy, and I opened a bottle of red wine. I didn't want to ask again, hoping she'd simply take control, but she seemed oblivious, chatting away casually, so we were on our third glasses before spanking was even mentioned again.

'It feels nice, going knickerless,' she said as she got up to pour herself a glass of water. 'Have you ever been made to go bare after a punishment?'

'Sometimes, yes,' I admitted. 'It's a good way of keeping your feelings strong.'

She reached back, to squeeze her bottom through her skirt. A little shiver ran through her. 'That feels nice,' she sighed. 'Are you going to spank me again before bedtime? That's another thing I used to think about, being sent to bed with a smacked bottom, and now I can be ...' She trailed off, smiling, her eyes closed as she began to pull up her school skirt, showing her legs, and her bottom, round and bare, still a little pink from her spanking. 'Go on, do it again, Penny,' she sighed, 'just like you did before.'

I stood up, torn between the desire to respond to her need and my own. She stayed as she was, bare little bottom slightly stuck out, kneading her cheeks to show the little pink hole between and a hint of pussy. I put my arm around her and kissed her cheek. 'If you insist,' I told her.

'I do,' she answered, 'right now!'

I caught the change in her voice an instant before

she abruptly twisted around, grabbing me around my waist and hustling me quickly towards a chair, too taken aback to resist. Before I really knew it I was over her lap, my skirt was up and my bare bottom was sticking out at the kitchen window. She was laughing in triumph and glee as she began to spank me, and I melted immediately, overcome by the sheer, breathtaking humiliation of being so suddenly turned across her knee, Pippa's knee, my young cousin.

She was spanking me and calling me a naughty girl as my cheeks bounced and quivered to her smacks, every impact of her palm on my bum flesh and every word sending a shock right through me, to bring me higher so fast I was on the verge of submitting myself to the final indignity and spreading my thighs to come on her leg when she began to speak. 'I'm going to enjoy this, Penny. Do you have any idea how I felt while I was across your knee and you were saying all those things to me? Yes, of course you do, and now I'm going to get you back! Let me see – yes, you were really rude with me!'

She stopped, but only to take hold of my bottom and haul my cheeks apart, spreading me open, my anus flaunted as she went on. 'No modesty, you said. I better get used to having my bumhole on show, you said. I better get used to having my bumhole touched, you said! Now how do you feel, with your cheeks open? You've shaved too, haven't you? Normally you're all hairy down there.'

'I – I had to,' I managed. 'AJ and her friends dripped wax in my pussy hair –'

'Yes, you said. Now let's get your bottom spanked, shall we?'

She let go and began to spank me again. I'd given in, too high to be proud, now sticking my bottom up to the slaps in a state of submissive ecstasy. She

223

giggled and began to smack me under my cheeks, as I'd done when she came on my leg. I took the hint, and was about to spread myself over her knee when my phone went. She laughed, holding me in place as she reached back to pull it from my bag. 'Oh, this will be good! I hope it's somebody from your work or something, so you can talk to them while I hold you over my lap. Won't that be humiliating?'

'Yes, but, Pippa, you mustn't spank me, in case they hear!'

She just laughed as she put the phone to her ear. 'Jade? Hi – No, Pippa. Can't you tell the difference?'

I twisted around, reaching for the phone as Pippa listened to whatever Jade was saying. She pulled away, then shook a finger at me. 'Not right now,' she told Jade, 'she's busy – very busy – I'm spanking her. Yes, she was naughty, of course – yes, she's over my lap right now, with her bum stuck in the air, listen –'

I gave a squeak of protest as she put the phone close to my bottom and delivered a salvo of slaps, my face colouring as I heard Jade's answering laughter.

'You see?' Pippa said as she put the phone back to her ear. 'Yes, bare – No, she hasn't got any on. Yes – Yes. She's already roasted my bottom, and now I'm roasting hers – That'll be great – Will do. Bye, Jade.'

'What did she say?' I demanded.

'She and Sophie are coming up tomorrow, that you're a dirty little trollop and I'm to spank you hard!'

I squealed as she suited action to words, applying her hand to my bottom again, harder than before, and laughing as she punished me, which tipped me straight over the edge. To be spanked at all was bad enough, never mind to be spanked by a woman so much younger than me, my own cousin, with my skirt turned high and my fat pink bottom stuck in the air, my cheeks spread to show off my bumhole, my friend told what was being done to me, and now being laughed at as I was beaten.

My thighs came wide and I was rubbing my pussy on her bare leg, utterly wanton, utterly uninhibited, exactly what Jade had said I was, a dirty little trollop, spanked across my cousin's knee, the girl who called me Auntie had my panties off and my bare bum dancing, my legs kicking in pain and ecstasy, my thighs spread and my bumhole showing, my sopping cunt spread out on her thigh as I came to the sound of her mocking laughter.

'Oh you dirty thing!' she called out in open delight as I hit my climax.

I was squirming on her leg, bucking my bottom up and down to the smacks and calling out her name again and again, telling her I needed her, I loved her, now with tears streaming down my face, a blubbering, spanked mess as I slipped from her lap on to the floor. She'd stopped laughing as I quickly picked myself up, and took me in her arms immediately, kissing me and stroking my hair, just as I'd done when I'd punished her, but firm too, standing no nonsense as she tugged her school skirt up to sit bare bottom on the chair and began to ease me down towards her sex, and as my lips found the smooth soft lips of her pussy she told me she loved me too.

Nine

When I awoke the next morning with Pippa's head cradled on my shoulder it was hard to think of anything much beyond how happy I felt.

We'd let ourselves go completely, finishing the wine and climbing into bed together, stark naked, drunk and giggling. For the next couple of hours we'd alternately been rude and intimate, kissing and cuddling, but also spanking each other, going head to tail and between each other's thighs, exploring every detail of each other's body. Had I not been so urgent it might have been ruder still, but my urge to hold her and to come with her was too strong for anything elaborate.

As we padded around the house in nothing but our tops I was simply too high on what had happened between us for my guilt to be more than a minor irritation in the back of my mind. My own moral qualms were gone, Pippa now my lover and my equal in every way, at least until one or other of us was due for spanking. I was going to feel bad about Kate, but it wouldn't be the first time in my life I'd had to cope with difficult emotions. Besides that, I could now see the sense of fate in what had happened, and the irony.

The rest of Saturday morning was very relaxed, spent by the pool, swimming, lazing in the sun and chatting. Jade and Sophie arrived with some bits and pieces to make a salad for lunch, also two bottles of white wine. As we talked, the conversation grew gradually ruder, covering spanking, all sorts of lesbian play and even peeing games. Pippa took it all in, sometimes shocked, but constantly fascinated, almost worshipful, and clearly keen not to see anything we did as negative.

By the time we'd finished the first bottle I'd been passed around to go across their laps, ostensibly to punish me for seducing Pippa. The spanking left me warm and rosy, and I stayed as I was, with just a pair of spanking panties under a light top, to serve them lunch. As we ate and drank our way through the second bottle, Pippa and I told them everything, just about, leading to plenty of teasing and another session across Jade's knee for me.

By the time I got up my bum was glowing and I was in a very submissive mood indeed, drunk and aroused, but no more so than any of them. Jade had rolled my panties down and I left them like that, because it felt so nice to have my bottom hot and bare under my top, and to know my cheeks showed behind even if I bent over ever so slightly. Jade and Sophie were also enjoying my humiliation, especially in front of Pippa, who had been giggling with delight as I was spanked and was now copying them by relaxing on her towel as I scurried back and forth at their bidding with my feelings growing ever stronger.

'More wine, slut,' Jade demanded even as I was making a rueful inspection of my red bottom. 'Come on, run along.'

'Yes, Miss,' I answered her, and went quickly inside, followed by a silvery laugh from Pippa that left me tingling with humiliation.

There was a bottle of Viognier in the fridge, and I quickly opened it before padding outside once more. Jade extended her glass and I filled it, then Sophie's and Pippa's. I was about to do my own when Jade gave a pointed cough. 'Ahem, Miss Muffet, what do you think you're doing?'

'Pouring myself some wine, Miss,' I answered, my bottom cheeks tightening automatically at the thought of further punishment.

'Who said you could have wine?' she demanded.

'Nobody,' I answered, hanging my head, 'sorry Miss Jade.'

'Don't be mean, Jade,' Sophie cut in. 'Let Muffet have her wine, only not whatever this stuff is, but some nice, hot private wine.'

Jade laughed, then snapped her fingers, pointing at my glass. I wanted to do it, badly, but I wasn't at all sure of Pippa's reaction. A glance told me that she had no idea what was going on, but she look intrigued. 'What are you going to do?' she asked.

I was going to speak, but Jade raised a finger. 'Uh, uh, Miss Muffet, I think it's about time Pippa learnt just what a bad girl you really are. I'm going to pee in her glass, Pippa, and make her drink it.'

'Pee in her glass!' Pippa echoed, her voice so rich with disgust that the blood rushed to my face. 'That is so gross! Go on, do it!'

I just stood there, fidgeting with embarrassment and terrified we were going to scare Pippa off. Jade obviously didn't care, and had stood up to take my glass. 'Watch!' she instructed as she squatted down.

Pippa was giggling in disgust and delight as Jade pulled her bikini pants aside and pressed the glass to the plump, furry lips of her pussy. Her belly tightened and then she'd let go, rich yellow pee squirting into the wine glass with a hiss. She'd filled it in seconds, but she didn't stop, letting it bubble out around the rim, to wet her bikini and run down her legs, giggling happily as she soiled herself.

'You are so bad!' Pippa squealed. 'Go on, make her do it, make her do it!'

Her face was set in impish glee, as cruel as I'd seen her, maybe more, as Jade lifted the glass of piddle. There was a big puddle on the ground, and I had a nasty suspicion I'd be going in it before too long as I took the glass. Pippa's eye were burning as she watched me, making me feel small and used as I put the glass to my lips, sipping at the rich, sharp taste of Jade's piss.

One taste, and what was left of my pride had gone. I shut my eyes in bliss as I gulped down the glass, swallowing the pee, still hot from Jade's body. Most went down my throat, but some spilt down my front, to wet my top and stick the thin cotton on to my breasts. All three of them were laughing as they watched me, Pippa loudest of all, which inevitably encouraged Jade and Sophie.

'On your knees, slut,' Jade ordered, pointing at the ground.

I went down, right in front of the pee puddle, looking up to await my next order. For a moment the three of them were watching me and sipping their wine, relaxed and amused while I knelt with my smacked bottom showing and my mouth full of the taste of piss. My stomach was churning, my toes wiggling, as unsure of Pippa's eventual reaction as I was sure my face was going in the pee puddle.

'Lick it,' Jade ordered, her voice full of relish, 'go on, lick my pee up!'

Pippa gave a fresh giggle, so full of anticipation she was biting her lip, but there was revulsion in her eyes too, which was making it the harder for me, but I was doing it, face down in Jade's pee puddle, lapping up the pungent liquid with my tongue like a dog drinking from a pond. Pippa's immediate squeal of disgust went through me like a knife, but I was still licking, my mouth full of dirt and piddle, my mind dizzy with humiliation.

'Have you ever seen a wet T-shirt contest, Pippa?' Sophie asked, stepping towards me.

'In Ibiza once, last summer –' Pippa began.

'Not like this you haven't!' Sophie giggled. 'Sit up, Miss Muffet.'

'Sophie –' I began, but it was too late.

She'd already pulled her bikini bottoms aside and she just let go, all over me, deluging me in hot piddle, first over my head and in my hair, then down my front as I knelt up, plastering my top to my breasts, and at last in my mouth as I came forwards, unable to stop myself. I took my breasts in my hands, rubbing the pee-soaked cotton over them as I drank Sophie's piddle, hot and fresh from her cunt, swallowing it down to make my belly swell and leave me dizzy with drunken arousal.

'What are you like, Penny!' Pippa crowed.

'She's a disgrace,' Jade responded.

'Once you've got her excited, she'll do anything, just about,' Sophie said happily as she shook herself dry over my head.

'Like being given a swirly?' Pippa giggled.

'Yes,' Sophie assured her.

'Let's do it!' Jade laughed. 'Come on, Miss Muffet, heel. It's time you had your hair washed.'

'Should we?' Pippa asked.

'Why not?' Jade queried.

'It's – it's just such an awful thing to do to somebody!' Pippa answered. 'Just so cruel, I'm not sure I could –'

'She has a stop word,' Sophie pointed out, and turned to look at me.

I hesitated, badly needing to be used, but terrified of losing Pippa. Yet she already knew AJ had flushed my head in the toilet, twice, and she'd just laughed. She was cruel, sensitive, but still cruel, cruel enough to let it overcome her disgust for my behaviour. I shook my head.

'See?' Sophie.

Still Pippa hesitated, but Jade spoke up. 'Do you, or do you not want to see Muffet get bog-washed? Come on, you're one of us now.'

A flush of pride immediately crossed Pippa's face. She bit her lip, then nodded. Jade was closest to me, and reached down to catch the neck of my top in her fist, making a scruff. I was pulled behind her, crawling, my eyes flicking between the ground and the rotation of Pippa's and Sophie's bottoms in their bikini pants as they walked ahead. Indoors, we went straight to the downstairs lavatory, where Jade positioned me on my knees in front of the bowl. I was shaking badly, my pussy so wet the juice had began to run down my legs. They looked at one another.

'I'm done,' Sophie announced.

'Me too,' Jade agreed, 'looks like you're on the throne, Pippa.'

'You – you want me to go first?' Pippa asked. 'Before her head goes down?'

'Well, yes,' Jade pointed out. 'There's not much use flushing her in clean water, is there?'

Pippa glanced from one to the other, unsure of herself but obviously wanting their approval.

'Go for it,' Sophie urged.

I just hung my head, unable to speak for the prospect of being flushed in Pippa's pee, my whole body shaking, already sodden, already desperate to come, but awaiting that last, awful moment.

Pippa giggled. 'Oh, OK, but this is bad, bad, bad.'

She'd sat down, her bikini pants tugged down to her ankles, her pretty, freckled face full of nervous excitement. Her thighs were closed, her bottom pushed out, her cheeks and neck pink with embarrassment, but her muscles had tensed, and her mouth came a little open as she let go. I heard the splash of her pee in the water beneath her, and more as her tummy tightened, and she was giggling hysterically as she looked up at Jade and Sophie.

'I'm doing it – I'm doing it, lots – aren't I bad?'

'Very bad!' Jade agreed.

'Now make her kiss your bumhole,' Sophie suggested, 'then in goes her head!'

'Kiss my bumhole?' Pippa echoed. 'Isn't that a bit too dirty? I mean –'

'It's OK,' I managed. 'It's nice, too nice not to –'

She made a face, then spoke again. 'OK, I suppose – you're doing the kissing, your mouth, my bumhole. Hang on.'

She pulled off a couple of pieces of loo paper to wipe herself, an act so simple, so everyday, yet so dirty when my face was about to go down her used toilet. Twice more she did the same, before rising to turn around, leaning on the loo as she stuck her bottom out, giggling in embarrassment but also a truly wicked pleasure. 'Go on then,' she said, 'if you want to be dirty, do it.'

Her trim cheeks were well parted, the tiny pink and brown star I'd asked to kiss on full show, her pussy moist and puffy, with a single drop of pee hanging from the tiny hood of her clitoris, and her pixie face looking back over her shoulder.

'Lick her,' Jade urged, 'lick her clean.'

I didn't need telling. It was what I wanted to do more than anything else in the world. Pippa stuck her bottom out a little more as my body rocked forwards. My tongue poked out, and her drunken, mischievous giggles had broken to a sigh of pleasure as I began to lick her anus. As her thick, earthy taste filled my senses I'd put my hands to her cheeks, spreading them wide and smothering my face between, lost in bliss as I licked at my darling Pippa's bottom hole, cleaning her tight little ring for her, and about to be flushed down the toilet she'd used.

It was perfect, exactly how I should be treated by my friends, my panties pulled down, spanked and humiliated, used to mop up their piss, my tongue used to clean their bottom holes. I let go of Pippa's cheeks, still licking, my face pushed well in between and my tongue burrowed up her anus. She was moaning with pleasure and rubbing it in my face, no longer caring. Sophie and Jade had their arms around each other, watching in delight, as I slipped my hands down my panties, front and rear, to masturbate.

My own bumhole felt slippery and wet, giving immediately to my finger, my pussy wetter still, taking three fingers with ease, and four and I spread my sex lips under my palm. I was rubbing, lost in ecstasy, my tongue pushed as deep up Pippa's tight, rubbery bottom hole as it would go, about to come, as she took me by the hair, calling me a bad girl and a slut as she pushed my head down, deep into the lavatory bowl. For one awful, ecstatic moment what she'd done in it was right in front of my eyes, before I screwed them tight as my face was pushed into it with a soft, wet noise, and I was coming. I heard her laughter, a shriek of gleeful, drunken disgust as my muscles locked tight.

'Do it, Pippa!' Jade yelled, and the water exploded around my head.

My mouth was open, full of water and loo paper and mess, my entire face under water, my fingers pumping in my open, sloppy holes, my body jerking in orgasm, lost to everything but what was being done to me, my mouth still full of the taste of Pippa's bottom as she flushed my head down my own lavatory, and coming over it, so dirty, so filthy, and so good.

When I came down from my orgasm I really thought I'd destroyed everything I'd built up with Pippa since the day we'd met at the quarry. I was wrong, the sole problem my own insecurity. She was drunk, aroused and thoroughly enjoying herself, playing the bad girl she had always wanted to be. After I'd been put in the bath I was made to lick her, also Jade and Sophie, each time with the other two watching.

Far from feeling guilty, she seemed to revel in what she'd done, and in particular in the approval of Jade and Sophie, and myself. If anything, she was concerned that I would feel bad for her having been so cruel, kissing me and repeatedly apologising until I finally turned her across my knee, took down her bikini pants and gave her a firm spanking in front of the others.

I knew I was supposed to retrieve my car from Pangbourne and take Pippa home, but I'd had far to much too drink and ended up making an apologetic phone call to Kate, which was in itself a surreal experience after what had happened. Jade and Sophie also stayed over and went back in the morning, taking Pippa and leaving me exhausted but on a plateau of sexual pleasure that didn't seem to want to break. I went back to bed, alternately dozing and teasing myself to orgasm over what had happened.

No matter how many times I masturbated, I could not get the sheer joy of giving Pippa her virgin spanking out of my head, nor of her punishing me in return. Every moment and every detail was fixed in my head, from the moment I'd picked her up to my own final orgasm as I'd lost control over her knee. Only when my pussy had become uncomfortably sore did I stop.

I was supposed to be across the road with Elaine by five so that I could be punished before we drove down to my mother's for Sunday dinner. For once I didn't really need it, but it would hardly have been fair to deny her just because I'd been playing with Pippa, and I wasn't sure I would have been able to do so in any case. After four years, going across her knee when I was told to had become pretty much instinctive.

After waking up shortly after half-past four I had to hurry my way through a shower and pull on a blue summer dress over a pair of spanking panties in order not to be late. Elaine was waiting for me, and we went straight through to the kitchen garden, where she'd been reading a magazine and drinking sherry when I rang the bell.

'Dressed like a seaside tart again, I see,' she remarked, good humoured but a little stern. 'Does that mean you'd like it harder today?'

'Um, as you please, Aunt Elaine,' I answered, unsure of exactly what her remark implied and so unable simply to admit to being willing to kneel for her if that was what was expected of me.

'Perhaps I should,' she replied. 'Over you go then.'

As when she'd used her hairbrush on me, she was a little tipsy, making me wonder if it would be a good moment to try to discover a little more about her spanking history. 'Punish me as you see fit,' I offered as I laid myself across her lap.

'I shall,' she answered, and turned up my dress.

She took it right up, high on to my back and over my head, so that I could see nothing but a field of blue cotton, my own hair and the ground, while my breasts were hanging out. I braced myself on the ground, already shaking a little and full of shame for being in a position that never becomes easy to accept, however often I'm made to adopt it.

'You – you said once I should have been punished on Bray Beach,' I said, as she took hold of my panties.

'What I said is that you should know how it felt,' she reminded me, easing my panties down over my bottom.

'To be punished in public?'

'Exactly,' she said, tucking my panties down before taking me firmly around my waist, 'but sadly it would be impossible.'

'Were – were you ever –' I managed, and broke off with a cry of shock and pain as she brought the rolled-up magazine down across my bottom.

She began to beat me, stern and silent, smacking the magazine across my cheeks hard enough to set me kicking and wriggling immediately, also gasping for air. I could hear the heavy slapping noises, each one in time to a blow that jammed my whole body forwards, with the next landing far too quickly to let me recover. Just ten or fifteen and I was well into my spanking tantrum, shrieking my head off and kicking in my panties, both my shoes off and my bottom spread to the world, but it was only when I began to cry that she spoke again.

'Some things are better left unsaid, Penny. Let's

just say that I take a great deal of satisfaction in punishing you this way, and would take a great deal more if it could be done in front of a substantial audience, including the woman who used – to – spank – me!'

Elaine punctuated the last words with hard swats of the magazine, delivered full across the cheekiest part of my bottom. I didn't dare say what was in my head, but she'd confirmed it for me, the memory of a spanking session, many spanking sessions, bare-bottom sessions, and at least one in public. No wonder she liked to spank me.

The spanking went on, harder than ever, bringing my tantrum up to a truly pathetic state, and yet for all my pain I couldn't get the image out of my head, my aunt Elaine, always so stern and so prim, down across her big sister's lap with her bikini pants down and her bare bottom bouncing to the smacks in front of dozens of people, maybe hundreds. First I was giggling brokenly in between my gasps and yelps of pain, and then laughing, in hysterics for all the blazing heat of my bottom cheeks, for my shameful exposure, because it was nothing to what she'd been given.

'What's so funny?' she demanded as she stopped spanking.

'I – I'm sorry, Auntie,' I managed. 'I'm just a bit emotional, that's all, sorry –'

'I see,' she remarked. 'Yes, Penny, I think we understand each other. We all need somebody, and you have me.'

She went back to work on my bottom, no longer with the magazine but by hand, quite hard, but no longer as a punishment, just playing with my bottom. I stuck my hips up, taken over the barrier while I'd been laughing, and now warm and urgent behind.

Soon I was sighing with pleasure and trying to get my thighs open across her leg, lost to all sense of decency.

'If you must, I suppose,' she said softly, and she began to smack over my pussy.

A moment later she had hooked her leg in over my panties, spreading me on to her knee. All I could manage was a little, shame-filled groan and I'd began to rub, feeling thoroughly dirty as I began to bring myself up towards orgasm on my aunt's leg. My pussy was spread out on her stocking, my slick shaven skin painfully sensitive, with every smack to my bum bringing me that little bit closer.

I let my thoughts go, wishing she do would as she had threatened, and take me across her knee in front of my whole family, but not in revenge. She'd do it to punish me for seducing Pippa, hard, mercilessly hard, with her hairbrush before I was caned. Yes, that would be perfect, brought into her drawing room by my ear, with everyone watching, Pippa herself, already spanked by Kate, standing in the corner with her rosy bottom on show, Susan trying not to smile, Jeremy trying to hide his erection, Jemima giggling, and my mother in silent disapproval as she watched her own daughter's dress pulled up ... her own daughter's panties taken down ... her own daughter's bottom laid bare ... and spanked ... and spanked ... and spanked.

As my cry of ecstasy broke from my throat it was what I wanted more than anything else in the world, the supreme humiliation of me, Dr Penny Birch, given a panties-down, bare-bottom spanking in front of my own mother. An instant later my orgasm had shattered and it was the thing I wanted least in the world, but there was a bitter smile on my lips as I came slowly down, of resignation to my own grossly ambivalent feelings, little different to those of my aunt.

The following weekend was scheduled for my visit to Colonel Aimsworth in Worthing, but it had all become rather complicated. Pippa wanted to be with me as much as possible, but whatever might have happened between us I could hardly compound my behaviour by introducing her to a notorious dirty old man. Not that she'd have been interested anyway, which was a good reason for not telling her.

The other complication was an invitation from Susan for the Saturday evening, which included the whole family and could not be put off as she finally seemed to have found a man she could settle down with, which meant a three-line whip from Elaine, although sadly not a real one.

That meant I had to get back from Worthing in time to get to Susan's, so I excused myself by saying I had to work in the morning, and promised to meet them all at Paddington. Jade and Sophie wanted to go out as well, so I had to explain what was happening to them and promise I'd bring Pippa over to Turnpike Lane after dinner. In the end I was rather pleased with myself, having set up the whole day in a neatly organised manner that kept everybody happy.

Saturday was wonderfully warm, with just the faintest breeze, far too nice to bother with a bra even it did mean being referred to as a seaside tart. If anything, that was the way I wanted to feel, which was just as well. If my last visit was anything to go by I might end up doing something extremely dirty, even sucking spunk through my panties again, so it was best to be in a naughty mood from the first.

I chose the blue dress I'd worn for my spanking the previous Sunday, along with a pair of my usual panties. Just having the white cotton snug around my bum and tight over my still shaven pussy was a delight, and helped to keep me in the right frame of mind as I walked down to the station. As before, it was a slow journey, but I'd left plenty of time and arrived in Worthing early enough to take a walk along the front before making my way to Beach View and arguing my way past the nurse.

The Colonel was in his room, seated exactly as before, with a glass in one hand, his face a trifle red and a faint whiff of malt whisky in the air. I'd knocked but he hadn't realised it was me, his expression detached and somewhat melancholy until he saw who his visitor was. Suddenly he was beaming. 'Ah, Penny, my dear, splendid, so glad you could come.'

'My pleasure. Is it just me?'

'Absolutely,' he answered, rubbing his hands together in unconcealed glee as his eyes moved down my body.

'I thought it might be,' I admitted.

'You don't mind?'

'Not at all.'

He gave an understanding chuckle and hauled himself to his feet, unsteady enough for me to offer him an arm, which he waved away. 'I'm in rather fine fettle today, as it happens, so I don't need help from you,' he said, 'not that sort of help anyway.'

His hand closed on my bottom as he spoke, taking a good-sized pinch of flesh hard enough to make me squeak. It was going to happen, no pretence, no mock reluctance. I'd be wined and dined, then it would be back to his room and down with my panties, for whatever rude treat took his fancy. I ate lightly at lunch, listening to his reminiscences and making conversation that grew steadily less polite as we worked our way down the bottle of Champagne he'd ordered to celebrate.

By the time we'd finished, I was ready, a little drunk, with my fantasy running nicely in my head. Even walking back through the streets of Worthing was fun, arm in arm with a man considerably more than twice my age, my nipples and panties showing through my light blue dress, every inch the little tart being escorted by her paramour, back to his lodgings for some thoroughly rude sex in the old-fashioned style. Fortunately, nobody in Worthing knew me.

I was determined to play my part, allowing the humiliation of what I was doing to build up slowly until I was ready to bring myself to a peak. In his room I immediately locked the door behind us, causing his eyebrows to raise as he reached for the bottle of malt. 'Forward little thing, aren't you?' he remarked. 'So, ah, I take it this means you have a little something for me?'

'If you like,' I promised, 'as a birthday treat.'

'What a wonderful attitude you have! Yes, I would like that, very much. Just like last time? One other thing too, just a harmless little foible of mine, if you wouldn't mind.'

'What's that?'

He put down the bottle and went to open a drawer instead, and pulled out a little pot. The lid lifted to show a rich red paste within, rather like blusher, but enough to last a year or more all at once.

'Rouge,' he explained, 'or, at least, the closest you can get to it these days. Plenty of girls used to wear it in my day, to put a bit of colour in their cheeks.'

'Do you want me to make up in an old-fashioned style?' I asked. 'I would, but I'm not sure I know how and I'd need red lipstick, eyeliner, foundation even. All I have in my bag is a stick of lipgloss.'

'Oh no, my dear, it's not for your face. I want you to rouge your cunt.'

I swallowed, taken aback by the sudden demand, and how crudely he'd phrased it. He went on, oblivious, as I took the pot of rouge. A glance at the lid showed it wasn't make-up at all, at least not in the sense I was used to. It had been made by a theatrical supply company, and was intended as face paint. Not for me, it wasn't. For me it was to be applied to my pussy, my cunt, making me a clown as well as a tart, a vulgar, ridiculous image, utterly humiliating and irresistible.

'Splendid sight, a nicely rouged cunt,' he was saying, his tongue clicking on the rude word with deep satisfaction, 'especially from behind. Back in Paris, some of the girls in the speciality shows used to do it when they danced the can-can. No drawers, you understand, this wasn't the Moulin Rouge, just a line of fat white bottoms with fat red cunts peeping out from between their thighs.'

He gave a pleased sigh and settled into his chair, once more with the bottle of whisky in his hand. I accepted a glass and swallowed it quickly as he went on. 'That's what memories are made of, my dear. When you're my age it won't be your career you look back on, or your money, none of that. It'll be the fellow who first kissed you behind the bike sheds, or the first time you took a fellow's cock out.'

As he finished speaking he had suited action to words, casually opening his fly and thumbing down the front of his underpants to flop out his cock and balls. As he began to stroke them he gave me a nod. I responded, tight lipped, turning my back and sticking out my bottom. There was a mirror on his wardrobe door, and I could see myself clearly, my dark, bobbed hair, my blue dress loose on the curve

243

of my back and bottom, just the image I wanted, light and summery and rude, a little seaside tart showing off for her dirty old man.

His cock was already growing in his hand as I began to inch my dress up, showing off my bare legs, teasing him by stopping just before my panties came on show, giving him a wiggle, and right up. With my dress on my back the taut white seat of my panties was showing to him, and I held my pose, allowing him to admire the rude view I was providing as his cock grew.

After a while he gave a pleased chuckle and picked up his glass, sipping whisky. I stuck my thumbs into my waistband, ready to pull down my knickers. Again I turned to the mirror, enjoying the full curve of my body, my back well dipped in, my bottom stuck out, really quite fleshy – no, embarrassingly plump, my cheeks fat and round in my panties, the sort of bottom that would belong to girl who needed regular spanking. I began to push, watching the trim white panties slide down over my big white bum, showing off deliberately to the sound of Colonel Aimsworth's cock slapping in his hand as he brought himself to erection.

'By God, I like to like to see a girl's bare arsehole,' he grunted as my knickers slid down to let out the full meat of my cheeks, open to show the rude pinkish-brown hole between, just as he'd said.

I stuck my bottom out further still, making sure he could see every detail of my anus, deliberately humiliating myself. He gave a grunt of appreciation and changed his grip on his cock, now rolling the foreskin up and down over his bloated helmet and toying with his balls. I pulled my panties a little lower, to show him my pussy, and how wet I was, how excited he'd made me.

'That's the way,' he said, 'right down, show it all. Shaved your cunt, I see?'

'Yes, just for you,' I lied, and reached down between my legs to spread my sex lips open, showing him my ready hole in a deliberately vulgar display.

His cock was hard, as ready for me as I was for him, his face red as he spoke again.

'Now put on the rouge, in front of me.'

I nodded and quickly pulled off my panties to let myself cock a leg up on the table, spreading myself behind in a thoroughly dirty pose, the sort of pose that felt good for me, rude and open, ready to take a cock in my wet, shaven cunt, just as soon as I'd applied a little rouge to make myself ruder still. Then I'd be not just naked, but blatantly exposed, marked as what I was, a dirty little tart, clownish and silly, ready for fucking by any man bold enough to get me out of my knickers.

Having taken up the pot, I quickly twisted the lid free and pushed my fingers down into the thick red paste. It felt cool and slippery, and the instant I touched it I knew it would not just be my pussy that would get a coating. Scooping up as much as I could, I pushed out my bottom once more, right out, so that he could see every rude detail as I wiped the rouge on to my sex, with my fingers splayed to smear it on to my lips but leave the heart wet and pink, then together to coat the plump bulge of my naked mound.

It felt gloriously naughty, gloriously humiliating, to be making such a blatant display of myself, and for his benefit, a man of his age, a man who'd enjoyed taking dirty pictures of me for years, a man who saw me as a little tart. What had I done? Had I slapped his face? Had I reported him to the proper authorities? Had I given him a lecture on appropriate behaviour towards women? No, I'd pulled down my panties and rouged my cunt to give him something to toss off over, and more.

Definitely more. The thick, long cock in his hand was going up my pussy, in up my shaven, well-rouged cunt, and soon. As I dipped my finger back in the pot of rouge something came to me, something he'd said about the dancing girls in Paris – just a line of big white bottoms with fat red cunts peeping out from between their thighs. That was how I wanted him to see me, as purely sexual, an appalling thing to think, utterly unacceptable, and just how I wanted to feel, appreciated not for my mind, but just for my mouth and tits and pussy, as places for men to stick their cocks, and best of all, my bottom, my fat white bottom, bare and open, my anus rouged and ready.

I put my hand back, touching a rouge-laden finger to my bumhole, to paint my ring, smearing it on good and thick. It felt glorious, teasing my anus in front of a dirty old man, making myself ready, because I was going to offer him the chance to fuck my bottom, to sodomise me. He was quite big though, and as I slid my finger in with his eyes almost bulging from his head I was telling myself it was as much to get myself ready as because it felt so good. Inside I was quite full, but I was too far gone to worry. I wanted his cock up my bottom and that was that.

'Would you – would you like to do me up my bum?' I asked, my own words sending fresh shivers through me.

He didn't answer, but his Adam's apple bobbed in his throat and that was enough for me. I eased my finger out of my bottom hole, leaving myself open and sticky with rouge, ready for penetration, ready to be buggered. I stayed how I was, just moving my leg down so that I could stick my bottom out, my fat white bottom, with my cunt showing between my thighs, my lips painted vulgar, clownish red, and my bumhole the same, just showing off, but he took it as an offer.

'In – in my lap, my dear,' he grunted. 'Could never make it standing.'

I nodded my sympathy and quickly whipped my dress off, then came to him, not to sit in his lap, but to drape myself over his knees. 'Warm me up a little, please,' I asked. 'Spank me.'

He set to work immediately, rubbing his cock on the flesh of my midriff as he began to smack my bottom, calling me a naughty girl as he did it. I was already too high for it to hurt, and too into it, sticking my bottom up and giggling like the wanton little tart I am. It would have been good to stay like that for ages, having my fat white bottom gently spanked across Colonel Aimsworth's lap, just the sort of place I should be, but he was soon getting impatient, rubbing his cock on me so hard I was scared he would come and deprive me of my dirty treat.

'No, no, up my bottom!' I protested as he began to grunt with passion.

I stood quickly, to find his erection a straining, eager pole, sticking up above the heavy sac of his balls. My bottom felt hot and bigger than ever, spanked to readiness, my bumhole a slippery, open spot between my cheeks. I turned, grabbed hold of my bottom and spread myself open, showing off my full rear view. He took his cock, aiming it as I gently lowered myself down, until I felt his helmet press to my bumhole.

My mouth came wide in a heartfelt sigh as I felt my ring start to spread, opening gently to the pressure as I pushed out, taking him, my bumhole agape on his cock head, and wider still as he pushed it up me. It had been a while since I'd let a man up my bum, too long, and I was squirming with pleasure as I wriggled myself slowly down, taking inch after inch of his erection inside me.

At last I had that glorious, bloated feeling, as if his cock was about to come out of my mouth, with my bumhole spread wide on the very base of his shaft and his fat balls pressed to my empty cunt. I spread my thighs as I settled on to his lap and slipped a hand down, touching my pussy and the junction of his penis and my bumhole, his cock, Colonel Aimsworth's cock, rammed home in my straining bumhole.

He began to push, and to grunt, buggering me to a steady rhythm as I started to masturbate. It was perfect, a big cock up my bum, up my fat white bottom with my cunt and anus rouged, better still, my spanked pink bottom, the culmination of my dirty little routine. He was going to come, getting urgent, and so was I, running over what I'd done in my head; pulled up my dress and taken down my panties, rouged my cunt and bumhole, asked to be buggered and asked to be spanked.

I threw my head back as I started to come, gasping in ecstasy at the feel of my packed rectum and the thought of what I'd done. His hands came around me, to clutch at my breasts, bouncing them and groping them as he thrust up inside me, gasping and puffing, and suddenly silent as he gave me what I needed, to have him spunk in my rectum, a glorious indignity for a dirty, spanked little tart.

We'd come together, but I wasn't finished, holding myself right on the edge, teasing the slippery, rouge-smeared flesh of my pussy as I eased myself slowly off his cock. He lay back, gasping, his face the colour of beetroot, but his eyebrows still went up in surprise as I twisted around and sank to my knees.

His cock was filthy, smeared with rouge and spunk and worse. It went straight in my mouth, my head filling with the thick taste of my own bumhole as I began to suck him clean. I was masturbating again as my head bobbed up and down on his cock, and twisted a little too, so that I could see in the mirror, a view so unspeakably rude it set my pussy tight again immediately.

I knelt at his feet, stark naked but for my smart black shoes and frilly white ankle socks. My mouth was full of cock, glistening, slippery cock just pulled out from my bumhole. Better still, my bottom was stuck well out, my cheeks splayed to make them look as big and round as possible, my thighs apart with my well-rouged cunt showing between, and my bumhole, red and squashy, obviously just sodomised, with bubbles of the Colonel's spunk emerging from my hole.

The trip back from Worthing was hectic to say the least. I'd overrun my time a little bit, carried away with my dirty behaviour, and there wasn't time to do more than the simplest cleaning up and take a last swallow of his malt. I did at least look outwardly respectable, or at least as respectable as possible in my summer dress and fresh panties.

Underneath I was still more than a little uncomfortable, with both my pussy and bottom hole sticky with rouge, which had proved far from easy to get off. With no time to do anything effective, I simply put up with it, wishing only that the Colonel had warned me in advance.

By the time I'd reached Reading I knew I was going to be late, but only by twenty minutes or so, as a fast train came in at the same time as my own. I ran, and just caught it, making a few final adjustments to my appearance in the loo, so that by the time we pulled in to Paddington there was nothing to suggest I'd done anything more unusual than an afternoon's work. I'd come in on a different platform, but I saw my family almost immediately, clustered beneath the arrivals board, and somebody else I recognised – AJ.

She looked like she'd stepped out of some dyke nightmare of hell, in black army boots, combats, a singlet that left half her breasts showing and most of her tattoos and piercings. Her face was set in an angry scowl, she was swaying as she walked, and in one hand she held a can of extra strong lager, which she dropped as she saw me.

I hesitated, not really wanting to introduce her to the family, but unsure what else I could do. They'd seen me, Pippa waving enthusiastically, my mother walking towards me with her face set in that all-too-familiar expression of mild exasperation. I waved back, walking faster in the hope of speaking to AJ and moving on before my mother reached us, also wishing the rouge between my bum cheeks didn't feel quite so sticky.

AJ stopped, her eyes fixed on me as she spoke, her voice angry and slurred with drink. 'You, Muffet, they said you'd be here –'

'Are you all right?' I ventured.

'No I'm fucking not,' she answered. 'Dumplings tells me you and the moppet got dirty together? Is that right?'

'Well –' I began, panicking because my mother was maybe fifty paces away and closing fast.

'Bitch!' AJ spat, and her hand lashed out.

I had no chance at all, caught by my dress and wrenched forwards, completely off balance. All I could do was emit a squeal of horror and despair as she flopped down on a trolley, a squeal provoked by the certain knowledge of what she intended to do – spank me. I tried to fight, my mind burning with the twin images of my approaching mother and my fat white bottom with my cunt and anus smeared with rouge, but it was no good.

Over her knee I went, up came up my dress – and my panties came down in Paddington Station.

The leading publisher of fetish and adult fiction

TELL US WHAT YOU THINK!

Readers' ideas and opinions matter to us. Take a few minutes to fill in the questionnaire below and you'll be entered into a prize draw to win a year's worth of Nexus books (36 titles)

Terms and conditions apply – see end of questionnaire.

1. Sex: Are you male ☐   female ☐   a couple ☐?

2. Age: Under 21 ☐   21–30 ☐   31–40 ☐   41–50 ☐   51–60 ☐   over 60 ☐

3. Where do you buy your Nexus books from?

☐ A chain book shop. If so, which one(s)?

_____

☐ An independent book shop. If so, which one(s)?

_____

☐ A used book shop/charity shop
☐ Online book store. If so, which one(s)?

_____

4. How did you find out about Nexus Books?

☐ Browsing in a book shop
☐ A review in a magazine
☐ Online
☐ Recommendation
☐ Other _____

5. In terms of settings which do you prefer? (Tick as many as you like)

☐ Down to earth and as realistic as possible
☐ Historical settings. If so, which period do you prefer?

_____

☐ Fantasy settings – barbarian worlds

- ☐ Completely escapist/surreal fantasy
- ☐ Institutional or secret academy
- ☐ Futuristic/sci fi
- ☐ Escapist but still believable
- ☐ Any settings you dislike?

_____

- ☐ Where would you like to see an adult novel set?

_____

6. In terms of storylines, would you prefer:

- ☐ Simple stories that concentrate on adult interests?
- ☐ More plot and character-driven stories with less explicit adult activity?
- ☐ We value your ideas, so give us your opinion of this book:

_____

_____

_____

7. In terms of your adult interests, what do you like to read about? (Tick as many as you like)

- ☐ Traditional corporal punishment (CP)
- ☐ Modern corporal punishment
- ☐ Spanking
- ☐ Restraint/bondage
- ☐ Rope bondage
- ☐ Latex/rubber
- ☐ Leather
- ☐ Female domination and male submission
- ☐ Female domination and female submission
- ☐ Male domination and female submission
- ☐ Willing captivity
- ☐ Uniforms
- ☐ Lingerie/underwear/hosiery/footwear (boots and high heels)
- ☐ Sex rituals
- ☐ Vanilla sex
- ☐ Swinging

☐ Cross-dressing/TV
☐ Enforced feminisation
☐ Others – tell us what you don't see enough of in adult fiction:

_____

_____

_____

8. Would you prefer books with a more specialised approach to your interests, i.e. a novel specifically about uniforms? If so, which subject(s) would you like to read a Nexus novel about?

_____

_____

_____

9. Would you like to read true stories in Nexus books? For instance, the true story of a submissive woman, or a male slave? Tell us which true revelations you would most like to read about:

_____

_____

_____

10. What do you like best about Nexus books?

_____

_____

11. What do you like least about Nexus books?

_____

_____

12. Which are your favourite titles?

_____

_____

13. Who are your favourite authors?

_____

_____

14. Which covers do you prefer? Those featuring:
(tick as many as you like)

☐ Fetish outfits
☐ More nudity
☐ Two models
☐ Unusual models or settings
☐ Classic erotic photography
☐ More contemporary images and poses
☐ A blank/non-erotic cover
☐ What would your ideal cover look like?

_____

15. Describe your ideal Nexus novel in the space provided:

_____

_____

_____

_____

16. Which celebrity would feature in one of your Nexus-style fantasies?
We'll post the best suggestions on our website – anonymously!

_____

THANKS FOR YOUR TIME

Now simply write the title of this book in the space below and cut out the
questionnaire pages. Post to: Nexus, Marketing Dept., Thames Wharf Studios,
Rainville Rd, London W6 OA

Book title: _____

TERMS AND CONDITIONS

NEXUS NEW BOOKS

To be published in January 2006

THE ART OF SURRENDER
Madeline Bastinado

Jude Ryan expects obedience. And she always gets it. Fellow artist, Michael Read, believes he can persuade any woman to submit to him. And he can be very persuasive. In Jude he finds a sexual appetite to match his own and a power he can't resist. The kiss of the whip, the unforgiving caress of leather restraints and cold, cruel stiletto heels are the tools she uses to push Michael to erotic extremes and open his eyes to a whole new world of forbidden pleasure. In her dungeon he learns that bondage can set you free.

£6.99   ISBN 0-352-34013-4

BINDING PROMISES
G C Scott

When Harold sells his flat, he also exchanges another kind of contract with the new owner: an agreement that involves his complete domination of an attractive, older woman who adores extreme restraint and rope bondage. And so his dark and intensely erotic initiation to the far reaches of control and sexual power begins in the most ordinary settings, with the most ordinary equipment. And despite being shocked at how far Samantha needs to go, can he resist taking her there?

£6.99   ISBN 0-352-34014-2

LEG LOVER
L G Denier

You will soon hold in your hands the first novel written exclusively about a male leg fetish – the intense story of one man's total and lifelong enthusiasm for women's legs, feet and their accessories. A highly detailed and intensely erotic love story about shapely legs, painted toenails, sheer hosiery, high heels and the women who enchant and tease while presenting their legs to catch the eye and arouse the helpless devotee. This is not only an epic journey to the extremities of leg adoration, but the very first book in the new Nexus Enthusiast imprint: an original series that will explore, reveal and tantalise the reader with the most highly detailed fetish fiction actually written by genuine enthusiasts for genuine enthusiasts. As kinky as fiction can possibly get!

£6.99   ISBN 0-352-34016-9

If you would like more information about Nexus titles, please visit our website at www.nexus-books.co.uk, or send a stamped addressed envelope to:
  Nexus, Thames Wharf Studios,
  Rainville Road, London W6 9HA

NEXUS BACKLIST

This information is correct at time of printing. For up-to-date information, please visit our website at www.nexus-books.co.uk

All books are priced at £6.99 unless another price is given.

ABANDONED ALICE	Adriana Arden 0 352 33969 1	☐
ALICE IN CHAINS	Adriana Arden 0 352 33908 X	☐
AMAZON SLAVE	Lisette Ashton 0 352 33916 0	☐
THE ANIMAL HOUSE	Cat Scarlett 0 352 33877 6	☐
THE ART OF CORRECTION	Tara Black 0 352 33895 4	☐
AT THE END OF HER TETHER	G.C. Scott 0 352 33857 1	☐
BARE BEHIND	Penny Birch 0 352 33721 4	☐
BELINDA BARES UP	Yolanda Celbridge 0 352 33926 8	☐
BENCH MARKS	Tara Black 0 352 33797 4	☐
THE BLACK GARTER	Lisette Ashton 0 352 33919 5	☐
THE BLACK MASQUE	Lisette Ashton 0 352 33977 2	☐
THE BLACK ROOM	Lisette Ashton 0 352 33914 4	☐
THE BLACK WIDOW	Lisette Ashton 0 352 33973 X	☐
THE BOOK OF PUNISHMENT	Cat Scarlett 0 352 33975 6	☐
THE BOND	Lindsay Gordon 0 352 33996 9	☐

CAGED [£5.99]	Yolanda Celbridge 0 352 33650 1	☐
CHERRI CHASTISED	Yolanda Celbridge 0 352 33707 9	☐
COLLEGE GIRLS	Cat Scarlett 0 352 33942 X	☐
COMPANY OF SLAVES	Christina Shelly 0 352 33887 3	☐
CONCEIT AND CONSEQUENCE	Aishling Morgan 0 352 33965 9	☐
CONFESSIONS OF AN ENGLISH SLAVE	Yolanda Celbridge 0 352 33861 X	☐
CORRECTIVE THERAPY	Jacqueline Masterson 0 352 33917 9	☐
CRUEL SHADOW	Aishling Morgan 0 352 33886 5	☐
DARK MISCHIEF	Lady Alice McCloud 0 352 33998 5	☐
DEMONIC CONGRESS	Aishling Morgan 0 352 33762 1	☐
DEPTHS OF DEPRAVATION	Ray Gordon 0 352 33995 0	☐
DISCIPLINE OF THE PRIVATE HOUSE	Esme Ombreux 0 352 33709 5	☐
DISCIPLINED SKIN [£5.99]	Wendy Swanscombe 0 352 33541 6	☐
DOMINATION DOLLS	Lindsay Gordon 0 352 33891 1	☐
EMMA ENSLAVED	Hilary James 0 352 33883 0	☐
EMMA'S HUMILIATION	Hilary James 0 352 33910 1	☐
EMMA'S SECRET DOMINATION	Hilary James 0 352 34000 2	☐
EMMA'S SECRET WORLD	Hilary James 0 352 33879 2	☐
EMMA'S SUBMISSION	Hilary James 0 352 33906 3	☐
EROTICON 1 [£5.99]	Various 0 352 33593 9	☐

FAIRGROUND ATTRACTION	Lisette Ashton 0 352 33927 6	☐
THE GOVERNESS ABROAD	Yolanda Celbridge 0 352 33735 4	☐
HOT PURSUIT	Lisette Ashton 0 352 33878 4	☐
IN DISGRACE	Penny Birch 0 352 33922 5	☐
IN HER SERVICE	Lindsay Gordon 0 352 33968 3	☐
THE INDECENCIES OF ISABELLE	Penny Birch (writing as Cruella) 0 352 33989 6	☐
THE INDIGNITIES OF ISABELLE	Penny Birch (writing as Cruella) 0 352 33696 X	☐
THE INDISCRETIONS OF ISABELLE	Penny Birch (writing as Cruella) 0 352 33882 2	☐
INNOCENT	Aishling Morgan 0 352 33699 4	☐
THE INSTITUTE	Maria Del Rey 0 352 33352 9	☐
JULIA C	Laura Bowen 0 352 33852 0	☐
KNICKERS AND BOOTS	Penny Birch 0 352 33853 9	☐
LACING LISBETH	Yolanda Celbridge 0 352 33912 8	☐
NON FICTION: LESBIAN SEX SECRETS FOR MEN	Jamie Goddard and Kurt Brungard 0 352 33724 9	☐
LESSONS IN OBEDIENCE	Lucy Golden 0 352 33892 X	☐
LETTERS TO CHLOE [£5.99]	Stephan Gerrard 0 352 33632 3	☐
LICKED CLEAN	Yolanda Celbridge 0 352 33999 3	☐
LOVE JUICE	Donna Exeter 0 352 33913 6	☐

THE MASTER OF CASTLELEIGH [£5.99]	Jacqueline Bellevois 0 352 33644 7	☐
MISS RATAN'S LESSON	Yolanda Celbridge 0 352 33791 5	☐
NAUGHTY NAUGHTY	Penny Birch 0 352 33974 4	☐
NEW EROTICA 6	Various 0 352 33751 6	☐
NO PAIN, NO GAIN	James Baron 0 352 33966 7	☐
NURSE'S ORDERS	Penny Birch 0 352 33739 7	☐
ONE WEEK IN THE PRIVATE HOUSE	Esme Ombreux 0 352 33706 0	☐
ORIGINAL SINS	Lisette Ashton 0 352 33804 0	☐
THE PALACE OF PLEASURES	Christobel Coleridge 0 352 33801 6	☐
PALE PLEASURES	Wendy Swanscombe 0 352 33702 8	☐
PARADISE BAY [£5.99]	Maria Del Rey 0 352 33645 5	☐
PLAYTHING	Penny Birch 0 352 33967 5	☐
THE PUNISHMENT CAMP	Jacqueline Masterton 0 352 33940 3	☐
PENNY PIECES [£5.99]	Penny Birch 0 352 33631 5	☐
PET TRAINING IN THE PRIVATE HOUSE [£5.99]	Esme Ombreux 0 352 33655 2	☐
PETTING GIRLS	Penny Birch 0 352 33957 8	☐
THE PLAYER	Cat Scarlett 0 352 33894 6	☐
PRINCESS	Aishling Morgan 0 352 33871 7	☐
PRIVATE MEMOIRS OF A KENTISH HEADMISTRESS	Yolanda Celbridge 0 352 33763 X	☐
PRIZE OF PAIN	Wendy Swanscombe 0 352 33890 3	☐

THE PRIESTESS	Jacqueline Bellevois 0 352 33905 5	☐
PUNISHED IN PINK	Yolanda Celbridge 0 352 34003 7	☐
THE PUNISHMENT CLUB	Jacqueline Masterson 0 352 33862 8	☐
RITES OF OBEDIENCE	Lindsay Gordon 0 352 34005 3	☐
SCARLET VICE	Aishling Morgan 0 352 33988 8	☐
SCHOOLED FOR SERVICE	Lady Alice McCloud 0 352 33918 7	☐
SCHOOL FOR STINGERS	Yolanda Celbridge 0 352 33994 2	☐
THE SCHOOLING OF STELLA	Yolanda Celbridge 0 352 33803 2	☐
SERVING TIME	Sarah Veitch 0 352 33509 2	☐
SEXUAL HEELING	Wendy Swanscombe 0 352 33921 7	☐
SILKEN SERVITUDE	Christina Shelly 0 352 34004 5	☐
SILKEN SLAVERY	Christina Shelly 0 352 33708 7	☐
SINS APPRENTICE	Aishling Morgan 0 352 33909 8	☐
SLAVE ACTS	Jennifer Jane Pope 0 352 33665 X	☐
SLAVE GENESIS [£5.99]	Jennifer Jane Pope 0 352 33503 3	☐
SLAVE REVELATIONS [£5.99]	Jennifer Jane Pope 0 352 33627 7	☐
THE SMARTING OF SELINA	Yolanda Celbridge 0 352 33872 5	☐
STRIPING KAYLA	Yvonne Marshall 0 352 33881 4	☐
STRIPPED BARE	Angel Blake 0 352 33971 3	☐
THE SUBMISSION GALLERY [£5.99]	Lindsay Gordon 0 352 33370 7	☐

THE SUBMISSION OF STELLA	Yolanda Celbridge 0 352 33854 7	☐
THE TAMING OF TRUDI	Yolanda Celbridge 0 352 33673 0	☐
TASTING CANDY	Ray Gordon 0 352 33925 X	☐
TEASING CHARLOTTE	Yvonne Marshall 0 352 33681 1	☐
TEMPTING THE GODDESS	Aishling Morgan 0 352 33972 1	☐
TICKLE TORTURE	Penny Birch 0 352 33904 7	☐
TIE AND TEASE	Penny Birch 0 352 33987 X	☐
TORMENT INCORPORATED	Murilee Martin 0 352 33943 8	☐
THE TRAINING GROUNDS	Sarah Veitch 0 352 33526 2	☐
UNIFORM DOLL	Penny Birch 0 352 33698 6	☐
VELVET SKIN [£5.99]	Aishling Morgan 0 352 33660 9	☐
WENCHES WITCHES AND STRUMPETS	Aishling Morgan 0 352 33733 8	☐
WHEN SHE WAS BAD	Penny Birch 0 352 33859 8	☐
WHIP HAND	G.C. Scott 0 352 33694 3	☐
WHIPPING GIRL	Aishling Morgan 0 352 33789 3	☐

---------- ✂ ----------------------------

Please send me the books I have ticked above.

Name   ....

Address   ....

              ....

              ....

              .... Post code ....

Send to: Virgin Books Cash Sales, Thames Wharf Studios, Rainville Road, London W6 9HA

US customers: for prices and details of how to order books for delivery by mail, call 1-800-343-4499.

Please enclose a cheque or postal order, made payable to **Nexus Books Ltd**, to the value of the books you have ordered plus postage and packing costs as follows:

UK and BFPO – £1.00 for the first book, 50p for each subsequent book.

Overseas (including Republic of Ireland) – £2.00 for the first book, £1.00 for each subsequent book.

If you would prefer to pay by VISA, ACCESS/MASTERCARD, AMEX, DINERS CLUB or SWITCH, please write your card number and expiry date here:

....

Please allow up to 28 days for delivery.

Signature ....

Our privacy policy

We will not disclose information you supply us to any other parties. We will not disclose any information which identifies you personally to any person without your express consent.

From time to time we may send out information about Nexus books and special offers. Please tick here if you do *not* wish to receive Nexus information.   ☐

---------- ✂ ----------------------------